W9-BMY-362

ENIGMA OF CHINA

ALSO BY QIU XIAOLONG

FICTION

Death of a Red Heroine

A Loyal Character Dancer

When Red Is Black

A Case of Two Cities

Red Mandarin Dress

The Mao Case

Years of Red Dust

Don't Cry, Tai Lake

POETRY TRANSLATION

Evoking Tang: An Anthology of Classical Chinese Poetry

100 Poems from Tang and Song Dynasties

Treasury of Chinese Love Poems

POETRY

Lines Around China

PHOTOGRAPHY / POETRY

Disappearing Shanghai (with Howard French)

ENIGMA
OF CHINA

QIU XIAOLONG

ST. MARTIN'S MINOTAUR ⚊ NEW YORK

ENIGMA OF CHINA. Copyright © 2013 by Qiu Xiaolong. All rights reserved. Printed in the United States of America. For information, address St. Martin's Press, 175 Fifth Avenue, New York, N.Y. 10010.

www.minotaurbooks.com

Library of Congress Cataloging-in-Publication Data

Qiu, Xiaolong, 1953–
    Enigma of China : an Inspector Chen novel / Qiu Xiaolong.—1st ed.
        pages cm
    ISBN 978-1-250-02580-7 (hardcover)
    ISBN 978-1-250-02581-4 (e-book)
    1. Chen, Inspector (Fictitious character)—Fiction.   2. Police—China—Shanghai—Fiction.   3. Shanghai (China)—Fiction.   I. Title.
    PS3553.H537E55 2013
    813'.54—dc23

                                                    2013011920

Minotaur books may be purchased for educational, business, or promotional use. For information on bulk purchases, please contact Macmillan Corporate and Premium Sales Department at 1-800-221-7945, extension 5442, or write specialmarkets@macmillan.com.

First Edition: June 2013

10 9 8 7 6 5 4 3 2 1

*To the Chinese netizens who fight for their citizenship
in the cyberspace—unimaginable elsewhere—in the face of
authoritarian control*

ACKNOWLEDGMENTS

PART OF THIS BOOK was written in Shanghai, where I was helped by netizens who have to remain nameless, and I cannot thank them enough for their courageous efforts; part of the book was written during a residency at the University of New South Wales in Sydney, and I want to thank Cathryn Hlavka, Stephen Muecke, James Ronald, Richard Henry, Helen Geier, and Jeremy Campbell Davys for their kind and generous support; part of the book, particularly the verse quote in the narrative, was encouraged by Yesi, a Hong Kong poet friend who recently passed away; and all the other parts too numerous for me to acknowledge here.

I want to thank my editor, Keith Kahla, whose extraordinary, thoroughgoing work has made a real difference for the book; my copyeditor, Margit Longbrake, who is so careful as to find mistakes even in my Chinese spelling; and my Spanish editors, Beatriz de Moura and Carmen Corral, whose invitation and arrangement made it possible for me to study in the Madrid museum the painting by Salvador Dalí, *The Enigma of Hitler*.

ENIGMA OF CHINA

ONE

CHIEF INSPECTOR CHEN CAO, of the Shanghai Police Bureau, was attending a lecture at the Shanghai Writers' Association, sitting in the audience, frowning yet nodding, as if in rhythmic response to the speech.

"The enigma of China. What's that? Well, there's a popular political catchphrase—socialism with Chinese characteristics—which is indeed an umbrella term for many enigmatic things. Things that are called socialist or communist in our Party's newspapers but are in practice actually capitalistic, primitive or crony capitalistic, and utterly materialistic. And feudalistic, in that the children of high cadres—or princes—are themselves high cadres: the 'red trustworthy,' or the successors in our one-party system.

"In spite of the Party propaganda machines chunking away at full throttle, Chinese society is morally, ideologically, and ethically bankrupt, yet still going, going like the rabbit in an American television commercial."

After tapping his pants pocket, looking for a pack of cigarettes, Chen stopped and thought better of it.

It was one of those controversial yet permissible lectures. The speaker was a well-known scholar named Yao Ji, a research law professor at Shanghai Academy of Social Science. Not exactly a dissident, Yao was nonetheless considered a potential troublemaker because of his open criticisms of the problems in society. He had published a number of contentious articles and posted even more unpublishable articles on several blogs online. A gaunt, angular man, he spoke with his hands on the podium, his body leaning slightly forward, and his prominently balding head reflecting the light pouring in through the stained-glass window. He looked like a hallowed figure, as in a time-yellowed painting.

Chen happened to know a thing or two about Yao due to an internal blacklist memo circulated in the police department. But it wasn't his business, Chen told himself. He adjusted the amber-colored glasses along the ridge of his nose and pulled down the French beret just a little. He hoped he looked like anything but a cop. Here and now, it wasn't a good idea to be recognized, even though several members of the association knew him fairly well. For the moment, Chen found himself bugged by the word *enigma*. It somehow reminded him, distantly, of a painting he'd seen, though he couldn't recall the details. Professor Yao was producing a flurry of concrete examples.

"Indeed, what are the characteristics of China? There are so many different interpretations and definitions. Here are some examples that speak for themselves. A Beijing University professor tells his students: 'Don't come to me if you don't make four hundred million by the time you're forty.' The professor specializes in real estate development, advocating high-priced housing investments in return for the referral fees he receives from developers. For him, and for his students, the only value in the world of red dust is what shines in cash.

"In a reality show, where the participants were discussing how one makes a marriage choice, a young girl stated her manifesto: she would rather weep in a BMW than laugh on a bike. The message of that is unmistakable. A rich husband who can provide her with material luxuries—even if in a loveless marriage—is what she wants. In a recent drunk driving case, the accused actually shouted at the cops, 'My father is Zhang Gang.' Zhang Gang is a high-ranking Party official, in charge of the local police bureau. Sure enough, the cops were hesitant to arrest him, but a passerby recorded the scene with his cell phone and placed the clip on the Internet. Immediately 'My father is Zhang Gang' becomes an Internet catchphrase. . . ."

These were all examples of what was really happening in China, Chen thought. But what did they mean?

For the government, "stability" was the main priority. It was declared that the economic and social progress from China's reforms had been achieved because of that stability. Yet the Party authorities were finding it increasingly hard to maintain that stability, despite their efforts to cover up any "unstable" factors.

Professor Yao was coming to his conclusion.

"In a time when the government's legitimacy is disappearing and the Party's ideology disintegrating, I am, as a legal scholar, still trying to hold that last line of defense—a real, independent legal system—hoping against hope for the future of our society."

Chen, his brows knitted more deeply, joined in the applause. As a cop, he found it far from pleasant to listen to such a lecture.

Still, he would rather be sitting here than in a routine political meeting with Party Secretary Li Guohua and other officials at the bureau.

Li, the Party boss of the police bureau, was reaching retirement age, and Chen was unanimously seen as his successor. But for one reason or another, Li had been recently reappointed for another two years. As a sort of compensation, Chen was made the first deputy Party secretary of the bureau and a member of the Shanghai Communist Party Committee.

To those on the outside, it looked like a promotion for Chen, but not in the Party power structure. Some "leading comrades" in the city government, not considering Chen "one of them," didn't want him to be the head of the bureau. They were uncomfortable with the prospect of Chen's taking on such a key position.

So the meeting at the Writers' Association gave him an excuse to not attend the routine Tuesday political studies meeting at the bureau. It would only drive him nuts to sit there while Li mouthed all the political phrases from the Party newspapers.

The subsiding applause pulled him back from his wandering thoughts. Now came the question and answer period. After that, it would be time for the meeting of executive members that they had scheduled weeks earlier.

Chen got up and walked out of the conference hall and out into the building's secluded garden. The association was located in a mansion built by a wealthy businessman in the thirties, then seized by the Party after 1949. For many years, the mansion had been used as the office complex for the Writers' Association.

He walked through the garden, coming to a stop by a tiny pond. He gazed at the white marble angel posing in the middle of the water. It was nothing short of a miracle, he mused, that the statue had survived the Cultural Revolution.

It was all because of Old Bao, the doorkeeper for the association, who, as an ordinary worker, was "politically glorious" and trusted by the Red Guards back then. One dark night during the Cultural Revolution, he moved the statue home in stealth on a tricycle and hid it under his bed. When the Red Guards came to smash anything "bourgeois and decadent," the nude statue, which was on the top of their list, was inexplicably gone. They questioned everybody except Old Bao, who was wearing a red armband and shouting revolutionary slogans more loudly than anyone. The disappearance of the statue remained a mystery for more than a decade, until after the Cultural Revolution ended. Then Old Bao moved the statue back to its original site in the garden. When people asked him why he had taken such a risk, he simply said that it was his responsibility as doorkeeper to keep things in the mansion from being damaged or destroyed.

Looking up from the pond, Chen saw a man waving at him from the visitor registration desk near the building's entrance. It was none other than Young Bao, the only son of Old Bao. When the old man was about to retire in the midnineties, his son was without a job. Thanks to Chen's suggestion that the son succeed the father, Young Bao came to sit at the same desk, with the same register, with a cup of tea—possibly the same cup—just as Old Bao had for years.

Chen was waving back at Young Bao when he heard footsteps. He turned around to see An, the newly elected head of the association, approaching.

An was a swarthy, medium-built woman in her midforties. She had written a prize-winning novel portraying the vicissitudes of Shanghai from the point of view of an unfortunate, helpless woman who had fallen prey to the relentless changes of the time. The novel was made into a movie, but An had not done anything close to that level since then. Perhaps, Chen contemplated, it was no wonder. In her new position, she enjoyed the privileges of a ministry-ranking Party cadre. She wouldn't want to write anything that could jeopardize that.

"Party Secretary Chen," she said jokingly. It was conventional for people to add one's official title to one's name and to delete the *deputy* as well.

"Come on, An," he said. "I felt ashamed listening to that lecture as a policeman, let alone as a deputy Party secretary for the police bureau."

"You don't have to talk about that with me, Chen. Back in college, you intended to be a poet, not a cop, but when you graduated, you were state-assigned to the police bureau. It's a story that we all know well. Still, there's no denying that you've done well at your present position. There's no point discussing that, either."

What she did want to discuss with him was a series of lectures being sponsored by the association. All of them were to be delivered by its members, and given the excellent location of the association here, there was no worry about there being a decent turnout. Not only that, there was the possibility of collaborating with Shanghai Oriental TV. Recently, lectures about Chinese classics had become popular. People were too busy making money to read the classics, but when relaxing in front of the TV, they enjoyed lectures with easy explanations and vivid images in the background—like fast food.

"A critic compared these lectures to infant formula, which the audience swallows without having to digest," Chen pointed out.

"It's better than nothing."

"That's true."

"They will not only bring in additional revenue to our organization, but a much-needed boost to literature too. So as an executive member, you should be the one to lecture about the *Book of Poetry*."

"No, I'm not qualified to do it. I've written nothing but free verse."

Chen understood her reasons for promoting the lecture series. The government subsidy for the association was on the decline, and in spite of An's efforts to generate extra money, such as renting out the attached building to a wine importer in the name of "cultivating an exchange between Chinese and French culture" and breaking down a section of the wall along Julu Road to build a café, the association remained financially strained. Its members were constantly complaining of inadequate service and benefits, and An was under a lot of pressure.

A cicada started chirping, a bit early for the time of the year, during a temporary lull in their conversation.

Chen glanced up to see a young girl moving light-footedly toward them.

Slender, supple, she's so young, / the tip of a cardamom bud / in the early spring. He didn't think she was one of the members, having never seen her at the association before. She was dressed in a scarlet silk

Tang jacket, reminiscent of a delicate figure stepping out of a traditional scroll, with "spring waves" rippling in her large clear eyes as in a line of classical poetry, yet holding a modern camera.

"Hi, Chairman An." She greeted An before turning to him with a bright smile, "You're Comrade Chief Inspector Chen, aren't you? I've read your poems. You used to write for us."

"So you are . . . ?"

"I'm Lianping, of *Wenhui Daily*. I'm a new hand, covering the literature section for the time being. I would like to ask both of you to continue to give your works to our newspaper."

She handed over her business card, which beneath her name declared her to be "the number-one finance journalist."

Interesting. He'd never seen such a title on a business card. Still, her request was not an unpleasant one.

"Yaqing's out on maternity leave. So I'm stepping in to cover the literature section while she's away." Lianping added, "Please send your poems to me, Chief Inspector Chen."

"Of course, as soon as I have any time for poetry."

For the newspaper nowadays, poetry was nothing but a bunch of plastic flowers tossed into a forgotten corner of an upstart's mansion. Few paid any real attention to it.

Then, as if in response to the cicada, his cell phone started chirping. The number displayed was that of Party Secretary Li.

Chen excused himself and strode off, stopping under a flowering pear tree. Flipping open the phone, he heard agitated voices in the background. Li wasn't alone in the office.

"Come back to the bureau, Chief Inspector Chen. We're having an emergency meeting. Liao and Wei are with me at my office."

Inspector Liao was the head of the homicide squad, and his assistant, Detective Wei, was a veteran police officer who had joined the force at about the same time as Chen.

"I'm attending a meeting at the Writers' Association, Party Secretary Li."

"You are truly versatile, Poet Chen. But ours is a most special case."

Chen detected a sarcastic note in Li's voice, even though the phrase "a most special case" sounded like a typical cliché from the Party boss. Once a sort of mentor to Chen in bureau politics, Li now saw him more and more as a rival.

"What case?"

"Zhou Keng committed suicide while in the Moller Villa Hotel."

"Zhou Keng—I don't think I know who that is."

"You've never heard about him?"

"The name sounds familiar, but sorry, I can't recall anything."

"You must have been working too hard on your poetry, Chief Inspector Chen. Let me put you on speaker phone, and Detective Wei will fill you in."

The deep voice of Wei took over. "Zhou Keng was the director of the Shanghai Housing Development Committee," Wei stated. "About two weeks ago, he was targeted in a 'human-flesh search,' or crowd-sourced investigation, on the Internet. As a result, a number of his corrupt practices were exposed. Zhou was then shuangguied and kept at the hotel, where he hanged himself last night."

Another characteristic of China's socialism was its reliance on shuanggui, a sort of extralegal detention by the Party disciplinary bodies. The practice began as a response to the uncontrollable corruption of the one-party system. Initially, the word meant "two specifics": a Party official implicated in a criminal or corruption probe would be detained in a specific (*gui*) place and for a specific (*gui*) period of time. The Chinese constitution stipulated that all forms of detention had to be authorized in a law passed by the National People's Congress, and yet shuanggui took place regularly, despite never having had such authorization. Shuanggui also had no time limit or established legal procedure. From time to time, senior Party officials vanished into shuanggui, and no information was made available to the police or media. In theory, officials caught up in the extrajudicial twilight zone of shuanggui were supposed to merely make themselves available to the Party investigation and, once that was concluded, to be released. More often than not, however, they were handed over to the government prosecutors months or even years later for a show trial and predetermined punishment. The authorities claimed that shuanggui was an essential element of the legal system, not an aberration to be corrected. More importantly, shuanggui prevented any dirty details from being revealed and tarnishing the Party's image, Chen reflected, since everything was under the strict control of Party authorities.

A shuanggui case wasn't in the domain of the police.

"Because of his position and because of the sensitivity of the case, we have to investigate and conclude that it was suicide," Li cut in mechanically, as if suddenly a recording of readings from the *People's Daily* had been switched on. "The situation is complicated. The Party authorities want us on high alert."

"Since Liao and Wei are working on it, why am I needed?"

"As the most experienced inspector in our bureau, you have to be there. We understand that you're busy, so we'll let the homicide squad take care of it. Most of it. Still, you must serve as a special consultant to the investigation. That will demonstrate our bureau's serious attention to the anticorruption case. Everyone knows that you are our deputy Party secretary."

Chen listened in silence while he lit a cigarette and inhaled deeply. Then he remembered.

"Zhou. A crowd-sourced investigation. It was because of a pack of cigarettes."

"Exactly: 95 Supreme Majesty. A picture of it online started the investigation, which resulted in a disastrous scandal. We can spare you the details," Li concluded promptly. "You'll consult with the homicide squad."

"But I don't know anything else about the case."

"Well, you know about the background, and that's important, very important."

Chen had merely glanced at an article in a local newspaper. It was just out of curiosity that he even remembered the term "human-flesh search." It was something connected with the Internet; that had been about all he could figure out at the time. A considerable number of Internet terms had started popping up in Chinese, their meanings barely comprehensible to non-netizens like himself.

Apparently, the case was a political one. A government official who fell dramatically as a result of scandal and later died while in shuanggui. It was a case that could easily lead to wild and widespread speculation.

But what about Li's insistence that Chen serve as a consultant? Presumably it was a gesture on Li's part. Zhou had been a high-profile Party cadre, so assigning Chen to the case underscored the fact that the bureau was taking a major investigation seriously.

"You said that Zhou committed suicide in a hotel?" Chen said.

"Yes."

"Which one?"

"Moller Villa Hotel, the one on the corner of Shanxi and Yan'an Roads."

"Then I don't have to come back to the bureau. I'll go there directly. It's close. Are any of our people on the scene?"

"None of ours. But two teams are already there. One from the Shanghai Party Discipline Committee and a special team from the city government. They had checked into the hotel with Zhou at the very beginning of shuanggui."

That could be something. A shuanggui investigation was usually the job of the Party Discipline bodies. There was no need for both the city government and the Party Discipline Committee to have people stationed there, especially now, with the police department involved.

"Well—" Chen said instead, "When will you will be there, Wei?"

"I'm leaving right now."

"I'll meet you there."

Chen hung up and ground out the cigarette on a rock. He was ready to leave when he glimpsed the young journalist named Lianping walking around the pond, heading back into the hall, possibly for an article in *Wenhui* about the association meeting. She was speaking into a dainty cell phone.

There was a flash of a blue jay's wings in the light overhead, and Lianping's face blossomed into a bright smile. Chen was reminded of a poem by Lu You from the Song dynasty. It wasn't one precisely suited for the occasion, except perhaps for the lines, *The ripples that once reflected her arrival / light-footed, in such beauty / as to shame wild geese into fleeing.*

He shook his head in self-mockery at his thinking of romantic lines when he was starting a major investigation. Perhaps, as An had just teased, he wasn't meant to be a cop.

On second thought, he decided to go back to the meeting as he'd originally intended. After all, he was only a consultant to the investigation. There was no point in getting to the hotel before the homicide squad.

TWO

THE MOLLER VILLA HOTEL was one of the so-called elite hotels in Shanghai. It stood on the corner of Yan'an and Shanxi Road and was meticulously preserved because of its history.

Eric Moller, a businessman who had made his fortune through horse- and dog-racing in Shanghai, had the fairy-tale-like mansion built in the thirties. It was designed in accordance with a dream of his young daughter. It turned out to be an architectural fantasy. It sported a northern European style, with Asian elements blended in, such as glazed tiles, colorful bricks, and even a crouching-tiger-shaped attic window, like those commonly seen in Shanghai shikumen. After 1949, it was used as a government office. Eventually the mansion was turned into an elite hotel, at which point it was completely redecorated and refurbished, its interior design and original details painstakingly restored. A new building in the same style was added next to it.

Chen must have passed by this corner numerous times, but he'd never paid any real attention to it, despite its recent rediscovery in the collective nostalgia that gripped the city.

Two uniformed security men guarded the entrance, standing alongside a pair of crouching stone lions.

He walked in and through to building B, located at the back. This was the new building made in fastidious imitation of the original, a three-story red brick villa with arched attic windows. Another uniformed security man sitting at a desk asked Chen to show his ID. The guard looked up at Chen, at the ID picture, then recorded the ID number in a register and made a phone call to someone inside before letting him pass.

The atmosphere of a fairy castle seemed to be completely lacking.

"Room 302," the security man said. "They're waiting for you."

Chen went up to the third floor, which consisted of only six attic rooms, each sporting an art deco window in the original style. He stopped in front of room 302 and knocked on the door. Detective Wei opened the door for him, holding a mobile phone in his hand. There were two others, neither of them from the police department.

Chen hadn't worked with Detective Wei before, though they had known each other for a long time. A hard-working cop, practical and experienced, Wei hadn't had an easy time in his career, and on occasion Wei apparently spoke less than highly of Chen's work.

"This is Comrade Jiang Ke, of the Shanghai city government," Wei said, introducing a wiry man in his late forties or early fifties with a disproportionately wide forehead. "And this is Comrade Liu Dehua, of the Party Discipline Committee."

Chen shook hands with both of them. Jiang was the deputy director of the city government, known as a shrewd, scheming man and one of the most powerful confidants of Qiangyu, the first Party secretary of Shanghai. Liu was an elderly-looking man, short, feeble, bald, and with a slight suggestion of a limp. He seemed to be more self-effacing by contrast, possibly because he'd already reached retirement age.

Behind them was the body of Zhou, which had been taken down

14

from a noose dangling from an exposed ceiling beam. His face looked distorted, his mouth twisted as if in a sinister final question never to be answered, one eye still slightly open. Judging from the rigor mortis in Zhou's body, Chen guessed the time of death was late last night.

It was ironic, Chen observed, that in a city in which it was extremely difficult to find an exposed beam from which to hang oneself, Zhou happened to be detained in one of the few rooms with original beams "preserved" in the old style.

It's not you that chose the beam, / but the beam chose you. A couple of lines came echoing out of nowhere, but Chen failed to recall the author.

What thoughts would have come across Zhou's mind at the sight of the rope dangling in the last minutes of his life? It wasn't hard to understand the rationale behind his suicide. A Party cadre, at the peak of his successful career, tripped up because of a pack of cigarettes, had fallen headlong into an infinite abyss, from which he saw no hope for a comeback.

"I'm glad you're here, Chief Inspector Chen," Jiang said cordially.

Chen had met Jiang a couple of times at city government meetings but had never been formally introduced. Liu smiled beside him, nodding without saying anything. Chen had a feeling that Jiang was the one that dominated here.

"Both Liu and I have talked to the hotel night-shift staff," Jiang said. "Nothing suspicious or unusual was seen or heard the previous night."

"In such a well-guarded hotel," Wei commented, "people might have slept too soundly to notice."

Before there was any further discussion, the crime scene technicians arrived. Chen nodded to one of them he knew. The scene itself was compromised. Jiang and Liu had been there for hours, moving about, touching here and there, examining this or that. In spite of their expertise in shuanggui interrogation, they weren't cops. A considerable number of hotel people had been in the room too, helping to take Zhou's body down and move it to the floor.

Jiang led Chen and the others into another room—room 303—next to Zhou's on the same floor. It was an impressive suite, which turned out to be Jiang's.

When they were all assembled, Jiang started up with an air of authority. "Since each of us arrived at the scene at different times and from different angles, Detective Wei, you might as well sum everything up for the benefit of Chief Inspector Chen."

Wei started accordingly.

"Zhou checked into the hotel at the beginning of shuanggui, about a week ago. Since then, he never stepped outside. Shuanggui consisted of a strict routine. He got up around seven, with breakfast delivered to his room at eight, then he talked to Jiang or Liu about his problems or wrote self-criticisms in his room. Lunch and dinner were delivered to him the same way. He seldom talked to the hotel people, he never made any outside phone calls, and he wasn't allowed visitors.

"This morning, a hotel attendant came to his door with a breakfast tray as usual, but there was no response from inside. The attendant returned about thirty minutes later. Still nothing. After a while, he called another attendant, and they opened the door—only to see Zhou hanging from the beam.

"To the best of their memories, despite their being very flustered, there was no sign of a break-in or struggle, no indication that anything had been removed or was missing from the room.

"Liu, who had stayed overnight in the hotel, was immediately awakened. That was about eight forty-five or nine in the morning. As for Jiang, he was delayed by a special meeting of the city government the previous evening, so he'd gone home instead. Upon getting Liu's call, he rushed over less than twenty minutes later. They examined the scene together, and around nine thirty, Jiang called Party Secretary Li of the police bureau."

16

At the end of Wei's summary, Jiang stated emphatically, "We were going the extra mile in Zhou's case. Whoever was involved, we were determined to learn everything. But it wasn't easy to make him talk. We thought we could bring more pressure to bear by staying in the same hotel with him. For security reasons, there were only the three of us staying here on the third floor."

"To fight corruption in the Party," Liu echoed, "particularly among high-ranking Party officials, is a top priority for us. No one can question that . . ."

Chen listened to the official harangues. Though not really registering what they were saying, he nodded like a wound-up toy soldier, seemingly in agreement.

But Wei, not as accustomed to the official language, began losing patience.

"What about the security videotape?"

"There was nothing on the tape. I checked," Jiang said.

Liu took a small sip of tea in silence.

"We have to study it," Wei said.

Jiang said nothing in response.

"So nobody heard or saw anything unusual during the night?" Wei stubbornly went on.

"Both Liu and I have already talked to the hotel staff," Jiang said, ignoring his question. "And I will double check with them."

With the death of Zhou, Liu and Jiang weren't supposed to remain at the hotel anymore, since they could offer no help to the investigation. But they showed no sign of departing anytime soon or of leaving the case to the police. Chen supposed both of them might be waiting for new orders from above. As a result, the two cops were not in a position to proceed as they would have preferred.

"I think the two of us have to go back to the bureau," Chen said, rising. "Inspector Liao was collecting a file on Zhou. We'll study it with him. And then when it arrives, we'll study the autopsy report too."

Surprise flickered across Wei's face, but he didn't say anything.

"Contact me as soon as you find out anything," Jiang said, also rising.

"Yes, certainly," Chen said. "And I'll report to you too, Comrade Liu."

With that, the two cops took their leave.

Walking out of the hotel, Chen pulled out a pack of cigarettes and offered one to Wei.

"Oh, you smoke China," Wei said, reaching for one. It was an expensive brand, though not as exorbitant as 95 Supreme Majesty. "What do you think, Chief?"

"If it was suicide, we don't have to be here, but if it was murder, they don't have to."

"Well put," Wei said, taking a deep draw on the cigarette. "Besides, they were here much earlier, and have all the information we don't."

"So we'll have to go our own way."

"You're right about that. You're busy with so many other things, Chief Inspector Chen. Let me do all the legwork, and I'll keep you posted."

"You're the one in charge of the investigation, Wei," Chen said, wondering at the possible note of sarcasm in Wei's words. "I'm just a consultant to your team. You may call on me at any time, of course."

Wei took his leave and headed on; Chen stayed behind and smoked. As Wei's figure disappeared into the crowd around the corner, Chen looked up at the overpass ahead and pulled out a cell phone.

THREE

CHIEF INSPECTOR CHEN WAS sitting in his new office—a larger one assigned him because of his new position as deputy Party secretary—and was busy polishing off a stack of administrative paperwork. He usually put off such paperwork until the last minute, but today he was taking perverse delight in doing it.

Something from Professor Yao's lecture echoed in his mind. An enigma, the problems involved in the characteristics of China, he reflected as he skimmed through the documents on his desk—just glancing at the title more often than not—and signed them.

He wondered whether or not Zhou's death might be such an enigma. The chief inspector hadn't yet done much about the case. For one thing, Chen had practically nothing with which to work. The "folder of information" he had mentioned at the hotel was only an excuse to get away. There was no lack of pre-scandal information about Zhou. A pile of newspaper clippings sat on the corner of his desk, but all of them were from official media and were about his exemplary work as director of the Housing Development Committee.

Zhou had enjoyed a spectacular rise concurrent with the amazing transformation of the city. He went from being an ordinary worker in a small neighborhood production group in the late seventies to the director of the Housing Development Committee. Zhou launched an incredible number of new housing projects that, in fairness, dramatically changed the city's landscape. Even as a Shanghai native, Chen found himself frequently lost among the new skyscrapers, which had appeared like bamboo shoots after a spring rain. So it was surprising that a crowd-sourced investigation about a pack of cigarettes could have toppled a Goliath like Zhou.

According to Party Secretary Li, what was discovered on the Internet led to the disclosure of Zhou's other problems, which resulted in his detention. But all these details were totally missing from the pile of newspaper clippings on his desk. Chen tapped the pile and heaved a long sigh.

The Party authorities chose to punish its officials selectively and secretively, with few details made available to the public.

Chen tried to research Zhou on the Internet. To his surprise, access to several Web sites was blocked. Even on sites he could go to, no entry involving Zhou's case would load, showing up as an "error" instead. The only available information on Zhou consisted of two or three lines reposted from the Party media. State control of the Internet wasn't news to Chen, but the extent as well as the effectiveness of it was alarming.

He settled back into plowing through the boring paperwork, which eventually began to wear him out. He rubbed his temple with a finger, and then with two, his glance wandering over to a time-yellowed copy of the *Vajracchedika Sutra*, a Buddhist scripture his mother had given him. It was about how everything in this world was illusion, and it emphasized the practice of nonabiding and non-attachment. He wondered whether he could make some time to visit his mother in the hospital that afternoon.

He stood up to go over and pick up the scripture when Detective Yu barged into his office, not bothering to knock.

Yu was a longtime partner and friend. Nominally, Chen was the head the Special Case Squad, but since he was frequently away, Yu was in practical charge.

It wasn't the first time Yu had been in the new office. Still, he glanced around and took in the impressive furniture one more time before he commented on the twenty-five-inch LCD screen on Chen's steel desk.

"It's the same size as the one on the Party Secretary's desk, Chief."

"You didn't come here to talk about that, did you?"

"No. Peiqin just called, asking whether you could come over for dinner this weekend."

Yu's wife Peiqin was a wonderful hostess and cook. Chen was no stranger to her culinary skill.

"What's the occasion, Yu?"

"We're celebrating Qinqin's acceptance to Fudan University. We should have done it months ago."

"That's worth celebrating. A top university like Fudan will make a huge difference in his future prospects. But I'm not sure about this weekend. I'll check my schedule and let you know."

"That would be great. Oh, she also wants me to say that you're most welcome to bring anyone with you."

"Here she goes again." Chen knew what she meant—she wanted him to bring a girlfriend—but he chose not to dwell on it. "She's as anxious about it as my old mother."

"By the way, I ran into Wei this morning. He was just assigned a case, and he was saying that it should have been assigned to you."

"What case was he talking about?"

"A Party official who committed suicide during shuanggui."

"Oh, that one. We're actually both assigned to it, but I'm serving merely as a special consultant to the team."

"Is foul play suspected?"

"Not really; it seems to be only a matter of formality," Chen said. "Since we're on the topic, do you know anything about 95 Supreme Majesty cigarettes?"

"Have you never smoked them?"

"I have heard of the brand."

"But you've smoked Panda, haven't you?"

"Yes."

"In the eighties, Panda was the brand exclusively manufactured for Deng Xiaoping. It was the best in the world."

"And earlier, China was name of the brand manufactured for Mao," Chen said, nodding. "In ancient China, items like that were called imperial product—gongping—and were for the emperor alone."

"Nowadays, both China and Panda are available on the open market as long as you can afford them. Each of the provinces also manufactures a special brand of cigarettes designed exclusively for the top Party leaders in the Forbidden City, such as 95 Supreme Majesty. It's even more expensive than China and Panda."

"Yes, that makes sense. Think about the very name '95 Supreme Majesty.' The emperor complex inherent in the name works marvelously for an age of conspicuous consumption."

"But how is 95 Supreme Majesty connected to the case?"

"Zhou was exposed because of a human-flesh search—which is basically a crowd-sourced investigation—that was triggered by a picture of a pack of 95 Supreme Majesty sitting in front of him."

"Interesting. I think Peiqin was talking about this. A Party cadre who was shuangguied and saw the writing on the wall. It isn't too surprising that he chose to end his life."

"That's true," Chen said, without trying to elaborate.

"Let me know when you will be available," Yu said as he took his leave.

In the afternoon, Detective Wei came to Chen's office.

Sitting in a chair opposite Chen, Wei started his briefing with a slight hint of hesitation, which was uncharacteristic of the experienced cop. According to Wei, both Jiang and Liu were still staying at the hotel, supposedly continuing their investigation of Zhou's problems. It was a parallel investigation to the police inquiry into Zhou's death. That was making things difficult for Wei. Jiang and Liu were both further up in the Party hierarchy, so Wei was expected to comply with their investigation, rather than to collaborate with them or work on his own.

"Liu went back to the Party Discipline Committee this morning, but Jiang shows no sign of decamping. He won't give me any specifics about why they shuangguied Zhou. Yes, his corruption was exposed on the Internet, but what specifically triggered shuanggui? Jiang said that he'd been focusing on how the pictures came to be posted online in the first place, but he hasn't revealed anything to me."

Chen knew what Wei was driving at. In the case of murder, the perpetrator usually has a motive. Revenge, for example. The person who landed Zhou in the trouble on the Internet might be someone holding a grudge and could have been the one who murdered him at the hotel.

But with Zhou already shuangguied, why was the second step necessary?

"I don't know what Jiang really wants. Zhou's death could easily have been declared a suicide. Jiang didn't have to drag us into this."

Seeing that there was no point in trying to interject any observations for the moment, Chen sat back and listened.

"And the hotel itself is a very strange one," Wei went on. "From time to time, it will close to the public—either in part or entirely—in order to serve special needs of the Party. For instance, the need to temporarily house shuangguied officials. For them to isolate that particular floor where Zhou was staying, other guests had to be moved out. The hotel employees have been specially trained, and

23

visitors have to register before being admitted into the building, as you saw.

"I managed to talk to some of the hotel staff without the other two present. Zhou was last seen around ten twenty in the evening by a room service attendant who delivered a bowl of cross-bridge noodles to his room. His statement was supported by the videotape from a security camera on the third-floor stair landing. The video showed that no one came up after the attendant left."

"This level of extraordinary security isn't entirely incomprehensible for a shuanggui investigation. The Party always worries about the details of cadre corruption leaking out," Chen said. "Now, what about the autopsy?"

"A fairly large concentration of sedatives was found in Zhou's body. According to his family, he slept badly and he often took sleeping pills. He could have swallowed a handful of them before going to bed—"

"Yes?"

"But something doesn't add up here, Chief Inspector Chen. Zhou had noodles around ten, so let's assume he took the pills shortly after that. Call it ten thirty. Now, the time of death was estimated at around midnight, about an hour and a half later. With that amount of sedatives in his bloodstream, he should have been fast asleep at the time."

"Perhaps he took the pills before the noodles?"

"Who would take sleeping pills before ordering room service? What if he had fallen asleep before the noodles were delivered? A more likely theory is that he took them after eating the noodles."

"He still could have been unable to sleep, despite the pills—presuming he took them after eating the noodles."

"But could he, after having taken the pills to try and sleep, suddenly have jumped up, discovered a rope somewhere in the room, made a noose, tied it tightly to the beam, and hanged himself?"

"No, one isn't likely to find rope in a hotel room. On that point, you're right," Chen said. "But what other possible scenario do you suggest?"

"According to the hotel staff, Zhou didn't appear depressed or in any way different that evening. The hotel menu is of a very high quality, and he didn't seem to have lost any of his appetite. He had finished a large portion of Yangzhou fried rice with beef soup for dinner that night, and about three hours later, ordered a large bowl of noodles to be delivered to the room."

Now something began to dawn on Chen. From the very beginning, he assumed that the Party authorities wanted Zhou's death declared a suicide, which would be a plausible conclusion under the circumstances. For that, Chen hardly needed to do anything. The suggestion that a shuangguied official had been murdered would result in more headaches for the city government, yet that seemed to be the direction that Detective Wei was leaning. Publicly acknowledging that such a thing was possible could be seen as against the interests of the Party, which was probably why Jiang wouldn't collaborate.

But Wei was a cop, so it was his duty to look into the possibility. And Chen was a cop too.

When Detective Wei left the office, Chen went over his notes for a long time before he decided to call Detective Yu.

FOUR

PEIQIN WAS HOME ALONE, hunched in front of the computer, reading a blog entry about toxic pork being sold in the markets. She tried not to worry about politics too much, but she was concerned about practical matters, minor yet relevant to her family.

The blog entry was entitled "The Pig Farmer Eats No Pork." It revealed the shocking fact that most pigs were fed a so-called compound feed—in reality, it was an additive-laced feed, which included hormones to make the pigs grow faster, sleeping pills so they would sleep all day and gain weight faster, and arsenic to make them look pink and healthy. Among the various additives, one commonly used chemical compound was called lean meat essence: it consisted of ractopamine or clenbuterol, with which the farmers could both produce more lean meat and reduce the amount of feed. The pig farmers didn't care about the consequences for the consumers. For their own use, however, they would keep one or two pigs raised on natural feed.

Knocking on the table in frustration, Peiqin wondered how reliable the information was. What she knew for a fact was that pork nowadays tasted different.

She had heard, however, that for high-ranking Party officials, there was a secret supply of pork and other meat raised on special organic farms. Such meat could be expensive, but it was all paid for by the government. It was beyond the reach of ordinary people like Peiqin and Yu.

It wasn't only the toxic pork, Peiqin reflected, as she stood up to pour herself a cup of tea. The vegetables were sprayed with DDT, the fish raised in contaminated water, and even the tea leaves—at least some of them—were said to be painted green. She couldn't help gazing suspiciously into the cup.

"What's wrong with China?"

An article like that wasn't going to appear in newspapers like *Wenhui*. In the official media, there was only the good and great news about China. The authorities wanted to present a picture of a harmonious society and didn't permit any negative news or commentary. Like an increasing number of people, Peiqin felt she had no choice but to get more and more of her news online. In contrast to the official media, the Internet provided less-filtered information, though even it wasn't free from government control.

Peiqin used the computer Qinqin left at home for her Web surfing. The campus computers ran much faster, and Qinqin studied there most of the time. He only checked e-mail or played games at home on the weekend, so Peiqin could use the computer as much as she liked during the week.

She heard voices and footsteps approaching the door. She rose and opened the door and saw, to her surprise, not just Yu but also Chen standing there.

"What wind has brought you over today, Chief Inspector Chen?"

"He was talking to me about a case," Yu said, "involving Internet searches. I told him you're a pro—"

"So here I am," Chen said, holding high a bottle of Shaoxing rice wine. "A student's gift to his teacher, a must in the Confucian tradition."

"Don't listen to him," she said. "It's dinnertime. You should have told me earlier."

"I'm no stranger, Peiqin. That's why I've come without giving you advance notice. We'll just have whatever you've already prepared."

"But there's only one bowl of eight treasures hot sauce," she said, glancing over her shoulder at the table. "With Qinqin off at college, we sometimes have nothing but noodles with a spoonful of sauce on top."

"The sauce isn't bad," Yu cut in, "fried with diced pork, dry tofu, peanuts, cucumber, shrimp, and whatnot—"

"So it's called eight treasures," Chen said with a grin. "I know. It's a Shanghai specialty. Really delicious!"

"No, it won't do for a distinguished guest like you. We can't afford to lose face like that," Peiqin said in mock dismay. "But have a cup of Dragon Well tea first and I'll see what I can put together."

In less than five minutes, Peiqin was able to put two cold dishes on the table: tofu mixed with chopped green onion and sesame oil, and sliced thousand-year egg in soy sauce with minced ginger.

"Something for your beer," she said, putting a bottle of Qingdao and two cups on the table.

"Don't go out of your way for me, Peiqin."

"Let her have her way," Yu said, opening the beer bottle with a pop.

She put the sauce of eight treasures into the microwave and a bunch of noodles into a pot of boiling water. While those cooked, she stir-fried several eggs into an omeletlike dish called super crabmeat and roe.

Chen helped himself to a spoonful of the omelet the moment it was placed on the table. "It tastes absolutely exquisite," he declared. "You have to tell me the recipe."

"It's easy. You just need to separate the yolk from the white. Fry the white first, and then the yolk. Add a lot of minced ginger, Zhenjiang vinegar, and a generous pinch of sugar too."

She ladled out the noodles, placed them into bowls, and poured the sauce on top of them.

"Laomian style," she said before serving a soup of dried green cabbage.

"Wow, that's the soup I've been missing."

"The fresh cabbage was so cheap back in the early spring, I bought several baskets and dried it at home," she said. She shook out several drops of sesame oil onto the greenish surface of the soup.

"When I was a child, my mother used to dry cabbage at home, too. She would boil the cabbage, then air dry it on a rope stretched across our small room."

"Oh, we have not visited your mother for a while."

"Don't worry about her. She's doing fine for a woman her age."

Chen changed the subject: "I hear you've become quite Web savvy, Peiqin. Yu told me about it."

"She's absolutely hooked," Yu chipped in, adding another spoonful of the spicy sauce to the noodles. "She hurries to the computer the moment she gets home—before she even thinks of cooking or washing."

"You're always so busy with your work. What else can I do alone at home?" She turned to Chen. "I'm simply fed up with the newspapers. Just yesterday, I read about the exposure of another corrupt Party official. It served him right, but in the newspaper, it's always due to the great leadership of the Central Party authorities that a rotten cadre is exposed and punished. As to why and how it happened, we are never told anything. The former premier made his famous statement about preparing ninety-nine coffins for corrupt officials and one for himself. It was an unmistakable and heroic gesture promising to fight corruption, no matter the cost. He got a five-minute ovation for his speech. But did he succeed in rooting out the corruption? No. The situation has been getting worse and worse.

"That's why people rely on the Internet for detailed information on how these officials fatten themselves like red rats. The Web is also censored, but quite a number of sites aren't run by the government. Consequently, one or two fish may still, from time to time, escape the net. These are commercial Web sites, run for profit, so the contents have to be eye-catching and feature information that's unavailable in the Party newspapers."

"Thank you so much, Peiqin. That was a very helpful overview," Chen said. "But I have a specific question for you. What is a human-flesh search?"

"Oh, that. I hope you aren't the target of one, Comrade Chief Inspector Chen," she said, with a teasing smile. "I'm just kidding. When and where the practice of crowd-sourced investigation started, I don't know. Possibly in one of the popular, controversial Web forums, where users—or netizens—can post their own comments. They are called 'netizens' because the public space of Internet is a kind of nation, of which they are citizens. For many, it is the only space wherein they can act like citizens, with a limited freedom of speech. As for the term *human-flesh search*, it was originally used to describe an information search that is human-powered rather than computer-driven. The netizens—the most dedicated Web users—sift through clues, help each other, and share information, intent on tracking down the target information one way or another. But the popular meaning nowadays is that it is not just a search *by* humans but also a search *for* humans, one which plays out online but is intended to have real-world consequences. The targets of this kind of search vary, from corrupt government officials, to new Big Bucks who appear suddenly with surprisingly large fortunes, to intellectuals too obsequious to the authorities, or any other relatively high-profile figure you might imagine. However, almost always there is an explicit or implicit emphasis on sensitive political and social issues somewhere in the target's background."

"Can you give me an example, Peiqin?"

"Recently, there was one in Yunnan Province. An amateur hacker broke into a local Party official's laptop, downloaded his diary, and put it online. That official, named Miao, was the head of the county tobacco bureau. He wasn't a particularly high-ranking cadre, but he had a lucrative position. The contents of the diary proved to be very spicy. It included detailed descriptions of his extramarital affairs, his under-the-table deals done in the name of Party interests, his pocketing government funds, and his bribing others while others bribed him, all in a complex cobweb of connections. The diary reads like a novel, with the persons involved labeled only by initials—such as B, M, S, and so on—but with dates and locations too. You might think this would be no big deal, since no one could tell if the diary was true or not. But you know what? A crowd-sourced search started immediately. Netizens threw themselves into it wholeheartedly, like kids at a carnival. All the women mentioned as having been in a sexual relationship with the official were located. They even found photos of most of them. The same with the other Party officials connected to him. By relentlessly digging into the dates and locations, the forum members were able to establish the authenticity of the diary beyond question.

"Consequently, Miao was fired and jailed for being an official corrupted by the evil Western bourgeois influence."

"So these netizens did a good job of sorting out a rotten egg," Chen said. "On the other hand, who gave them the right to invade others' privacy?"

"No one did. But who gave the Party officials the right to do all those horrible things in the first place? China has a one-party system, with absolute power, absolute media control, and an absolute highway to corruption. People have to do something, right? No problem is really solved by conducting a crowd-sourced search like that. But exposing one Party official is better than none. These searches have now developed a pattern. When an official is first named on the Internet, he or she denies any wrongdoing, fights back, and threatens to take legal action against anyone posting about them online. The government, meanwhile, supports the targeted official while, it goes without saying, remaining in the background. But the ongoing search inevitably brings up new hard evidence, irrefutable, of corruption and abuse of power, much to the embarrassment of the government. The government then has no choice but to shuanggui the official thus exposed."

"I've heard about the role played by these netizens in bringing the melamine-contaminated milk powder scandal to the nation's attention," Yu chipped in again. "The local government tried to suppress the stories because the milk powder company was important to the local economy, but once they were on the Internet, the stories spread like wildfire. There were statements and pictures posted online of some of the victims of the contaminated milk powder. Ultimately, the Party authorities had no choice but to put the head of the company in prison."

"Back to these crowd-sourced 'human-flesh' searches, Peiqin," Chen said. "Have you heard about what happened to an official named Zhou—and all because of a pack of cigarettes?"

"Oh yes, the pack of 95 Supreme Majesty. It was just the rottenest luck for that guy."

"What do you mean, Peiqin?"

"Let me begin by telling you something about a small store close to my restaurant, Chief Inspector Chen. The store specializes in buying back and reselling expensive cigarettes and liquors. As you may know, Party officials of a certain rank usually are given one or two cartons of cigarettes per month for their so-called socialist business needs. The cigarettes they are given may not be as pricey as 95 Supreme Majesty, but they sell for at least five or six hundred yuan a carton."

"Yes, I have to admit, I get a carton every month," Chen said, "but I always finish it before the end of the month."

"But nonsmoking officials also get them as a perk of their Party positions; they get cartons and cartons as 'gifts.' Because the gift isn't cash, they have nothing to worry about. They could never finish all those cigarettes, even if they did smoke. Instead, they sell the cartons back to stores like the one next to my restaurant and pocket the cash. It's no secret."

Chen couldn't think of a response. He, too, had such "gifts" pushed onto him occasionally, though he'd never tried to sell them back for cash.

"As expensive as 95 Supreme Majesty may be, it is not surprising or scandalizing in itself. The Chinese people have seen too much. You know the term *socialism with Chinese characteristics*, do you? A big shot like Zhou would have surprised people more if he smoked a less expensive brand."

"Then why was Zhou chosen as a target for a crowd-sourced search?"

"The picture of the pack of 95 Supreme Majesty showed up after he spoke at an important meeting. Do you know what the speech he made that day was about?" She went on without waiting for an answer. "It was about the absolute necessity of keeping the housing market stable. What does that mean? It means prices cannot be allowed to fall. At present, a square meter at Lujiazui costs a 130,000 yuan. I would have to work for four or five years to earn enough to buy one square meter. Now, for our family, the present situation is not too bad. We have one and half rooms in an okay location assigned to us through the state housing quota, thanks to your help. But what happens to Qinqin after he graduates college? He will need an apartment for himself. How can people like us possibly afford a place to live if housing costs don't come down? It's more than probable that he will have to live like we did before we moved here. Remember, we lived with Old Hunter for years, with three generations squeezed together in one wing unit."

"Don't worry about the distant future, Peiqin," Yu said, with a lame smile.

"You think only about your cases, but I have to think about our son. In today's Shanghai, a young man with no apartment means no possibility of dating a young woman, let alone marrying her. People are all so realistic in this materialistic age," she said, frowning, and turning back to Chen. "Back to your question, do you know why the housing prices keep rising?"

"Because of greedy developers."

"No. Because of the even more greedy Party officials. The land belongs to the government. Under their control, it is sold off through a so-called auction system where the rights go to which-ever developer has the highest bid. Rising revenue from the sale of the land keeps pushing up the city's GDP, which the city officials point to as proof of their hard work—without mentioning that a substantial amount goes into their own pockets. Who gets the land, how, and at what price—it is all the result of shady dealings. Not too long ago, the premier made a statement about cooling down the overheated real estate market. Some developers, nervous about a possible downturn in the market, offered to bring prices down a little. Zhou, worrying about a snowball effect, highlighted the importance of keeping the market stable in his speech that day. He said that if some companies reduced prices irresponsibly, the government would punish them for causing economic trouble. Not only was this reported in several newspapers, they also ran a picture of him tapping a pack of cigarettes. That was the pack of 95 Supreme Majesty.

"That speech was like kicking a hornet's nest. Zhou was support-ing the interests of the city government, or the Party officials, but not those of the ordinary people. That picture of the 95 Supreme Majesty pack, once it was posted online, provided a perfect excuse for people to vent their anger and frustration."

"Well done, Peiqin," Chen said, raising the cup of Qingdao beer, "I'll drink to that. Please go on."

"Now, according to the official propaganda, a Party cadre is the 'people's servant' and earns about the same as an ordinary worker. For one in Zhou's position, the monthly salary would be about two or three thousand yuan. But a carton of 95 Supreme Majesty costs more than that. A photoshopped version of the picture showed up on the Internet with the retail price of a pack written underneath. It was posted as the evidence of an official living extravagantly beyond his means. It was both a legitimate criticism and an implied question: How could Zhou, if he wasn't corrupt, afford that pack?

"The original post drew a flood of responses in no time. As if responding to a call to arms, the offers to help with a crowd-sourced search swamped the Internet. If Zhou could afford the cigarettes, what else?

"It seemed justifiable for people to approach the search from this angle. Before Zhou could come up with an explanation for the cigarettes, another picture popped up. This time he was wearing a Cartier watch. Then, in breathtaking succession, more and more pictures were posted online as irrefutable evidence of Zhou's decadent lifestyle. Those were shots of the three luxury cars registered in his name—two Mercedes and one BMW—and of his son studying at Eton, a private school in London, and driving an Audi there. There were also more than five properties in the city under his name. Some capable hackers even managed to get hold of copies of the title deeds to his properties. Soon it was impossible for Zhou to defend the wealth he had amassed in the last five or six years."

"I'm beginning to understand, Peiqin. It was a master stroke, that crowd-sourced search."

"Yes, it really backed the government into a corner. They knew only too well why Zhou was being targeted. But with so many people protesting, without a legitimate excuse for his sudden wealth, and with the irrefutable evidence of it all, they found it hard to shield him anymore. They realized it was more important to protect the Party's image, so they put Zhou into shuanggui—over a pack of 95 Supreme Majesty."

"Thank you so much, Peiqin. You've thrown much light on the background of the situation."

"So it's a case you're investigating?"

"No. Not exactly," Chen said with a wry smile. "Shuanggui is not the territory of the police. It's believed that Zhou committed suicide while under detention at a hotel. I'm simply serving as a consultant to the team investigating the cause of death."

"Zhou's dead?"

"Yes. It will be announced in the newspapers soon."

"This will cause another storm on the Internet. Suicide while under detention. How will people online react?"

"Your guess is as good as mine."

"You've been talking so much about Internet searches, Peiqin," Yu said, changing the subject, "but what I'm searching for is the dessert."

"Sorry, I forgot," Peiqin said, rising in haste. "A friend from Beijing brought me some green bean–paste cakes, supposedly from Fangshan, the Forbidden City."

"That restaurant in the North Sea," Chen said, "on the island where chefs used to prepare all the delicacies for Dowager Empress Cixi toward the end of the Qing dynasty. The name of the restaurant alone, Fangshan, is more than enough to evoke the imperial majesty complex and its privileges from China's collective unconscious. It's just like the brand name of 95 Supreme Majesty."

"Don't worry, Chief. I'm not a Party official. The green bean cakes are just a gift from an old friend."

"I know who it is," Yu said with mock seriousness. "He was a secret admirer of Peiqin from the days when we were educated youths during the Cultural Revolution. He's not an official, just an ordinary clerk in the Beijing Travel Bureau, otherwise I would be really worried."

"But I am worried," Chen said, putting a tiny cake in his mouth. "If the government is anxious to conclude that Zhou's death was suicide, then why was I chosen to consult on the investigation?"

"You've conducted several high-profile anticorruption cases, which a lot of people know," Peiqin said, putting the remaining green bean–paste cakes into a box for the departing guest. "So if you're involved, people will believe the official report."

"Having you on the case is an endorsement of their conclusion," Yu cut in again.

"Thank you, Peiqin and Yu, for the meal, for the cake, for the lecture about the Internet and crowd-sourcing, and for everything else," Chen said, rising. "Now I have your endorsement, I think, for what I'm going to do next."

FIVE

AS A SPECIAL CONSULTANT, Chief Inspector Chen wondered about his role in the investigation: what was left for him to do, and what was not. As the old proverb says, there's no point in or justification for cooking in another's kitchen. Detective Wei, on the other hand, didn't seem to mind that much.

But Wei wasn't the one and only chef in there. Jiang was another, and he was following his own recipe. Then there was the city Party Discipline Committee team, even though it looked like Liu wasn't at the hotel most of the time.

Chen began to have second thoughts about this assignment after his dinner with the Yus.

The city government might not be able to convince people with just an announcement that Zhou had committed suicide. A police investigation into his death could be a necessary show, one that had best be performed in convincing earnestness. So as Yu had put it, Chen's role as a consultant could simply be to endorse the conclusion.

If so, Chief Inspector Chen was in no hurry to do anything.

What made the situation even more complicated was the divergent investigations of Wei and Jiang.

Judging from his discussions with Wei, the stubborn detective was more and more inclined to conclude that Zhou had been murdered. This persistence had to be an annoyance to Jiang, who, to protect the interests of the city government, wanted a conclusion of suicide.

Chen didn't think that he had to confront Jiang right away. Still, he felt compelled to do something on the case, so he settled on a visit to Zhou's widow.

The Zhous lived in Xujiahui, just a block away from the Oriental Commerce Center. For a Party cadre with Zhou's position, their three-bedroom apartment might not be considered too luxurious—that is, if one didn't take into consideration the other properties he owned.

Mrs. Zhou opened the door in response to Chen's knock. She was a fairly buxom woman in her early forties, and the way she was leaning against the light-flooded doorframe was suggestive of something soon to go out of shape, like a full blossom at the end of the summer. She was wearing a white blouse and white pants, with a black silk crepe on her sleeve. She looked Chen up and down with undisguised hostility.

"How many times are you cops going to snoop around here?" she snapped. "Why aren't you out trying to catch the real criminal?"

How could she tell that he was with the police before he even said anything? There must be something that tipped people off about him, whether he was in uniform or not.

"My colleagues have already talked to you, I believe."

"Yes. Several of them," she said, then added in mounting frustration, "Different groups of them. They searched the apartment repeatedly, turning the whole place upside down. And what did they find? Nothing."

There was nothing surprising about searches having been conducted here. The first one was probably right after Zhou was put in detention, and then they continued after his death.

"I was just assigned to the case," Chen said, taking out his business card. "My colleagues may not have told me everything. In fact, I'm only serving as a consultant to the team. But first let me express my sincere condolences, Mrs. Zhou."

She examined his business card; then a visible change of expression came over her face.

"Oh, come on in," she said, holding the door for him. "It's so unfair, Chief Inspector Chen. Zhou did a great job for the city. All this happened because of a pack of cigarettes. I just don't understand."

Chen sat down on a black leather sofa in the spacious living room, and she perched herself on a chair opposite.

"I must have met Zhou at some government meeting, but I didn't know him personally. Nonetheless, there's no denying all the work he did on new construction in Shanghai," said Chen.

"But no one has taken that into consideration. People talked about nothing but that pack of 95 Supreme Majesty. It was given to him by an old friend. He told the Party Discipline officials all about it. They should have let him explain to the public, but instead they rushed him into shuanggui. No one would help him. All those buddies of his in the city government only wanted to save their own necks. The police did nothing."

"Shuanggui is not within the police force's domain, " he said, somewhat taken aback by her unconcealed resentment. "I wasn't in a position to do anything about it. The discipline team and the city team had moved into the hotel with him days before I was told anything about the case."

"If there was anything improper or wrong about his decisions at work, it shouldn't have been reported as his responsibility alone. He worked directly with the people above him, and without their approval, he couldn't have done anything. You know how much of the city's GDP last year was due to the real estate sector alone? More than fifty percent."

"It's huge, I understand," he said vaguely, wondering about the accuracy of her claim.

"People are complaining about housing costs. Zhou knew that only too well. But if the property price fell dramatically, it could have a domino effect that would be disastrous for the economy of the whole city. So Zhou emphasized the market stability, but it was in everybody's interest."

Apparently, she was aware that the pack of 95 Supreme Majesty wasn't the real issue.

"I haven't paid much attention to the fluctuations in the real estate market, but I agree with you, Mrs. Zhou, that it wasn't fair for Zhou to have been targeted just because of a pack of cigarettes. Now, I just have some routine questions for you. For starters, did you have any contact with him during the last few days of his life?"

"They didn't permit me to visit him at the hotel. The phone there was tapped, and most likely, so is the one here in the apartment as well, and he knew better than to call back regularly or talk too much."

"When did you last talk to him?"

"Sunday. The day before his death. He hardly said anything, except that he was fine, and that I'd better not call the hotel or talk too much."

"Did you notice a drastic change in his mood?"

"It was such a short conversation, it would have been difficult for me to tell. I don't remember noticing any change."

"When did you last see him?"

"The day before he was shuangguied."

"How was he?"

"He was terribly upset at being targeted on the Internet. It was a cold-blooded lynching."

"Did he say anything specific about it?"

"He wondered how the government could allow mobs on the Web to go on like that. He thought the government should have exercised total control over the Internet."

"What did he mean by that?"

"He thought they should order all the Web sites to shut up about

95 Supreme Majesty, and delete all posts about it. If the authorities had really wanted to do that, they could have. In fact, they've taken actions like that on previous occasions. But they were unwilling to do this for him."

"Well, it could be difficult," Chen said vaguely. He didn't know what else to say.

"'When the rabbit is caught, the hound will be stewed too,' Zhou always said, quoting an old saying. I know for a fact that particular speech that started his trouble had been approved by the people above him. It's not fair that he shouldered all the blame."

Her complaining didn't surprise Chen, but the object of her complaints did.

"You mentioned that many people have come to your place. Can you tell me more about them?" Chen asked, shifting the focus of the conversation.

"Yes, various teams showed up over many weeks. I was too shocked to remember their names. They looked through the things Zhou left behind, then took away the computer and other stuff that they claimed was possible evidence."

"Did they find what they were looking for?"

"I don't know. Zhou hadn't left anything valuable here." After a short pause, Mrs. Zhou continued. "We do own several apartments in the city, but it was my decision to buy them. Zhou hardly ever talked to me about his work, but he would get many phone calls. From what I overheard, I thought housing prices would keep going up, so I borrowed heavily from banks for the various down payments. I am still paying off those mortgages. Please don't believe all the Internet stories about how wealthy our family is."

It wasn't up to him to look into the wealth of the Zhous, but Chen couldn't bring himself to believe anything she was telling him about how their real estate was acquired.

"They were back again the day before yesterday, combing through the apartment one more time."

That was after Zhou's death, Chen thought.

"What did they say to you?"

"Jiang, the head of the group, kept demanding that I turn over what Zhou had left behind. I didn't know what he was talking about. As I've said, Zhou seldom talked to me about his work at home, and he didn't give me anything related to it."

"Did they have a search warrant?"

"No, but they went ahead without one. Didn't you say shuang-gui is beyond the police bureau's control? They didn't have to follow any procedure. They just turned the place upside down."

"That's not right."

"They even forbid me to talk to anybody about it. I was told I couldn't say a single word to the media or to other people. You're different, I know. You're the only one I've talked to."

Chen couldn't help feeling a wave of sympathy for her. In China, as long as a Party official was in his powerful position, he had everything. But once he was out of power, everything was gone.

That was why Mrs. Zhou appeared so helpless. Her husband was gone, her home had been repeatedly searched, and no one would ever lend a hand.

That was probably why Party Secretary Li had been hanging onto his bureau position so desperately, making things difficult for Chen.

"It has been just like a dream shattered to pieces," she said, then started sobbing inconsolably. "Last night, I wished I wouldn't wake up, and would instead stay lost forever in the dream."

It is nothing but a dream, / in the past, or at the present. / Whoever wakes out of the dream? / There is only a never-ending cycle / of old joy, and new grief. / Someday, someone else, / in view of the yellow tower at night, / may sigh deeply for me.

But was there something else to Mrs. Zhou's complaints?

It was an elusive thought. Chen told himself not to jump to anything like a conclusion. There was a lot more for him to check out first.

SIX

THE FIRST THING CHEN did when he got back to his office was turn on his computer, almost exactly the way Yu had described Peiqin.

Chen was struggling with something he had heard before Peiqin filled him in more fully.

On the Internet, anything politically sensitive would be "harmonized" into nothing through a keyword search by specific Web control mechanisms. So Chen wasn't exactly surprised when his search for the phrase "95 Supreme Majesty" repeatedly drew a blank. With each search he got the inevitable error message.

After repeated attempts, he changed tactics by typing in "top brand cigarettes," and this time he was able to find some related content. A lot of questions were being raised about Zhou's alleged suicide. Speculation about his death was rampant. Posters on various Web forums were devoting an incredible amount of energy and time discussing possible clues, analyzing them, and advancing one possible scenario after another.

Chen spent a couple of hours going through the Web posts and blogs. One of the bloggers was particularly sharp—his tone was satirical, and his conclusion caught Chen's attention.

"A house isn't built in one day, nor by one man. Think of all the new houses in the city. Zhou knew too much, so he was harmonized out of sight."

Chen realized that there was an antigovernment sentiment among the dedicated Web posters and that their reactions were justified. For a detective, however, generalizations like that weren't the way to conduct an investigation.

Chen moved on from reading about Zhou's death to some general background information about the housing market.

As a rule, government control of Web content applied there as well. But complaint or criticism seemed to be permissible to an extent. Perhaps the government was aware that it would be useless to try to totally suppress it since the housing problem affected too many people. On the other hand, the Web forums and blogs where it was discussed seemed to be run by people clever enough to avoid direct confrontation with the authorities. Chen particularly liked a bit of doggerel he found titled "Calculation":

It would take three million yuan / to buy an apartment of one hundred square meters / in an acceptable location in Shanghai, / therefore, for a farmer tilling three acres, / at the average income of eight thousand yuan per year, / he would have to work from the Ming dynasty to the present, / not calculating in the possibility of natural disasters; / for a worker, with a twenty-five hundred yuan monthly income, / he would have to work from the Opium War in the Qing dynasty, / with no holiday, weekend, or any break whatsoever; / for a white collar, with sixty thousand as his yearly salary, / he would have to start working in 1950, / without eating or spending anything; / and for a hooker, she would have to fuck ten thousand times, / every day, with no interruption / even during her period, moaning, groaning, writhing, / from the day she turned sixteen to the age of fifty-five, / and all that without including the necessary expenses / for decoration, furniture, and electronics for the room.

That explained why these "netizens" threw themselves into the search campaign that brought Zhou down, but as another post pointed out, Zhou wasn't an isolated case.

Zhou's actions wouldn't be possible without the long, long chain of corruption behind him—link after link, circling the whole city. Behind all the propaganda, housing reform is in reality a huge scam, benefiting only Party officials, and inflating the economy into an impossible bubble. Theoretically, the land belongs to the people collectively, but now it's sold to them—and only for seventy years. The seventy-year limit is a long-sighted regulation or calculation. Not only can the current officials sell the land, but their sons and grandsons can sell it all over again . . .

The phone rang and interrupted Chen's Web browsing, bringing him back to the reality of his office. It was Jiang, the investigator for the Party, who was still staying at the hotel. He was the one the police were supposed to report their progress to.

"Is there anything new, Chief Inspector Chen?"

"Not really. Detective Wei is in charge of the investigation. We just compared notes this morning. It seems to him that there are some questions raised by the autopsy."

"What questions?"

"According to the autopsy, Zhou took a fairly large dose of sleeping pills that evening."

"We checked into that. He had trouble falling asleep. It wasn't unusual for him to take that many pills. He told me he took them every night at the hotel. He was under a lot of stress in those last days."

"But it's rather unusual for a man to take sleeping pills shortly before hanging himself. "

"Perhaps, in spite of the sleeping pills, he was too worried to fall asleep that night. Then, in the darkness, he thought of suicide. It isn't unimaginable."

"I visited his widow," Chen said, "who complained about the repeated searches of their home, and the confiscation of his computers and all other documents. Was there anything found on his computer?"

"Nothing. He had deleted all the files."

Chen wondered whether Jiang was telling the whole truth, but there was nothing the chief inspector could do about it.

"What else did she say to you?" Jiang asked.

"She kept repeating that Zhou had worked so hard for the city, and it wasn't fair for him to bear the responsibility alone."

"How could she say that?" Jiang asked after a short pause. "The city government has asked us to reach a conclusion as soon as possible regarding Zhou's death. So far, you haven't found anything really suspicious about the circumstances of his death. I think it's reasonable to presume suicide."

"I understand the situation. It's complicated. I'll discuss it with Wei and report to you again."

Putting down the phone, Chen decided he did need to have another talk with Detective Wei, but for a reason he wasn't going to tell Jiang.

SEVEN

THE NEXT DAY AT lunch, Chen sought out Wei in the bureau canteen.

"How about a cup of coffee after lunch?" Chen said, holding a bowl of barbecue pork and rice.

"I'm not a coffee—" Wei broke off, leaving the sentence unfinished. After a brief pause, Wei said, "That would be great, Chief."

Fifteen minutes later, they walked out of the police bureau together.

"We could go to Starbucks or any other place you like, Wei."

"I know nothing about coffee," Wei said, "but my son talks a lot about a place called Häagen-Dazs."

"Yes, let's go there. There is one on Nanjing Road, near the corner of Fujian Road, next to the Sofitel."

It might not be such a good choice, Chen thought. Häagen-Dazs was a brand of ice cream, but in Shanghai, it was something fancy. It was a status symbol, and a number of the Häagen-Dazs specialty stores were marketed as luxurious spots for young people. There was even a popular TV commercial where a pretty girl declared: "If you love me, take me to Häagen-Dazs."

But the Häagen-Dazs store on Nanjing Road also served coffee, which turned out to be quite decent, though Chen would still have preferred a regular café. They chose two seats on a sofa, facing the window looking out on an ever-bustling pedestrian street.

"Tell me how you've been progressing," Chen said, taking a sip of the coffee.

"We have to conduct a thorough investigation before we are able to conclude it was suicide, right?"

"That's right. You remember what Party Secretary Li said the first day we were assigned to the case: 'Investigate and conclude it was suicide.' But don't worry about him. Let's go over what you've done."

Detective Wei gave him a quick look of surprise, having caught the sarcastic tone about Party Secretary Li, then addressed his question.

"It's difficult because we know so little about the background. Zhou was shuangguied a week before his sudden death. Jiang is not sharing any information he got prior to our arrival at the scene. Why?"

That wasn't a difficult question for Chen. From Jiang's perspective, the details of Zhou's shuanggui case had to be covered up to protect the image of a harmonious society, even at the expense of the police investigation.

"Now, for the sake of argument," Wei continued, without waiting for Chen's response. "Let's suppose that it's a murder case. Hypothetically. What could be the motive?"

"Have you found one?"

"Perhaps more than one. In our investigations, it's common to focus on people who would directly benefit from the death, isn't it?"

"That's true. In this case, I don't think such a list will be too long. It's definitely worth checking out."

"Also, I have a hunch that the list may be connected to the picture that started everything."

"Explain that to me, Wei."

"When the picture first appeared in the newspapers, no one paid any attention to it. Then it showed up in a Web forum where the original crowd-sourced search started. According to Jiang, the manager of the Web forum was sent an electronic file of the picture along with a note about the pack of cigarettes."

"Who sent the photo?"

"We don't know yet. The sender used a one-time, fake e-mail address and logged in from an Internet café."

"So the sender applied for the e-mail address while he was at the café, and then never used it again."

"Jiang checked into it with the Internet café, but he drew a blank. He concluded that the troublemaker must have calculated all the possible consequences of initiating the crowd-sourced search. That's why Jiang has been focusing on that angle—"

"Hold on a moment, Wei. Does Jiang think the sender could be the murderer?"

"No. For Jiang, it's suicide. A foregone conclusion. So the reason for his focus is beyond me."

"What about you?"

"I'm not saying that the sender is necessarily the murderer—we don't know if the person benefited from the death of Zhou. But it's not that difficult to see that some people did benefit from it, Deputy Party Secretary Chen."

The Party title sounded extremely awkward coming from Detective Wei. In fact, it was the first time Wei had chosen to address Chen as such, and Chen didn't miss the implication. What Wei was implying was that the people after Zhou's position would be on the top of the list of suspects.

"Have you been to Zhou's office?" Chen asked, ignoring Wei's statement.

"Yes. The day Zhou was marched away from his office, a team headed by Jiang did a thorough search. There was nothing of value left behind. I talked to the deputy head, Dang Hao, for more than an hour, but didn't learn much that was useful. You know how a Party cadre can talk on and on in politically correct language. Dang simply kept on denouncing Zhou, just like an editorial in *Wenhui Daily*."

"When a wall is shaky, people will all push. Especially the one next in the line for the position," Chen started, then cut himself short, realizing that he too was a Deputy Party Secretary. "What else did he say?"

"While Dang was critical of Zhou, he defended the work of the office. He admitted that Zhou's job was a complicated, difficult one, considering how much the Shanghai economy relies on the booming housing market."

"In other words, Zhou wouldn't have delivered that speech without the approval of the city government?"

"On that, your guess is as good as mine" Wei said. "Dang did confirm that the photo was approved by Zhou himself, then given to his secretary, Fang, to send out to the media."

"Interesting. Usually providing photos would be the job of a newspaper photographer."

"Zhou cared about his public image and made a point of personally selecting which picture would be given to the media."

"But someone had to take the pictures. For instance, a journalist."

"That's what confused me. According to Jiang, he checked through Zhou's e-mail files but didn't find one that indicated from whom Zhou had received that picture."

"He might have deleted the e-mail and the file. But Jiang's people are pros. If it was on his computer, they would have found out one way or another."

"I think so too," Wei said. "Of course, looking at possible motives could point us in a different direction. In that speech, Zhou mentioned a particular company that was trying to bring down real estate prices in an irresponsible way. Zhou didn't name any names, but people knew which company he was referring to. It was Green Earth. Before the 95 Supreme Majesty scandal broke, Teng Jialiang, the general manager of Green Earth, was under a lot of pressure."

"That might be something, Detective Wei. Did you check him out?"

"I did. Teng was cooperative, and he gave me quite a few details on the background of Zhou's speech. Since last year, the Beijing authorities have been talking about needing to curb the housing prices for the sake of harmony in our socialist society. Teng thought reducing prices a little would be seen as a well-meant gesture and, at the same time, increase his company's market share. But out of the blue, Zhou targeted Green Earth as a troublemaker who was damaging market stability. Teng was in a tight spot. While other developers saw him as a greedy suck-up looking to curry favor with the Beijing authorities, the city government actually pressured him to back off."

"Well, I remember reading in the *People's Daily* just last week that it's a top priority to ensure that ordinary people are able to buy property."

"Teng put it well. The *People's Daily* is in Beijing, but Zhou represented the interests of the Shanghai government. What's more, there's also a personal reason Zhou had for targeting him."

"A personal reason?"

"Teng's project is located not far from one being developed by Zhou's cousin, or under his cousin's name. So Teng's proposal to reduce prices posed a threat to the profitability of Zhou's or his family's project."

"Does Teng have an alibi?"

"He wasn't in Shanghai that night, but he's well connected, both in the white way and the black way."

"I see," Chen said. The white way referred to the aboveground—or legal—connections, and the black way to the criminal, such as triads or gangsters. Chen understood why Wei brought up the two ways here. "But Zhou was already shuangguied. Do you think Teng would take such a risk as to kill him at the hotel?"

"You have a point," Wei said, then took a gulp of his coffee, "Oh, it's damned bitter."

Apparently Wei wasn't used to coffee. Chen waited, saying nothing, and taking a deliberate sip of his own coffee.

"Now, regarding the circumstances of Zhou's death at the hotel: there are puzzling aspects about it. Oh, I almost forgot—I managed to talk to the hotel attendant without letting Jiang know. Here's the record of that interview. The attendant's name is Jun."

Wei pulled a mini recorder out of his pocket, set it down, and pushed a button. He raised his coffee cup without taking another sip.

WEI: Please try to remember in detail what you did, saw, and heard that night, Jun. It could be very important to our work.
JUN: I'm a just a hotel attendant. I've already told everything I know to your people.
WEI: Well, let's go over it one more time.
JUN: I was on the night shift, from six p.m. to six a.m. Usually, it's not busy after midnight, so I can take a nap, and occasionally I can nap up until morning. All last week, there were only three guests staying on the third floor, so there wasn't much for me to do.
WEI: In other words, of the six rooms, only three were occupied.
JUN: Yes. That was due to a special arrangement with the hotel. We didn't ask questions. Among other things, we were told that the guest in room 302 was to have every meal delivered. The other two were just like other guests. They might eat in the dining hall in building A, but they could also order room service.
WEI: Now tell me what happened Monday night.
JUN: Well, around six fifteen I delivered dinner to room 302. It was fried Yangzhou rice and the soup of the day.

WEI: Did you go into the room?

JUN: No, not exactly. I knocked on the door; he opened it and took the tray from me.

WEI: Did you notice anything unusual about him?

JUN: No, I wasn't aware of anything. After that, I went to the other two rooms to turn down the beds. Both of them were in, and both of them told me not to bother. So I returned to my room.

WEI: Then?

JUN: Around ten twenty that evening, I was told to bring a bowl of cross-bridge noodles and a bottle of Budweiser to the guest in room 302.

WEI: Hold on, did you know that it was Zhou who was in room 302?

JUN: No, at the time I had no idea who he was. But guests at the hotel aren't ordinary people, and we know better than to ask around.

WEI: At the time, had you heard anything about Zhou?

JUN: No. Nothing before that night.

WEI: When you delivered the noodles, did you notice anything unusual about him?

JUN: He looked all right to me. He was smiling, and he didn't forget to give me a five-yuan tip. According to the hotel regulations, we're not allowed to accept tips, but if a customer insists, we don't refuse.

WEI: Did you take the noodles into the room or just to the door?

JUN: I went into the room because it was a bowl of special cross-bridge noodles. We usually spread out all the tiny dishes and sauces on the table and then tell the guest how to add the toppings, though it may not be necessary if the guest has had cross-bridge noodles before.

WEI: So was he alone in the room?

JUN: Yes, I'm positive.

WEI: Did you say anything to him?

JUN: I asked whether he wanted me to open the beer for him, and he nodded.

WEI: Nothing else?

JUN: Nothing—oh, he did pick up a slice of Jinhua ham as soon as I placed the dishes on the table. He said that it was his favorite, and that he would like some more in the next day or two. It's genuine Jinhua ham that the hotel gets through a special supply channel. A lot of our guests really like it.

WEI: A different question, Jun. You went from picking up the noodles from the kitchen directly to his room?

JUN: Yes, directly to his room. The soup had to be served hot.

WEI: Anything else? Anything that struck you as unusual?

JUN: Nothing I can recall. Once he started to put the toppings into the soup, I left the room. Sorry, but that's about all I can tell you.

"Not much," Wei said and pressed the stop button. "Jiang must have talked to the hotel people earlier, but he doesn't want me to approach any of them without his prior approval. As a result, I had to talk to Jun in a small teahouse on a side street not far from the hotel. At the same time, Jiang keeps asking me to update him on our progress."

"It's a game two can play, Wei." Chen said, "From now on, you don't have to tell Jiang anything unless he is cooperative. Jiang and Liu were in charge of shuanggui, and we are in charge of the investigation into Zhou's death. So it's up to them to tell us what they know about Zhou."

"Liu has hardly been to the hotel in the last two days. But Jiang is the representative of the city government."

"If Jiang makes things difficult for you, you may say I told you to report only to me. Tell him it was my special instruction."

"Thank you, Chief," Wei said, looking him in the eye. "When you were first promoted, some of us believed that it was because of your educational background, that it was simply a lucky break coinciding with the Party's new cadre promotion policy. Some also said it was because of that article in *Wenhui Daily* written by your journalist friend—"

Chen gestured to stop Wei from going on. It was true that he had been promoted for a number of reasons not relevant to police work, such as his education and the image he presented to the public, both of which happened to serve the propaganda needs of the Party.

"Lots of things could have been said about me, and some of them were true. For instance, my degree in English had nothing to do with my job with the police bureau. Even today, I still can't help wondering if I should have pursued a different career. I know it might not be fair for others in the bureau."

"All I want to say is that I'm glad to work under you, Chief. I'll consult you about every move I make."

"Remember," Chen said, "you're in charge of the investigation, not I. Whatever move you decide to make, you don't have to consult me first. You know that proverb; 'A general fighting at the borders doesn't have to listen to the emperor sitting far, far away in the capital.'"

"So you mean—"

"You have a free hand. If anything happens, I'll take responsibility—"

Chen was interrupted by his ringing cell phone.

"Hi, Chief Inspector Chen. It's Lianping, the journalist from *Wenhui Daily*. Do you remember me? I've just read something about you."

"Of course I remember you. What's the news, Lianping?"

"Let me read it to you. 'According to Chief Inspector Chen, so far there's no evidence whatsoever to suggest that Zhou's death could be anything other than suicide.'"

"That's absurd," he said. "Who gave that irresponsible statement to *Wenhui Daily*?"

"Jiang, of the city government."

"The investigation hasn't been concluded. That's all I can say to you today."

"Jiang's statement is vague about that, but it reads as if you have already concluded your investigation."

"That's wrong, but thank you so much for calling me, Lianping. We're still following possible leads. I'll let you know as soon as we do conclude our investigation."

"Thank you so much, Chief Inspector Chen. Please don't forget the poems you promised me for our newspaper. I'm a huge fan of your work."

The statement released by Jiang wasn't exactly a surprise to Chen. On the contrary, it was more or less what he had anticipated.

Next to him, Detective Wei was standing up, a grin on his face. "I have to go back to work, Chief Inspector Chen," Wei said.

Chen was known among his colleagues as a romantic poet and for having had an affair with a *Wenhui* journalist. Wei might have overheard that the caller was from *Wenhui* and guessed it was that female journalist calling.

But Chen had said what he wanted to say to the journalist. He began thinking about their conversation at the Writers' Association, and what lines she reminded him of that day, as she came tripping over from the garden path, a blue jay's wing flashing in the light.

EIGHT

AFTER WEI LEFT, CHEN stayed at the café. The chief inspector had to sort through all the bits and pieces of information he had just learned.

He ordered another cup of coffee, which tasted better than expected. The soft sofa seat was comfortable, its tall back providing a sense of privacy, and the window commanded an ever-changing view of the pedestrians out on the street.

Chen sat and stirred the coffee with a small spoon.

Something in the interview of the hotel attendant fluttered across his mind, but the hunch was an elusive one. It was gone like a rice paddy eel before he could grasp it. He knew that Detective Wei might not have told him everything—not directly, at least. If so, it was understandable. High-ranking officials could be involved, lurking in the background, and that would be too much for an ordinary cop like Wei. Especially since he didn't have any solid evidence or leads at present. But Chen thought he understood what Wei was driving at.

Chen took a small, measured sip of the coffee and mentally reviewed some of the details Wei had mentioned. For one, if a man talked about eating Jinhua ham again in a couple of days, it was hard to conceive of his committing suicide an hour or two later.

The photo that started it all was another puzzle. Could Zhou have taken it himself? If so, he was truly hoist with his own petard.

Detective Wei was determined to move the investigation in a direction that Jiang wouldn't like. Of that, Chen had no doubts. As Wei's colleague and consultant to the investigation, Chen was supposed to back him up.

Still, he was in no hurry to confront Jiang.

If the authorities were really anxious to close the case, they could do so with or without Chen's "endorsement," let alone Wei's opinion of their conclusions. A Party member must, first and foremost, act in the interests of the Party, and Chen had to speak or shut up accordingly. But in spite of the statement that had been given to the media, Jiang was still staying at the hotel, allowing the cops to continue investigating, and constantly checking in with them. There was no point in going to the hotel, Chen concluded. If anything, it would be better to try and maneuver around it.

On his way out of the café, Chen bought a hundred-yuan gift card, which he thought he would give Detective Wei for his son.

Near He'nan Road, Chen slowed down at the sight of a towering building still partially covered in scaffolding. Already, several top brands had their logos displayed proudly at the construction site, with a billboard declaring, "Open for business soon." It was going to be another high-end department store.

For some reason, there weren't any workers there that afternoon, nor were there machines hustling and bustling around.

Standing by the construction site, Chen pulled out his phone and called Mr. Gu, the chairman of the New World Group. It wasn't a long talk, but it was long enough to confirm what Wei had told him regarding Teng Jialiang, chairman of the Green Earth Group.

At the end of the conversation, Chen accidentally pressed the wrong button on the phone, which brought up the message function. He thought about writing a text—to himself—detailing the possible clues before he forgot them, but it was awkward to walk and write at the same time. So he looked up and walked over to the Eastern Sea Café, which was a little farther east. In his experience, writing down the random thoughts that passed through his mind sometimes helped him straighten out his thinking.

Eastern Sea Café, a survivor from the days of the Cultural Revolution, looked shabby, overshadowed by the new buildings that surrounded it. There he sat down and had his third cup of coffee of the afternoon while he composed a text to himself.

Teng had reason to hate Zhou, possibly enough reason for Teng to retaliate. While Teng might not have been at the meeting, people from his company were there and could have seen the pack of cigarettes. So the Internet frenzy started by the photo of the pack of 95 Supreme Majesty could well have been Teng's revenge.

But what about after the downfall of Zhou?

The chief inspector didn't think that after Zhou was disgraced, there was any motive—or, at least, not enough for Teng to murder Zhou at the well-guarded hotel. It was technically possible, since Teng was connected to the triads. If Teng really wanted to get rid of Zhou, however, it would've been easier before Zhou was shuangguied.

Chen saved the text, finished the coffee, and dialed the number for Jiang as he walked out of the café.

Chen managed to convey the simple message that it was too early to draw any conclusions regarding Zhou's death. He didn't say anything specific about the news in *Wenhui Daily* and Jiang knew better than to talk about it. Chen did not say much else, except to make sure that Jiang would remain at the hotel for the day.

Chen cut across to Jiujiang Road, where he hailed a taxi at the back of the Amanda Hotel. About five minutes later, he arrived at the office of the Housing Development Committee, which was in the Shanghai City Government Building near People's Square. He didn't have to take a cab for such a short distance, but a man walking up to the City Government Building might be taken by the security guards as another troublesome "complainer."

He got past security and headed straight to the office of Deputy Director Dang of the Housing Development Committee.

On Detective Wei's list of possible benefiters, Dang was at the top. Dang was also at the fateful meeting, seated next to Zhou at the rostrum, capable of seeing the cigarettes at close range. It was a common scenario in Party power struggles: the number two succeeded the number one after the latter fell from grace.

So Dang had motive, but he also had an alibi: Dang had been at a hotel in the county of Qingpu for a business meeting, where he then spent the night, at least according to the hotel register. Still, Qingpu was not far—he could have sneaked out after dark, if he'd known which hotel Zhou was in, or he could have hired a professional.

Passing Zhou's office, which was still locked with an official seal, Chen came to Dang's, which was right next door.

Dang was a tall, robust man in his early forties with beady eyes, bushy brows, and a ruddy complexion. He greeted Chen affably, then, after an exchange of a few polite words, came to the point.

"You're not an outsider, Comrade Chief Inspector Chen, so I won't give you the official response. Zhou meant well. It's easy for people to complain about the housing bubble, but once the bubble bursts, the economy will collapse. So when Zhou saw signs of instability in the market, he tried to forestall them. Unfortunately, he underestimated the pent-up frustrations of those who couldn't afford housing. In a pack of cigarettes, they found a convenient outlet for their anger. We certainly can't rule out the possibility that some people used this as an opportunity to smear our Party's image."

"Yes, we are looking into all the possibilities," Chen responded, almost mechanically.

"I don't know about Zhou's other problems under shuanggui investigation. If all that was exposed on the Internet was real, then it served him right. In the office, Zhou alone had the final say, making most decisions without discussing them with any of us," Dang said casually, picking up Chen's card. "Oh, you're deputy Party secretary. Then you know how things can be. A lot happens in the office without my knowledge. As far as the pack of 95 Supreme Majesty is concerned, however, that was just Zhou's luck. You'll have to find the root of the trouble, Chief Inspector Chen. It wasn't anything directed against Zhou personally, but against the Party instead. We can't allow those people on the Internet to go rampaging like that anymore."

Chen nodded. Such a demand from Dang made sense. The Internet couldn't go on uncontrolled like that: the next target could be Dang.

"Now, I have a question about the actual photo, Dang. Do you have any idea who took it?"

"Jiang asked me the same question," Dang responded with a sigh. "During the meeting, several of us were sitting with Zhou next to the podium. It would have been out of the question for any one of us to disturb the meeting by taking pictures. There were many other people sitting in the conference hall who could have taken photos, though. So the short answer is that we don't know. We do know, however, that Zhou himself e-mailed the picture to his secretary, Fang, who wrote the press release and sent it with the picture. It's possible that Zhou had someone taking the pictures with his own camera, and then downloaded them onto his own computer. If it had been e-mailed to Zhou from somebody else, Jiang would have discovered the sender when they searched his computer."

Chen nodded, noting the subtle subject change from "I" to "we" in Dang's explanation, without making any comment. Still, Dang had basically confirmed Wei's account.

"Needless to say, none of us here had access to his computer before the scandal broke," Dang went on. "Then Jiang's team took it away, along with all the CDs and disks in his office."

"Is it possible that Zhou had several e-mail accounts, some of them unknown? Or perhaps he deleted some e-mails or files?"

"That's possible, but I don't see how. Jiang's people wouldn't have discovered that. They are computer experts. If Zhou had received the picture from somebody else, they would have ferreted that out one way or another."

"So his secretary sent the text out to the media along with the picture per his instruction."

"That's correct," Dang said, then added, "as far as I know."

"Is that a rule—that all press releases and attachments have to be approved by this office?"

"Anything about the housing market can be extremely sensitive. A careless remark from someone in our office can cause panic among the sellers and buyers. That's why a rule was instituted: for an important speech like Zhou's, Zhou himself would review the text, and sometimes the pictures as well, before his secretary sent them out to the media."

"Can I talk to her—the secretary, I mean?"

"Fang's not in today. She called in sick early this morning. Jiang talked to her, though, and she told him that she merely sent out the things Zhou gave her, and only under his specific instruction. She's just a little secretary."

"A little secretary," Chen repeated reflectively. The term could mean a mistress—usually much younger—serving under the guise of being a secretary. There was nothing about that in Wei's folder. Chen didn't push. Dang didn't elaborate. Still, Chen asked for her name, address, and phone number before he took leave of Dang.

Back out in the People's Square, Chen saw a group of elderly people exercising to loud music blaring from a CD player. It was a song that was familiar to him, played often during the Cultural Revolution. "Generation after generation, we will always remember the great deeds Chairman Mao has done for us."

It was one of the rediscovered "red songs," popular again because of the dramatic change in the political environment. But for these people, it was perhaps just a melody they could energetically dance to.

Chen hailed a taxi back to his own office, feeling exhausted.

NINE

IT WASN'T UNTIL FIVE past nine that evening that Chen got back home.

The hours spent in front of his office computer had yielded little. He was worn-out, and his muscles were sore, as at the beginning stages of the flu. He rubbed his eyes, yet felt far from sleepy.

He opened his notebook to the page he'd been working on, which had a list of details, like a jumble of dots awaiting connection to point in possible directions. But he couldn't see how to connect those dots.

Chen hadn't learned anything new from the interview with Dang that afternoon, though it was possible that Dang was involved in some way that no one was aware of.

What puzzled Chen wasn't the fact that Zhou himself gave the picture to his secretary for the press release but rather who had taken the picture and how Zhou had obtained it.

There was no record of anyone sending him the picture after the meeting. Jiang had checked Zhou's computer, as Dang had just confirmed.

Zhou might have downloaded the picture from a camera, his or somebody else's. Apparently nothing found on his camera either confirmed that possibility or ruled it out.

A more plausible scenario was that the picture came from a camera that belonged to somebody else. But if so, who could have put it onto Zhou's computer—or given Zhou a camera or something else for Zhou to save the picture on the computer himself?

The people in the Housing Development Committee. Dang in the office next door, and others on the same committee. Possibly the secretary, or the "little secretary" too.

Chen glanced at his watch, felt the beginnings of a throbbing headache in addition to the muscle pain, and dialed Wei's number.

"I've thought about that, Chief," Wei responded readily, "I've talked to the secretary—her full name is Fang Fang. I've also done some research on her."

Wei then launched into a detailed narrative about Fang, checking his notes from time to time. Listening, Chen could also hear the occasional rustle of Wei turning pages.

"Fang started working for Zhou about two years ago. Quite different from the conventional little secretary, she's middle-aged, already in her early thirties, and a bit too thin to be really considered attractive. An official of Zhou's rank could easily have hired one prettier and younger. There were stories around the office that Zhou went out of his way to give the position to her. It was considered a fantastic position, secure and well paid, not to mention all of the possible gray money, and more than a hundred candidates applied. Zhou, giving his reasons for choosing her, said he hired her because Fang studied in England for three years, majored in communication, and spoke English well, which would be important in her work for the city of Shanghai, a major international city. Fang was very grateful for the position, having failed to find a job in England after she graduated and having remained unemployed for more than a year after she came back to Shanghai. At the Housing Development

Committee, she was soon promoted to the position of director's assistant, responsible for all the clerical work, including the press releases. On that particular occasion, Zhou reviewed the material before turning it over to her. She declared that she didn't pay any special attention to either the text or the attached picture. It was merely part of her daily routine, and the photo didn't stand out. After all, Zhou smoked that particular brand most of the time. As for the other corruption charges, she didn't know anything. Zhou never really discussed those deals or decisions with her. So far, Jiang and his team don't consider her a likely suspect, but they seem to have put a lot of pressure on her to speak out against Zhou.

"As for that Monday night, Fang was at home with her parents. They had a relative from Anhui visiting, so her alibi's solid," Wei concluded after checking his notes again. "Now she's really worried about her job. It's only a matter of time before she gets sacked. Dang will definitely not keep her in such a crucial position."

It was a long conversation. Chen wiped the sweat off his forehead with the back of his hand. Detective Wei had done a good, thorough job, and like Jiang, he didn't see Fang as a likely suspect. She had no motive.

Chen wondered whether it would be worthwhile for him to interview Fang. What the *Wenhui* journalist had said earlier in the day came back to him, echoing ironically in his mind as he sat in the solitary stillness of his room: *There's no evidence whatsoever to suggest that Zhou's death could be anything other than suicide.*

It was supposed to be a direct quote from Chief Inspector Chen, who hadn't said anything close to that. Still, it didn't appear to be that far from the truth. At least, not at the moment.

He got up to pour himself a small cup of whiskey, from a bottle he had brought back from the United States as a souvenir. He hoped that it would somehow reenergize him a bit, but he wasn't a drinker. He took just one small sip and began coughing almost uncontrollably.

Another wasted day. He realized, looking back, that Lianping's mention of poetry in her phone call was perhaps the only bright spot in a dismal day. That, however, was a fleeting moment: most of the conversation had been about his "statement" about the investigation.

He felt fatigued. A couplet by Du Fu came to mind: *My temples frost-streaked through adversities, / Too worn out even to drink from the shoddy wine cup.*

In his college years, Chen hadn't liked Du Fu, who seemed to be too much of a Confucianist poet, telling rather showing, too serious and always worrying about the woes of the country in grandiose lines.

Time really flies. How long had it been since Chen started working as a policeman after graduation? At first, however reluctant to be a cop, he was still idealistic. What about now? Perhaps existentialist at best, like a mythological figure in an ever-repeating process of rolling a boulder uphill, only to watch it roll down. His reveries were interrupted by another call, this one from Detective Yu, who never hesitated to phone, despite the late hour.

"Look out, Chief. Internal Security has come into the picture."

"The ones who police the police. Why are they now involved?"

"Well, you would know better than me."

The fact was that Chen didn't know, having been away from the bureau for most of the afternoon. Still, the appearance of Internal Security meant things had become too sensitive for the police bureau, or too sinister.

Or Internal Security had been brought in to watch over the cops.

Whatever interpretation was correct, it was an ominous sign.

And he felt really sick.

TEN

HIS MIND IN TURMOIL, Chen sat hunched in the bureau car, sweating profusely, making one phone call after another.

He had been sick all weekend and the following Monday, lying miserable and alone in bed most of the time, with the phone shut off.

Then Tuesday started with the news that Detective Wei had died the previous day in a traffic accident.

The chief inspector had no choice but to take a handful of aspirin, put a small packet of them in his pants pocket, and hurry out.

The bureau driver, Skinny Wang, a self-proclaimed fan of the chief inspector, invariably mixed up the real-life man with the one in his imagination, the result of having devoured many mystery novels. Wang had heard of the death of Detective Wei, and with one hand on the wheel, he was having a hard time restraining himself from asking Chen questions.

According to the report from Ruijin Hospital, Wei had been rushed to the emergency room as an unidentified victim of a traffic accident on the corner of Weihai and Shanxi Roads. He wasn't carrying any ID on him or wearing his uniform. He died there shortly afterward. It wasn't until after some traffic cops arrived the following morning that one of them noticed among his possessions a tie pin given by the police bureau. The officer believed he saw some resemblance between the corpse and Detective Wei and started making phone calls.

Wei's wife had called the bureau about his not returning home the previous night approximately fifteen minutes before the homicide squad heard from the traffic cop.

According to Wei's wife, Wei had left home the previous morning at eight a.m., wearing a beige jacket, a white shirt with a tie, and dress pants—which was too formal for a detective on duty. Still, he would occasionally go out of his way to dress well if an investigation called for it.

"It wasn't an accident," Wang managed to interject the moment Chen put down the phone. "Not in the very middle of his investigation."

"Traffic is terrible and the city is teeming with reckless drivers. There are so many accidents every day. Don't jump to any conclusions."

"That's true. Still—"

But Chen was already dialing Liao, the head of the homicide squad.

"I have no idea what he was up to that morning," Liao said. "We discussed the case just the day before. He was inclined to believe it was murder, as you know, but he had nothing substantial to support it. So he could have been planning to push on in that direction."

"That's possible," Chen said, thinking of Wei's attire that day. Wei could have planned another visit to the hotel, this time in disguise. "I think you might be right, Liao. And I'll discuss it again with you soon."

As the car turned onto Shanxi Road, Wang started in again. "I heard something about the hotel. Yesterday, when I was driving Party Secretary Li, he got a phone call from someone above him."

"How do you know?"

"Li has two phones. One white, one black. The first one he seldom uses, except for important or inside calls. Few know the number, I bet."

"That's probably true. I know of only one number."

"I can tell from the immediate change in his tone when he picks up the white phone. To someone with a higher Party position, Li can be so obsequious. I'm afraid that's why you are still only the deputy Party secretary, Chief Inspector Chen."

"In that conversation, Li mentioned the hotel several times and also something about a Beijing team coming there, which I pieced together from his repetition of the other man's words. Also, Zhou's name came up in the middle of it. Li spoke cautiously and most of his responses were simply 'yes.' It was difficult for me to follow without knowing the context. Toward the end of the conversation Li said, 'I understand. I'll report to you and to you alone.'"

Earlier that morning, after he had been given the news about Wei, Chen had been told about a team from the Central Party Discipline Committee in Beijing. Nobody had contacted Chen about it in advance, and he wasn't even in a position to inquire into it. Was the arrival of the team connected to the Zhou case?

"Drop me off at the corner near the Writers' Association," Chen said, having an abrupt change of mind. "You may go back to the bureau. I don't know how long I'll be here."

"No problem. I can wait. You can just call me whenever you need me."

"I think I'll take a taxi from here. Don't worry about me. But if you hear anything new, let me know."

"Of course, Chief Inspector Chen."

Chen got out and walked to the association.

Young Bao, the doorman in the cubicle near the entrance, poked his head out and greeted Chen cordially.

"I have some fresh Maojian tea today, Master Chen. Would you like to have a cup?"

Chen had no particular business at the association that morning, and he liked a cup of good, refreshing tea. Chen's visit was merely a pretext, a way to keep Wang from knowing what he was really planning to do. The bureau driver could be very talkative.

"Thanks." Chen said, stepping into the cubicle. "But don't call me Master Chen. I've told you that before."

"My father told me you're a master. He's never wrong."

Young Bao handed him a cup. Chen savored the unique fragrance rising from the green tea.

"It's not too busy here?"

"No, not busy at all. In less than a month I knew all the people working here. Of course, they don't have to sign the register when they arrive. Most of the members who come here from time to time know the rules, and they sign the register without my having to ask them."

Chen nodded, taking another sip of tea.

"In Old Bao's days, he said it was quite busy. There were a lot of visitors, especially young visitors—the so-called literature youths. Nowadays it would be idiotic for people to call themselves literature youths."

"That's true, unfortunately."

"So I sit here all day, with not much to do. You can see that from the register. Less than ten pages have been used this month."

At the Writers' Association, Chen reflected, there wasn't much for security to do, but for a time-honored government institution, the presence of Young Bao and the register was still indispensable.

"The other day I was at the Moller Hotel," Chen said, "and the doorman was busy all the time."

"That's a special hotel. Weiming, the doorman there, is a friend of mine. His register is at least three or four times thicker than mine," Young Bao said, chewing a tea leaf reflectively. "But I have nothing to complain about, Master Chen. Among all the doormen in the city, I'm probably the only one who can read during work without worrying about the consequences. In fact, both An and you have encouraged me to read as much as possible. After all, it is the Writers' Association, and it has a library of its own. "

"I'm glad to learn that you enjoy reading so much."

"Weiming, the Moller doorman I just told you about, is another bookworm. He comes to me for books—it's much more convenient than going to the public library—and in return, he sells me canteen coupons for the hotel. The food there is excellent but still inexpensive due to the government subsidy and the high-ranking cadres who stay there."

Chen didn't immediately respond, being reminded of a metaphor: China was turning into a huge cobweb of omnipresent correlations, with every thread connected and interconnected, however thin or insubstantial, visible or invisible.

"Guess what I've been reading lately. Detective stories. Some of them were translated by you. That's another reason I have to call you a master. Not just because of your literary work, but also because of your police work."

"I have to cut my visit short, Young Bao. The tea is really excellent," Chen said, draining the cup, "but I have to go now."

"I'm glad you like it. I'll keep the tea here for you—it'll be here anytime you come over."

Chen walked back to Shanxi Road. He remained depressed, in spite of the refreshing tea, but he no longer felt so exhausted. He headed straight to the hotel, though not without looking over his shoulder a couple of times.

A flower girl standing by the street corner greeted him with an engaging smile.

"Buy a bouquet, sir?" She spoke in a non-Shanghai dialect, a basket of dazzling white jasmine flowers at her feet.

Thinking of Wei, he paid for a budding jasmine blossom as small as a button decoration and put it in his blazer pocket.

Yesterday, Wei could have been on his way to the hotel, turning the same corner, with, or without, the flower girl standing here with her basket.

The scenario of Wei going to the hotel would account for his formal dress that morning. He would have been going on his own, trying to make sure no one recognized him as a cop. Wei would have had to be cautious, since the city team was still stationed there.

Now there were people from the Central Party Discipline Committee from Beijing involved as well, and they were probably not coming just for someone like Zhou. Beijing wouldn't send a team just for him. Chen had to be more cautious.

Still, he thought he would try not to worry about the Beijing team too much: its work would be considered none of his business, and Chief Inspector Chen had enough on his hands.

He slowed down, strolling at a leisurely pace, like a tourist, and pulled out his cell phone. Chen called a retired cop nicknamed Encyclopedia.

Filling him in briefly, Chen asked, "Why have all these people chosen the Moller Hotel? Can you tell me something about the history of the hotel?"

"Oh, it used to be Moller Villa. After 1949, it was turned into offices of the Shanghai Communist Youth League. It operated both under the city government and under the Central Communist Youth League in Beijing. Quite a few of today's high-ranking leaders in the Forbidden City started out in the Youth League, which makes them a most powerful faction in the Party power structure."

"Thank you so much, Mr. Encyclopedia," Chen said. He said his good-byes and hung up.

It occurred to Chen that the current Central Party general secretary had also been a cadre from the Communist Youth League. He and his closest allies were sometimes called the Youth League Gang. There was also a Shanghai Gang, as it was sometimes called, consisting of cadres who rose to the top through the city government. That group was headed by the Shanghai Party boss, Qiangyu, and it was said the Shanghai Gang stood in opposition to Beijing's Youth League Gang.

The arrival of the Beijing Central Party Discipline Committee team in Shanghai, and at this particular hotel, could be a sign of an intensifying power struggle at the top. Chen couldn't tell whether or not it was in any way connected to the Zhou case.

Actually, that struggle might have been another factor in Chen's not being promoted to Party secretary of the Shanghai police bureau. Chen was rumored to be closely connected to major figures in Beijing, such as Comrade Zhao, the ex-secretary of the Central Party Discipline Committee, even though Chen himself knew that it wasn't true. For one thing, Comrade Zhao had not contacted him in quite a while. For another, no message had been sent to Chen about the Beijing team being dispatched to Shanghai.

The chief inspector decided to take a few extra precautions on this visit to the hotel. Instead of going to Jiang's room in building B of the hotel, Chen approached the hotel front desk. He didn't have to sign a register to do that.

"Sorry, but there's a special meeting going on at the hotel," the desk clerk said as Chen walked in. "It is no longer open to tourists."

"What a pity! I've heard so much about this legendary hotel," Chen said. He picked up a brochure, adding, as if an afterthought, "But what about the people already staying here?"

"They will have to move out, and as soon as possible."

So there was something going on here. Perhaps there wouldn't be an exception made for Jiang, and he too would have to leave the hotel, but Chen wasn't sure.

Walking out of the hotel like a disappointed tourist, Chen looked around before he crossed the street and went to a new restaurant. The restaurant was called Northeast Family, and it sported a row of red lanterns in front of its rustic façade. He walked in, and then went up to the second floor, where he was surprised to see several kangs—or table-and-seat units shaped like kangs—by the windows overlooking Shanxi Road. He went over to one out of curiosity.

A waiter hurried to his side, saying apologetically, "Sorry, this is a table for six people."

Sitting at this table, however, Chen could easily keep the hotel in sight.

"What's the minimum charge to sit here?" Chen asked.

At some restaurants, a private room had a minimum charge attached: it was possible this restaurant had a minimum for desirable tables.

"Usually, we charge six hundred. Our northeast cuisine is not expensive, so you can have a banquet for that. One person alone wouldn't be able to finish that much." The waiter paused. "Well, let's make an exception for you and waive the minimum expense, sir," he said considerately. "We have eating girls here. For just one hundred yuan she'll sit at your table and introduce you to the specialties of our cuisine."

"Fine. I'll pay for her company, but I want to sit by myself for a while first. "

"Whatever you want, sir. I'll brew you a pot of Dragon Well tea first."

He secured the table against the window. It wasn't that comfortable to sit on the kang. A real kang was a long earthen bed with coals burning underneath, the people sitting above with their legs comfortably crossed under them, and with a small table in the middle during mealtime. Here he saw only a resemblance of one, but he took off his shoes, climbed on, and started keeping watch on the hotel.

Across the street, the hotel shimmered in the sunlight. It didn't take long for him to realize that the hotel looked different that morning. For about fifteen minutes, he didn't see anybody walking in or out. There were only a couple of luxury cars that drove in, their curtains drawn, and not a single taxi. The hotel must have been converted into a "political base."

A young eating girl came over, dressed not unlike someone from the northeast, and managed to speak with only a slight suggestion of a northeast accent.

"Shark fin is a specialty of our restaurant, sir."

"Shark fin is advertised as the special in every restaurant. I don't have to order it here, but I'll have the rest of the specials on the menu."

"You certainly know how to order," she said in agreement. She perched herself on the edge of the kang and kicked off her slippers. He wondered whether she would sit with him like that through the entire meal, as if they were in some movie scene of a couple in the northeast countryside.

"Thank you," he said, taking out a ten-yuan bill. "Here's a small tip for you, but I want to sit by myself for the moment."

"Whatever you like, Big Brother," she said, standing up, clutching the bill. "Whenever you need anything, just call me. We have all sorts of service available. And service for you afterward in a private room too."

"I'll let you know."

Soon the dishes he'd ordered arrived on the kang table. Northeast cuisine, known for its homely style, was not considered one of the major cuisines in China. He helped himself to a piece of pan-fried tofu, took a sip of tea, and took out a notebook.

Chen started drawing up a timetable in his notebook of the events surrounding Wei's accident the previous day. One probable scenario was that Wei—dressed like a tourist—was going to check into the hotel, incognito, in the hope of learning something that had eluded him in his official capacity. But was the hotel already closed that day due to the arrival of the mysterious Beijing team?

79

Whether the hotel was closed or not, Wei, leaving home around eight that morning, should have been somewhere near this location around nine. He made his way to the scene of the accident three or four hours later, though it was no more than a five-minute walk from the hotel. So, where had Wei been during the interval?

Wei could have sat here by the window, just as Chen was doing today, keeping an eye on the hotel. It was eerie to imagine—to imagine himself turning into Wei—

"Big Brother, the dishes are getting cold," the eating girl said, returning to the table.

It was true. He hadn't even touched some of them. He wondered how long he'd been sitting here, lost in thought.

"They are quite good, but I've somehow lost my appetite," he said apologetically. He pointed at several dishes. "Sorry, these are not even touched."

"Don't worry. I was supposed to eat with you, and now I'll have to finish it all by myself."

He asked for the bill, which came to a little more than three hundred, including the fee for her. She added her name and number to the receipt.

"Next time, call me directly."

On his way out, he looked at his watch. It was almost twelve thirty.

It wasn't pleasant to climb the steel steps of the overpass, but he did. He'd hardly done anything all day, yet he couldn't shake off a feeling that he was burning up. He wiped his sweat-covered forehead with the back of his hand. Passing under him, the traffic flowed like a turgid river.

It reminded him of a stone bridge he'd crossed long ago, the fallen leaves crunching under his feet, the water murmuring under the arch . . . It was an elusive scene in his memory, flashing into his consciousness for a split second, and then fading into confusion.

He labored down to the other side of Yan'an Road. A high-rise loomed in the afternoon sunlight—the Wenhui Office Building on Weihai Road. It housed not only the *Wenhui Daily* newspaper but also the *Xinmin* evening newspaper and *Shanghai Daily,* an English-language newspaper, along with several smaller newspapers, all under the umbrella organization of the Wenhui-Xinmin Group, or Wenxin Group, for short.

The scene of the accident was near the intersection of Shanxi and Weihai Roads. Because of the constant flow of traffic at that location, there was no yellow tape cordoning off the area. Nor was there any sign of a policeman on duty.

Chen decided to take a walk around the area first. As if in mysterious correspondence, his cell phone rang: the traffic cop who had dealt with the accident was calling him back.

"Detective Wei was run down on Weihai Road as he turned in from Shanxi Road, heading east. Several witnesses claimed that's what they saw. There's no ruling out the possibility that he had walked past the Wenhui Office Building first and then was turning back, but it's not likely. As for the vehicle that hit him, it was a brown SUV that was parked one block down on Weihai Road. Apparently it started up suddenly, sped west, hit him, and took off. It happened so fast that nobody saw anything clearly. According to one witness, the SUV seemed to slow down after hitting Wei, but only for a second, then it sped away and turned onto Shanxi Road. The driver might have slowed to take a look, but must have realized it was too late."

"The SUV hit him head-on?" Chen asked.

"Yes. At a high speed."

"But that means the SUV was in the wrong lane."

"Drunk driving, Chief Inspector Chen. Luckily, it wasn't right after school had let out, or it could have been much worse."

"Thank you. Would you fax a report to my office? Provide as many details as possible. I'll be back there soon."

For the next half an hour, however, Chen continued to walk back and forth along Weihai Road, his phone clutched in his hand. There was something not right about the accident.

Weihai was a two-lane street. A westbound car wouldn't have ended up in the lane alongside the Wenhui Building, unless the driver was drunk or someone's car spun out of control during a too-swift left turn. Chen thought the chances of such a dramatic, disastrous turn of events were slim.

Once again, he walked past the Wenhui Office Building, this time catching sight of a makeshift noodle stall on the sidewalk. The stall consisted of two pots of boiling water and soup on portable propane gas heads, along with a variety of meat and vegetable toppings on display in a glass case. The chef-proprietor appeared to be a local resident, cooking and hawking his wares with a flourish as if he was in a Hong Kong gourmet documentary. He dipped a ladle of noodles into the water, took it out almost immediately, and added the topping.

Chen went over to the stall and sat at a rough wood table. He noticed there were two or three beers in an almost empty crate nearby.

"A bottle of beer, the roast duck as a cross-bridge dish first, and then the noodles."

"We don't serve beer at lunchtime. Those are for myself. But if you really want one, twenty yuan. It's normally served Hong Kong style, but I'll make an exception for you and serve the topping separately."

"That's great. That you serve cross-bridge, I mean," Chen said.

"Do you know the story about it?" the proprietor asked good-naturedly and went on without waiting for an answer. "In the old days, a scholar was preparing for the civil service examination on a secluded island in Yunnan. His capable wife had to carry his meals across the bridge to him. Among his favorite foods was a bowl of rice noodle soup with assorted toppings. But because of the time it took to deliver them, the noodles lost their flavor, having sat too long in the soup. So she put the steaming hot chicken soup in a special container, the toppings and noodles in two others, and then mixed them after arriving at her husband's place. That way, the noodles and the toppings still tasted fresh. Revitalized by the delicious noodles, the scholar threw himself back into his preparations and eventually passed the examination. So it's called cross-bridge—"

"How interesting!" Chen nodded, though he already knew the story.

"And here is my modification. Instead of putting the toppings on the noodles, I serve them separately, so the customer can have the topping as a cross-bridge dish."

"Good idea," Chen said, producing a pack and handing the chef a cigarette.

"Wow—Panda."

Chen wanted to talk with him or, failing that, to sit and observe from the stall. A bowl of noodles wouldn't give him much time, but a bottle of beer could make the difference.

"So business is pretty good here," Chen said, slowly pouring himself a cup from the beer bottle.

"Not at this time of day. But during lunchtime, quite a number of journalists come here from across the street. Or in a couple of hours, it's kindergarten time. It's not the rich parents who wait in the cars for their kids, but drivers and maids."

"I see. The roast duck is really fresh and nice. I'd love to have another portion, but I'm full today." The compliment was true. The duck tasted delectable, its succulent skin crisp, its meat juicy. It wasn't placed on top of the noodles but in a separate white saucer, its scarlet color making a pleasant contrast to the green vegetable in the soup. "So, are you here all day?"

"Seven in the morning to eight or nine at night. I live in the lane just behind this street. My wife prepares all the toppings at home and delivers them here every two or three hours. They are guaranteed fresh. Those young journalist girls can be fastidious, and they won't come back if they're even slightly unsatisfied."

Chen noticed that several people were now walking around the scene of the accident near that intersection, pointing, commenting, and shooting pictures. They could be journalists, or maybe cops in plainclothes. Chen turned to the proprietor.

"What are they doing over there?"

"There was a hit-and-run accident yesterday."

"There?"

"Yes, I saw it with my own eyes."

"That's something. Tell me about it. And another bottle of Qingdao, please."

The proprietor eyed him in mild surprise. Presumably he thought Chen was one of those eccentric Big Bucks who would choose to hang out and talk at a plain sidewalk noodle stall, passing out Panda cigarettes, willing to pay twenty yuan for a bottle of Qingdao, which he promptly knocked open on the edge of the table.

"It happened shortly after lunchtime, I remember. The street was relatively quiet. But all of a sudden, I heard a car roaring down the street. It was a brown SUV, and it hit the man right on the corner—"

"Hold on a minute," Chen said. "The man was walking on the same side as the Wenhui Office Building, right?"

"Yes, it's the driver's fault. He must have been dead drunk."

"Didn't he stop?"

"He slowed down and reached out, but he saw the victim was beyond hope. So he fled the scene like a wisp of smoke."

"So the driver can't have been that drunk."

"Now that you mention it, there was something strange about it. The brown car was parked not too far away. No more than a hundred meters or so. It was the only car in the neighborhood at the time, of that much I'm sure. I don't know how long it had been parked there, but at least a couple of hours. I first noticed it when I took a break around ten thirty. It was an expensive SUV, and the driver appeared to be dozing inside. So how could he be that dead drunk after dozing there for a couple of hours?"

A group of young people walked up and interrupted their talk.

Chen took out his wallet and counted sixty yuan. "Keep the change. I'll be back. The noodles are excellent."

"My name is Xiahou. I'm here, seven days a week."

"Thanks."

As Chen headed back to the corner where the accident occurred, he dialed the number for Party Secretary Li. He didn't have to report in to the Party boss daily, but he decided to do so that afternoon.

"Any new discoveries, Chen?" Li asked, after he picked up.

"Nothing from me. How about Wei?" he said. "Did Wei talk to you yesterday?"

"He may have called me that day or the day before, but he didn't have anything important to say. Wei was a good comrade."

"Did he talk to you about taking a special approach to his investigation?"

"Not that I remember. It was just a routine briefing."

"Did he mention his plans for the day?"

"No, nothing like that. He was just bringing me up to date. You're the special consultant on the investigation, not me."

Li sounded vague, cautious, and irritated.

"This case is directly under your supervision, Party Secretary Li, just as you said that first day. Like Detective Wei, I have to report in to you regularly."

Another thought crossed Chen's mind. If Wei had called Li that morning, Wei must have had his cell phone with him. But in the report submitted by the hospital, there was nothing on Wei's body to identify him. If they had found his cell on him, they could have identified him easily.

Was Wei making a call when he was run down? Was his cell phone knocked out of his hand and out of sight?

There was something else Chen had to do. He took a deep breath, then pulled the tiny jasmine blossom out of his blazer pocket and tossed it toward the accident scene.

A gray pigeon was flying by, its whistle trailing in the air. Chen looked up, but it was already out of sight.

He was reminded of a couple of lines in a Song dynasty poem, which he had thought about not too long ago, in the garden of the Writers' Association.

But what made him think of those lines here and now was something else. Another person and another life. In the days when he'd just been assigned to the bureau, *Wenhui Daily* was in another building, one near the Bund. There Chen met with a journalist who later went to Japan.

How far you have traveled, / I don't know. Whatever I see / fills my heart with melancholy. / The further you go, the fewer / your letters for me. The expanse / of the water so wide, no message-carrying / fish in sight, where and whom / can I ask for your news?

That was the first stanza of a poem composed by Ouyang Xiu in the eleventh century. At that time, people still liked the romantic legend of fish carrying messages across rivers and seas for lovers. Having to wait weeks or months for communication was something almost unimaginable now, in the age of e-mail.

Chief Inspector Chen turned and walked into the newspaper's current office building, trying to pull himself together. It was a most magnificent lobby, like that of a five-star hotel. In the middle of the hall, he noticed a black and white photo exhibition, and past it, a small café, which seemed to be a convenient place for journalists to relax or meet with their visitors.

ELEVEN

LIANPING STARTED HER DAY with a visit to Yaqing, the literature editor of *Wenhui Daily*, who was on maternity leave. Yaqing lived in a high-end apartment that was about a five-minute walk from the newspaper office building.

Yaqing answered the door with a smile, standing slender, suave in a red silk robe embroidered with a golden phoenix, and in soft-heeled leather slippers. A huge diamond dazzled on her finger. She looked like an elegant, high-class lady, and Lianping didn't immediately recognize her.

Her place was a huge two-story apartment overlooking a small man-made lake. Ji Huadong, Yaqing's husband, was one of the "successful elites" in the city, dealing in exports and imports.

A nanny served them Dragon Well tea in the spacious living room, along with a platter of fresh lychee.

"This is this year's new tea," Yaqing said, breathing lightly into the cup. "Before the Rain."

"It smells so refreshing. How is Little Ji?"

"A wet nurse is feeding him in the nursery."

"That's so nice. I won't take up much of your time, Yaqing. I just wanted to catch you up on how things are going with the literature section of the newspaper."

"Don't worry about it, Lianping. At *Wenhui*, the literature section is symbolic at best. Few people read it, and that's why our boss didn't bother to bring in another editor to work on it while I'm out on leave. I know it has added so much to your workload. I'm sorry." After taking a sip of tea, Yaqing resumed casually, "I may or may not come back to the newspaper after my leave. I haven't yet told anybody at the paper, but Ji thinks it's not worth it. He's been so busy with his work, and when he comes home, he wants me to be there for him."

"But what about your journalist career? It's hard for me to imagine an intellectual like you living the life of a full-time wife. For a couple of months, perhaps, but in the long run, wouldn't it be boring?"

"No, not at all. At least, not for me. With his business expanding, Ji has a lot of social obligations that require my attention and company," Yaqing said, and then changed the subject. "Your boyfriend Xiang has an even bigger family business. Remember that tide and time wait for no man—or no woman."

"There you go again."

"I'll tell you what. I just received the officially approved list of 170 new expressions compiled by the Beijing Education Ministry. According to it, if a girl hasn't married by the age of twenty-six, she'll be called a 'leftover.' And at age of thirty, a 'senior leftover.' And after thirty-five, 'a leftover saint,' which is a sarcastic reference to the Monkey Saint from *Journey to the West*."

"That's so cruel."

"But so realistic. Even our Education Ministry has approved the phrases. What's the use of saying anything against it?"

"Well, not everyone is as lucky as you," Lianping said, trying to change the subject again.

"You can say that again. On the day of our son's birth, Ji bought me a Lexus SUV. But you aren't doing so bad, either. You got a Volvo from Xiang, right? You definitely deserve it. You'll make a perfect match for him. You're pretty, highly educated, and intelligent."

"Come on, Yaqing. Xiang just loaned me the down payment. I have to pay all the installments and repay the loan from him as well."

Actually, Xiang had tried to insist on buying the car for her, but he wasn't exactly her boyfriend, and she declined his offer. She hadn't made up her mind about the relationship. Neither had he, apparently. He was traveling with his father on business in Guangdong. She'd been expecting a phone call from him but hadn't heard anything so far.

Because of his family background, she'd been keeping the budding affair secret, except among close friends like Yaqing. She was concerned what people might say in this materialistic age. Perhaps, as a newly popular saying went, finding a good husband was far more important than finding a good job.

She did not consider hers a good job, though it was secure, with a decent salary, and extra income when her writing was reprinted elsewhere. *Wenhui* had a contract with Xinhua Agency, syndicating news articles to foreign agencies, with the only requirement being that everything had to be politically acceptable. That requirement was what bothered her.

For a girl from outside of Shanghai, she was considered to be doing fine for herself in the city. Thanks to a down payment made by her entrepreneur father, she'd been able to buy an apartment just a couple of blocks behind Great World, a well-known entertainment center in the middle of the city on Yan'an Road. Still, she was feeling the increasing pressure of the mortgage payments. It was the same with her car, not to mention the other necessary expenses required for her to maintain a "successful" image in her professional circle.

"Come on, I know he offered to buy the car for you," Yaqing said, "but you insisted on accepting the down payment only as a loan. Actually, that was so clever of you—"

Lianping's phone rang, which prevented her from explaining, though she wondered why Yaqing thought she'd been clever. She picked up the call.

"Hello, this is Lianping."

"Hi, I'm Chen Cao. We met at a meeting of the Shanghai Writers' Association not long ago. You later called about some poems for your section in *Wenhui*. Do you remember?"

"Oh, yes, of course I remember, Chief Inspector Chen. Do you have your poems ready for me?"

"Well, I haven't forgotten your request."

"I knew you would write for us."

The fact was, however, she hadn't thought he would. The high-ranking cop was far too busy, and she'd asked for his poetry perfunctorily, only because of her temporary position.

But she'd heard about him, as far back as her college years—not about him as a professional writer but as the legendary chief inspector. When she started working for *Wenhui*, she heard even more about him, particularly from her colleagues covering crime or politics in Shanghai. When she met him at the Writers' Association, though, she wasn't exactly impressed. He seemed to be a bit too reserved, not at all like the romantic poet she'd once imagined. For an emerging Party cadre, however, such a pose made sense, and she thought she could understand it.

"I tried to dig out some of my old poems."

"Please send them to me. You have my e-mail address. I can't wait to read them."

"Actually, I'm in the lobby of your office building right now. I'd like to discuss with you—"

"Really, Chief Inspector Chen! I'll meet you there in five minutes," she said. "How about meeting me in the café on the fifteenth floor? It'll be more comfortable for us to sit talking there."

As she flipped the phone closed, she saw Yaqing eyeing her incredulously.

"No wonder," Yaqing commented. "You have Chief Chen Cao waiting for you in the lobby—no, in the café."

"I saw him the other day at a meeting of the Writers' Association. It was all just to cover your section, you know." She stood up in a hurry, "Sorry, I have to get back to the office."

"He's surely a character! A rising Party official with several major investigations to his credit, and connections to the top echelon in the Forbidden City. Not to mention that he's a poet in his own right at the same time. We've published his work in the Pen column. Believe it or not, he's said to have dated one of our journalists years ago, written poems for her, which she then published in the newspaper."

"That's incredible. But it didn't work out between them?"

"No, but I don't know the details. Her name is Wang Feng and she left for Japan. Which is all I know. He's really something, an enigmatic Party cadre."

"Isn't he? As an official of his rank, I expect he can pick and choose when it comes to girls. He must have quite a number of them waiting around. By the way, do you remember the title of those poems?"

"I think I still have a copy of the newspaper somewhere."

"Great. If you can find it, take a good photo of the text and send it to my phone."

"Certainly, but why?"

"So I can talk to him about it."

"I see. No problem, then. It might be a plus for you to publish his work in our newspaper. He's now the deputy Party secretary of the city police bureau, but it's just a matter of time before he's the number one, according to Ji," Yaqing said, nodding. "What a glutton you are! You have one full bowl in front of you, and you have your eye on another."

"Come on, Yaqing. I'm merely interested in his poems."

"But he's a wild card," Yaqing said, accompanying her out to the elevator. "And complicated too. You never know what he will come to you for. Your present boyfriend Xiang is a safer bet."

Lianping, too, started to wonder about the reason behind Chen's visit as the elevator started to go down. He didn't have to come to the office to talk about his poems. A phone call or an e-mail would have been more than sufficient. And any of the official newspapers in the city would be eager to publish his work.

Five minutes later, she spotted him as she stepped into the lobby hall of the Wenhui Office Building.

"I have to show my ID and sign the register here," he said. "I thought it might be easier for you to bring me through security as one of your authors."

That was considerate of him. An official visit from the police might cause speculation, but no journalist would worry about having a professional connection such as Chief Inspector Chen.

He was wearing a light gray blazer, white shirt, and khaki pants that morning. He certainly didn't look like a cop, but he didn't look like one of those long-haired romantic poets, either.

"I'm so glad you could make it over today, Chief Inspector Chen. Let's go on up. It's much quieter, and it has a better view."

"Thanks. Please just call me Chen. For one thing, having a cop around might not be so popular in your office."

"But a high-ranking policeman like you is certain to be popular anywhere, particularly so at our Party newspaper."

"Well said," he remarked, apparently appreciating the repartee.

They took the elevator up to the café on the fifteenth floor, where they chose a table by the window.

He ordered a cup of freshly ground coffee. She ordered herself a cup of fresh jasmine tea, breathing onto the water, making the white petals ripple out against the green, tender tea leaves.

Everything is possible but not necessarily plausible, she reflected, a jasmine petal between her lips.

"I really appreciate your support of literature, Lianping. It's an age when few people read poetry," he started, taking a sip of coffee. "But my pen is rusted. I happened to be passing by the *Wenhui* building this afternoon and I thought of you. So I decided to drop in and discuss it with you."

She couldn't help feeling flattered. At least he'd taken her request seriously.

"So what poems have you brought me today?"

"Sorry, nothing yet. I have a special case on my hands, so I'm really busy at the moment. But I would like to talk to you about what topics would be appropriate for *Wenhui*."

"Let me see, I may still have the poems you wrote for us earlier."

She pulled out her phone and pressed a button. Sure enough, Yaqing had sent over the text. She then turned the phone over to Chen.

He took a quick look at the screen and handed it back with an embarrassed expression on his face.

"Wow, that was written years ago," he said.

It was a group of poems entitled *Trio*, which she hadn't read. She started reading the first piece, entitled "Tenor":

Straw-stuffed, caught in the rain, too / saturated to shake in the wind, to be / is to be constructed: plastic buttons / for your eyes to keep the horizon / high-buttoned in a shroud of drizzling mist, / a carrot nose, half-bitten by a mule, and a broken ancient music box for your mouth, / wet, eccentric, repeating / Ling-Ling-Ling / to the surrounding crows at dusk. / Setting afire a straw-yellow / photograph, murmuring "Let bygones / be bygones," as if whistling alone, / in the dark woods, I open / the window to the sudden sunlight. / Another day, when it begins to rain, / I am you again—

"Please don't read any more, Lianping."

She found it hard to juxtapose the persona in the poem with the Party cadre sitting opposite, stirring his coffee with a spoon. Could it be the poem that was written for Wang Feng, or was it for another girl, perhaps named Ling? Stories about the chief inspector circulated among her circle, and it would be difficult for people not to speculate.

"You are so romantic," she said, looking up from her phone.

"That is a too-sentimental piece," he said, seemingly self-conscious. "But it will never do to mistake the persona for the poet. To use T. S. Eliot's words, poetry is impersonal. I dashed off those lines after watching a Japanese movie, conjuring up the agony of the protagonist, and saying what he does not say in the movie. An objective correlative, so to speak. With creative writing, using such a persona may have a liberating effect."

"I see. What about an ordinary cop's persona, then? Of course, you are an extraordinary one. But you could choose to focus on an unextraordinary cop, like one of those working under you, where there is a lot of sacrifice but no flower or limelight. That would be a subject appropriate for a Party newspaper like *Wenhui*, and naturally you are familiar with the details."

He didn't respond immediately, but he seemed genuinely intrigued, nodding and sipping at his coffee again.

"Yes, you've made a good suggestion, and a politically correct one too. I'll definitely think about it, Lianping. So, have you been in charge of the literature section for a long time?" Chen asked.

"No, it's actually not my section. I normally edit the finance section."

"You majored in finance?"

"No, in English."

"Oh, that's interesting," he said, though he chose not to follow up on it. "Finance is far more popular today."

"What do you mean, Chief Inspector Chen?"

"According to a novelist who was popular in the eighties, it's far more popular nowadays to be a businessman, so he's become a prosperous CEO and no longer writes."

"Oh, that's Tieliang. I watched that TV interview with him. What a shame! He made a fortune running a chain of clubs for officials—all in the name of literature and art." She added more hot water to her cup and said, "But he's not alone. You might remember a sentence in *Dream of the Red Chamber*: 'Except the two stone lions crouching in front of the Jia mansion, nothing else is clean.'"

"Well, you simply need to swap 'the Jia mansion' with 'socialism with Chinese characteristics.'"

"Wow, that's quite something for a Party cadre to say."

"May I smoke, Lianping?"

"Go ahead," she said, realizing she'd been carried away by the conversation. After all, it was a senior police officer who was sitting opposite her, and she wondered what he really wanted to talk to her about. "Oh, I heard that you've published a collection of poetry, and it sold out."

"I, too, thought it sold quite well. As it turned out, however, a Big Buck bought a thousand copies from the publisher, and then gave them out as gifts to his business associates. While it was done as a favor to me, and without my knowledge, it came as a blow to my self-esteem as a poet. And as a cop, too, since I failed to detect that trick with the sales. But then again, I didn't graduate from the police academy, so perhaps that can be counted as a factor in my defense."

She enjoyed his subtle touch of self-irony. At least he knew better. Then it was her turn to speak in a self-deprecating way.

"I didn't major in finance. But for a girl from Anhui, any job in Shanghai was worth grabbing. My major in English did give me one advantage, though. In today's financial world, a lot of new terms have to be translated from English. For instance, *mortgage* and *option*. These terms were nonexistent in the state economy. So I was offered the position at *Wenhui*."

"That is quite a coincidence. I was assigned to the job at the police bureau due to similar considerations—I was needed to translate a handbook of police procedures."

"In my situation, there's also a material difference between a literature journalist and a finance journalist."

"Enlighten me, Lianping."

"For example, at the meeting at the Writers' Association, what I was given there was a cup of tea. And not high-quality tea, for that matter. But at a meeting of real estate professionals, a journalist might be given all sorts of things. One time, I was even given a laptop."

"No wonder Tieliang no longer writes," Chen said. "But still, your job is important. It helps people understand the financial world in which they live, a world that would otherwise make no sense to them."

"Well, it might be necessary for us to make sense of it in a politically acceptable way. As Zhuangzi put it, 'He who steals a hook will be hanged; he who steals a country will be made a prince.' Our job is to justify the practice of country-stealing."

"Yes, corruption runs like an unbridled horse through this one-party system of ours."

"People all know about it, but can we write about it? For instance, consider all the shady deals in the housing market. One of the developers of the Xujiahui, Mr. Tao, used to be a dumpling peddler, but now, three or four years later, Tao is a billionaire. How? It's said that a high-ranking official in the city government took a fancy to Tao's wife after he saw her ladling out dumplings in their curbside stall. Needless to say, the official both gave and took in an incredible amount from her dainty hand—money for access—after they enjoyed cloud and rain in the dark night."

"You know a lot about these things, Lianping."

"I'm a finance journalist, and I have a friend whose father is a developer. I hear about all the manipulations and fluctuations of land prices done in the interests of the Party," she said, with an embarrassed smile. "Sorry, I'm getting a bit carried away."

"No, I'm grateful for your insight. I have to admit, by catching the 'last bus' during the housing reform, I was assigned to a three-bedroom apartment. Supposedly I got such a large place because of my mother, even though she refused to move in with me."

"You don't have to say that. For a Party official of your rank, a three-bedroom apartment would be nothing. Nor has there been anything like 'last bus.' Just half a year ago, the head of *Wenhui* got a villa rent-free, the theory being that he would then be able to work better for the Party newspaper."

"Well, in terms of social Darwinism, it's the successful—whether businessmen or Party officials—versus the unsuccessful, the ordinary people."

"But can we write about or report on them? No. That's why Party newspapers, like *Wenhui* or *Liberation*, are really struggling. They only survive because of the mandatory subscription policy in the city. That also explains the popularity of Internet blog writings. They're watched by the government, but not that strictly or that effectively."

"Well, I happened to be in the neighborhood," he said, abruptly changing the subject. "One of my colleagues had an accident on the street corner around here."

"Oh," she said, slightly disappointed. He wasn't here because he'd thought of her—or about the poems he'd promised her. "Those reckless drivers are impossible."

He then took another sip in silence.

"But it's strange," she said. "Usually, cars drive slowly around here. What day was this?"

"Monday."

"So that's—" She didn't finish the sentence. "Yes, I remember hearing something about it."

"Detective Wei was killed—right there and then."

"Killed. That's impossible." Shocked, she stood up and pointed out the window. "Look at the snaillike traffic."

Chen followed her gesture and waited for her to go on.

"This is a busy street. It's not like the highway, but it has its own terrible traffic. Sometimes the traffic is in a total snarl. On the fifteenth floor, you might not hear that much noise, but one definitely can in my office."

"Because it's a busy intersection with many people coming and going?"

"Do you know how many people come to *Wenhui* every day? A large number of the journalists have their own cars. Then there are the taxis for the visitors. Sometimes there are so many that the taxis form a long, curving line in front of the building. There is also the kindergarten across the street."

"The kindergarten? Yes, I remember seeing one across the street. But what about it?"

"You should see it around three thirty. There are even more cars lined up and waiting then. It's a private kindergarten. One of the best in the city—the best location, the best reputation, and the best history. The enrollment cost alone is thirty thousand yuan per year. The annual donation parents have to make on top of that comes to around another ten thousand."

"Wow, that's more than an ordinary worker's annual salary."

"But those aren't ordinary parents. That's why, starting around three in the afternoon, you'll always see a long line of cars there—chauffeurs and nannies, waiting in private luxury cars."

"But what about the other times of the day?"

"There are still quite a lot of people. The kids might not arrive on time, or their parents may have them picked up earlier for one reason or another. The kindergarten aside, there are many people coming to *Wenhui* at any time of the day," she said, shaking her head in disbelief. "Some of the visitors here are government Big Bugs. That driver must have totally lost his mind to drive so recklessly along Weihai Road."

"You mean that a driver along here should know better," he said, taking out a notebook.

"I can't say for sure. Anything could have happened. Is this the case you're working on?"

"No, I'm only a consultant on that case, but Detective Wei was a colleague of mine."

"Is foul play suspected?"

"I just heard about it, but I can't help wondering how it could have happened right in front of Wenhui Office Building."

"I'll ask around and let you know. Some of my colleagues may have seen or heard more about it."

"You're really helpful."

"I've also had the pictures from the meeting at the Writers' Association developed." She pulled out an envelope containing photos. They started looking through them together.

"That's a good portrait," he said, picking out a shot of himself. "Someday I may use it on a book cover."

"That would be fantastic."

"I'll see to it that you get credit."

"Don't worry about it. I take a lot of photos, especially for the finance section. Credit or no, it's just a routine part of the work. I'll e-mail you the file too."

"Thanks. By the way, you asked me about the Zhou case the other day. Have you heard or read anything about the photo of the pack of 95 Supreme Majesty? A *Wenhui* journalist is sometimes better informed than a cop."

The question didn't come as a surprise to her. In fact, it would have been a surprise if the chief inspector hadn't asked the question.

"First, let me tell you something, Chief Inspector Chen, something that happened to a journalist friend of mine in Anhui. He wrote an article exposing a major state company's falsified sales figures right before it applied to go public. Do you know what happened? He was listed by local police as one of the 'most wanted' for slander, despite the fact that the article was well researched and documented. The head of the company turned out to be the nephew of the public security minister in Beijing. Even today the journalist has to hide in another province because of his 'crime.'

"Now, a job at a Party-run newspaper is generally considered a good one. It's secure and decently paid, as long as you know when to shut your mouth and to close your ears. So in terms of the picture in question, what can a journalist say except what can be read in an official newspaper?"

"That's what disturbs me," he said.

"I'm responsible for finance and new business news. So I'm supposed to attend meetings like the one in which Zhou made his speech, and then write a story about it, whether I agree with what's said or not. However, I didn't go to the meeting that day. Why? I was told that the Housing Development Committee would send preapproved text along with pictures, which I could publish by simply adding some adjectives and adverbs. Which was what I did.

"People active on the Internet, and not working for *Wenhui* or other Party newspapers, might be able to tell you more about it," she said cautiously. "I've heard that the human-flesh search was started on a Web forum run by somebody named Melong, but that's about all I know."

"Melong?" An inscrutable expression flashed across his face, as if he was hearing the name for the first time. It was probably a deliberate response. To a high-ranking cop in charge of the investigation, that couldn't have been news, she thought.

"For Melong, the search that started with Zhou's picture might have been intended as a smart protest, but what it then led to went way beyond his expectations or imagination," she said. Then she added, "Perhaps I could make some inquiries for you in financial circles."

"That would be a great help, Lianping. I'd really appreciate it. I'm still a layman, standing outside the door of the Web world."

"Oh, I also keep a blog. Nothing official, you know," she said, writing down the blog address on a Post-it. "It's called *Lili's Blog.*"

"Why Lili?"

"That's my real name, the one my parents gave me. But for a journalist, it sounds too much like a pet name. So I changed it to Lianping."

"I'm going to read it," he said. He drained the coffee, which was already getting cold, and stood up. "And I'll send you my poems as soon as possible. Thanks for everything, Lianping."

TWELVE

CHIEF INSPECTOR CHEN WENT to the bureau the next morning as usual.

Being a special consultant to the Zhou case didn't absolve him of his responsibility for the Special Case Squad. He was still the head of the squad, though Detective Yu was, effectively, in charge.

After taking a quick look at an internal report, Chen put it down with a lingering bitter taste in his mouth. It was about a dissident artist named Ai, who was said to be stirring up trouble with some of his postmodern exhibitions, which consisted of distorted nude figures done in an absurdist fashion. Chen decided not to take it on as a potential case for the squad. Not because he knew anything about Ai's work but because he didn't think it was justifiable to open an investigation of an artist like Ai simply for the sake of "a harmonious society."

There was a message from Party Secretary Li about a routine meeting around noon, but Chen chose not to return the call.

Instead, he kept brooding over the suspicious circumstances of

Wei's death. An abandoned brown SUV had been found in Nanhui. It had been stolen from a paper company several days ago. The abandoned SUV added to the possibility of its having been a premeditated assault, but at the same time, it was also a dead end. Despite his hunch that Wei's death was connected to his investigation into Zhou's death, Chen knew better than to discuss it around the bureau, not even with Detective Yu. The chief inspector felt utterly abysmal about not helping more with Wei's work. He had a splitting headache coming on.

Then he remembered that Lianping had given him the address of her blog. Taking a break from thinking about Wei, he turned to his computer and typed in the address.

What she had posted there seemed to be quite different from her articles in the newspaper. The title of a recent piece immediately grabbed his attention: "The Death of Xinghua."

Xinghua was a poet and translator of Shakespeare who died during the Cultural Revolution. He was little known among the younger generation, so Chen wondered why she chose to write about him.

A first-class poet and scholar, Xinghua translated Shakespeare's Henry IV, *edited and annotated the complete translation. That's about all that people would learn about him if they happened to turn one or two pages in the* Complete Works of Shakespeare. *What could be more tragic than a forgotten tragedy!*

As early as the Anti-Japanese War in the forties, Professor Shediek at Southwest United University considered Xinghua one of his most promising students, as gifted as Harold Bloom. Xinghua soon made a name for himself with his poems and translations, but his career was abruptly cut short. In 1957, he was labeled a rightist during the nationwide antirightist movement. He was condemned and persecuted in the subsequent political movements, and he died in his midforties at the beginning of the Cultural Revolution. When an article about him appeared in the official newspaper in the late seventies, the circumstances of his final days were not mentioned at all, as if he had simply died a natural death.

I happened to get in touch with his widow, who told me about all that he had suffered toward the end of his life. At the beginning of the Cultural Revolution, he was subjected to the most humiliating mass criticism and punishment. His home was ransacked by Red Guards, and his almost completed translation of The Divine Comedy *was burned on the street. That summer, he was forced to work in the rice paddy field from six in the morning to eight in the evening for "ideological transformation through hard labor." Xinghua was sweating all over, thirsty, and hungry, but he wasn't allowed any water or food; toward the end of the day, he had no choice but to wet his lips with a handful of water scooped up from a dirty creek. At the sight of that, a Red Guard rushed over and fiercely pushed his head into the contaminated water, holding it under for several minutes, while another Red Guard kicked him violently in the side. Soon Xinghua fell sick with a swollen belly and fainted in the field. Less than two hours later, he died there of acute diarrhea. The Red Guards insisted, however, that he had committed suicide, and required that an autopsy be performed. Why? Because suicide was said to be another crime—a deliberate act against the efforts of the Party and people to save him. Xinghua's family begged, but to no avail. His body was cut open; fortunately, the autopsy report proved that he had died of having swallowed contaminated water, and his family was spared the posthumous label of counterrevolutionary.*

But why did the details of his tragic death never come out in the official media? Why were the Red Guards never punished? It is said that the Red Guard who pushed Xinghua's head into the creek was from the family of a high-ranking cadre, and the one who kicked Xinghua became a high-ranking Party cadre himself. It was said that they simply, passionately believed in Mao, and with Mao's portrait still hung high on the gate of Tiananmen Square, what really could be done? Although the Cultural Revolution was officially declared a well-meant mistake by Mao, there is still an unofficial rule that all writing about the Cultural Revolution should be "contained." In other words, vague, short, euphemistic, and as little as possible.

After all, who remembers Xinghua?

It's by chance that I came across a poem by Xinghua. A stanza of it reads:

Trying to grasp a blade of grass, a piece of wood, to secure / the present moment, to avoid the flight of time, / to hold on, to fix oneself, / but in the distant mountains, autumn spreads out at the peaks, / storing infinite joy and sorrow. / After failure comes a stroke of luck.

It is a sad poem. Not only because one's self has to be maintained by grasping a blade of grass or a piece of wood, but contrary to the heartrending wish in the last line, no stroke of luck came to the poet in the end.

Chen lit a cigarette, waving out the match forcefully. It wasn't perhaps one of the blogs that would appeal to a large number of people. Most of them had probably never heard of Xinghua. The number of hits on the page spoke to that. But Lianping nonetheless did her research and wrote emotionally. It wasn't just about one man's suffering during the Cultural Revolution, it was also about today's society.

Chen liked the poem quoted at the end of the article.

Now, what about his own luck as a policeman? Chen picked up the phone and called Jiang at the hotel.

At his insistence, Jiang confirmed one thing. The original post that landed Zhou in trouble appeared in a Web forum managed by a man named Melong, though Jiang appeared to be surprised that Chen had learned this through his own channels.

Chen then called Lianping.

"I want to thank you for your blog post on Xinghua. It's a good piece. It's a pity few remember him today."

"I majored in English too. Don't forget that."

"So you must know a lot about blogs and blogging."

"They aren't difficult, but blogs aren't uncensored. Web sites have to take a piece down the moment they get a notice from the netcops. Fortunately or unfortunately, Xinghua isn't a name on their radar."

"By the way, you mentioned someone named Melong yesterday. Do you post on his forum?"

"He runs a popular forum, and he's asked me to write for him, but I choose not to. His forum is a bit too controversial, if you know what I mean."

"So you know him well?"

"No, not well. I've only met him three or four times. But he's clever and resourceful, a real computer wizard. That's how he was able to start his Web forum single-handedly."

"Is there anything else you can tell me about him?"

"Not offhand, but let me make some phone calls."

"That would be great. Thank you in advance, Lianping." Chen then said his good-byes.

Afterward, Chen tried to talk to Detective Yu, but Yu was out of the bureau with some other officers. Chen left a note for his long-time partner, saying that their squad shouldn't take on any new cases during his absence. It was a rather unusual request. Yu was more than competent, but what could the squad possibly do with a case like the one on the artist Ai?

The time for the department meeting drew near, but Chen wasn't in any mood for it. He decided instead to skip it and sneak out of the bureau. Being a special consultant at least gave him an excuse.

He didn't request the services of a bureau car. On the corner of Yan'an and Sichuan Roads, he boarded bus 71, which was crowded, as always. The bus crawled along patiently in heavy traffic. Chen paid little attention to the changing scene outside, lost in a tangle of thoughts. Instead of getting off at the stop on Shanxi Road, he remained on the bus, standing, holding on to a strap overhead. The bus was heading toward East China Hospital, where his mother was.

She'd been there for weeks, recuperating from a minor stroke. His failure to take proper care of her was unforgivable, he couldn't help telling himself again. He was sweating profusely, bumping up against an ovenlike, overweight woman as the bus lurched down the street.

He hadn't visited his mother in several days, though on the phone she'd repeatedly assured him that everything was all right.

East China Hospital was located on West Yan'an Road, in a large compound enclosed by high red walls. It was a hospital for high-ranking Party cadres, with the most advanced equipment, utmost security, and privacy. It was accessible only to those of a certain rank—a rank higher than that of chief inspector.

His mother's private ward was on the second floor of the European-style building. At the carpeted landing of the staircase, an elderly man in a white shirt and green army pants nodded to Chen formally. It was a gesture out of an old movie. Chen didn't recognize him, but he nodded back.

Chen's mother wasn't in this hospital because of his position, which by itself was far from enough, he reflected as he knocked gently on the door. It stood ajar, with the afternoon sunlight peeping in through the windowpanes across the corridor. There was no response. He waited a moment or two before he pushed open the door. She was alone in the room, taking an early nap.

Quietly, he drew a chair to the bedside, gazed at her sleeping face, and touched her hand.

Who says that the splendor / of a grass blade can ever prove / to be enough to return / the generous, radiant warmth / of the ever-returning spring sunlight?

These were the celebrated lines by Men Jiao, an eighth-century Tang dynasty poet, comparing his mother's love for him to the warmth of the ever-returning spring sunlight. Chen was lost in memories . . .

A young nurse walked down the corridor, stopped, and poked her head in without entering or saying anything. She smiled and left, moving out of sight like a pleasant breeze in the early summer.

The room appeared bright and clean, with a window overlooking the well-kept garden in the back. It was much nicer than the old, overcrowded neighborhood in which she still lived. She might as well stay here a little longer.

His glance then fell on the presents heaped on the nightstand. Most of them were expensive. Swallow nests, ginseng, organic tree ears, royal jelly . . . To his astonishment, he also saw a bottle of hajie lizard essence, supposedly bu or nutritious to the yang, according to traditional Chinese medical theory. But he wondered if it could be beneficial to an old woman in her present condition. These gifts were probably from Overseas Chinese Lu or Mr. Gu, both of whom were prosperous entrepreneurs and were making a point of showering her with expensive presents. They hadn't even bothered to tell him that they had visited.

In the amazing drama of China's economic reform, it had been only a matter of years before the two had become billionaires. Had Chen listened to Lu's advice back when Lu was just starting his restaurant chain business, Chen could have become one as well.

But he, too, was successful as a Party official, though he tried not to see himself as one like Zhou. There was no denying, however, that he enjoyed some of the same "gray privileges" the others did.

One of those gray benefits was a large discount on the hospital bill. His mother's arm had been broken by a Red Guard during the Cultural Revolution. No compensation had been offered at the time. All these years later, however, she was suddenly classified overnight as "handicapped," a status that entitled her to more medical benefits, in accordance with a new regulation. Not to mention the fact that she'd been allowed to stay here during her recovery and had been provided with a single room.

Ironically, in order for him to be a filial son, he had to be a loyal Party official, supporting the government that had injured her.

His mother stirred, opening her eyes with a surprised smile at the sight of him sitting by the bed. She looked ashen, shrunken, but she managed to reach out an emaciated hand.

"You didn't have to come to visit. This hospital is much better than a nursing home."

"How was lunch today?"

"Good. They served well-cooked soft noodles with sliced pork and green cabbage."

She gestured at a menu on the table. Unlike other hospitals, there seemed to be quite a variety from which to choose here. It was almost like a small fancy restaurant. Her choice of dish was probably due to her teeth. She'd lost several of them, but she refused to bother with the ordeal of dental treatment at her age.

He got up to mix a cup of green tea and American ginseng essence for her.

"Our relatives and friends all say good things about you," she said affectionately. "I've long given up trying to figure things out in China today. It's all too much of an enigma for me, but I know that you always try to do the right thing."

"But I haven't been taking good care of you. When you get out of the hospital, please come and stay with me. Nowadays it's quite common for people to hire a live-in aide."

"No, I'm fine. I'm a contented woman. If I left the world today, I would go with my eyes closed in peace, except for one thing I'm still concerned about. You know what I'm talking about."

That happened to be one thing about which he had nothing to tell her. Chief Inspector Chen remained single. *Confucius said, "There*

are three most unfilial things in the world, and to go without descen-
dants is the worst."

"White Cloud came by the other day," she went on. "A really nice
girl."

"I haven't seen her for a while."

He was to blame, he admitted to himself, for the distance between White Cloud and himself. The shadow of her dancing in the
private karaoke room seemed to always accompany her, or perhaps it
was nothing more than the shadow swirling in his mind.

The water flows along, the cloud drifts away, and the spring is gone. /
It's a different world.

He tried to straighten up the things on her nightstand here, as if
the effort could somehow make him feel less lousy. He was interrupted by a noise at the door.

"Hello, Chief Inspector Chen. Nurse Liang Xia told me that you
were here today. You should have told me you were coming."

Chen looked up to see Dr. Hou striding into the room, beaming
from ear to ear. Hou Zidong, the head of the hospital, was wearing
a white smock over a black suit with a red tie.

"Dr. Hou, I want to thank you for everything you've been doing
for my mother. You're a busy man, I understand, so I didn't call you."

"Auntie has been doing well. No need to worry. We'll make sure
that it's just like home here."

"Dr. Hou has done a fantastic job, as I have told you many times,"
she said, looking at Chen with a light of pride flashing in her eyes.

Chen understood. It was all because of a "case" Chen had helped
with in the late eighties. The "suspect" in question was none other
than Hou, a young doctor newly assigned to a neighborhood hospital. While in college, Hou had been involved in a so-called foreign
liaison case. According to an inside control file, Hou had visited an
American medical expert staying at the Jinjiang Hotel and had
signed his name in the hotel register book several times. The American was alleged to have connections to the CIA. So Hou was put on

a blacklist without knowing it. After Hou's graduation, there was an international medical conference in New York, and the head of the Chinese delegation picked Hou as a qualified candidate—someone with several English papers published in the field, whose presence could help to "contribute to China's image." But for Hou to join the delegation, it was necessary to investigate his involvement with the American. Chen was assigned to listen to the recordings of the phone conversations between Hou and the alleged American spy. As it turned out, they talked about nothing but their common interests in the medical field. In one phone call, Hou did urge the American to be more careful, but judging from the context, he was referring to the American's drinking problem. It was ridiculous to put Hou on a blacklist because of that, Chen concluded. He transcribed and translated the taped conversations carefully, submitted a detailed analysis to the higher authoritities, and proposed that Hou's name be cleared.

No longer a suspect, Hou was allowed a spot in the delegation, his speech was well received at the conference, and his luck since then had been incredible. It wasn't long before he was transferred to East China Hospital, one of the most prestigious in the city, where eventually he became the head of the hospital. About a year ago, Hou had learned of Chen's help from a high-ranking cadre who stayed at the hospital. The next day Hou came to the bureau, declaring Chen was the "guiren" in his life—the life-changing helper who had come out of nowhere.

"I knew somebody helped, but I didn't know it was you, Chief Inspector Chen. Ever since then, I've always tried to be a conscientious doctor. Do you know why? I wanted to be as conscientious as my guiren. There are so many problems in society today, but there are still a few good Party cadres like you. Now, if there is ever anything I can do for you, just say the word. As in the old saying, for the favor of a drop of water, one has to dig out a fountain in return."

Dr. Hou kept his word. When Chen's mother was sick, Hou took it upon himself to handle everything. It was impossible for ordinary people to get into the prestigious East China Hospital, but Hou made an exception for her and arranged a special room, in spite of the fact that she had suffered only a minor stroke. He insisted that she stay for her convalescence as well.

"You've really gone out of your way for her, Dr. Hou."

"For me, it's as effortless as a wave of my hand. Auntie may stay here as long as she likes. She doesn't owe the hospital any money. To be frank, we need cash-rich patients like her in our hospital. Lu, one of your buddies, insisted on depositing a large sum against the account of his auntie."

"Overseas Chinese Lu is impossible," Chen said with a wry smile, glancing at the presents on the nightstand again. Lu might not be the only one.

Dr. Hou's cell phone rang. He looked at it without answering it.

"I've got another meeting. I have to go. But don't worry, Chief Inspector Chen. I'll come by regularly."

Chen's mother sat up and watched the doctor walk out of the room, then turned to her son.

"You go back to your work too. People don't speak so highly of the police, but my son is conscientious, I know. That comforts me more than anything else. Good things do not go unrewarded. It's karma."

Chen nodded.

"Oh, before I forget, there is a gift card from another of your buddies. Mr. Gu. You know how to deal with it, I think."

He picked up the gift card and frowned at the amount. Twenty thousand yuan.

The money meant nothing to Gu, who was a business tycoon. He'd helped Chen in an earlier investigation, and Chen had also proved helpful to Gu. Gu had since claimed to be a friend of the chief inspector, and he, too, called Chen's mother his "auntie."

The expensive gift card would have been acceptable for a real aun-tie, but as it was, it was just another way for Gu to grease the con-nection. Still, it was considerate of Gu. What made it difficult for Chen was that the gift card came not to him but to his mother. It wouldn't be that easy for him to return it.

"I'll take care of it, Mother," Chen said, putting the card in his pocket.

His cell phone rang. It was Detective Yu. Chen excused himself and stepped out into the hall.

Yu called to fill Chen in on the meeting that had just finished in the bureau. Among other things, Party Secretary Li had been sur-prisingly adamant in refusing to acknowledge that Detective Wei's death happened while he was on duty. Wei was killed during the investigation, but no one knew what he was doing there at that par-ticular intersection, at that particular moment. Li claimed that Wei might have been there for himself, checking out some evening courses at a night school around the corner.

To Chen, the change in Li's attitude was not too surprising. Initially, Li must have been shocked and saddened, like everybody else in the bureau. Wei was a veteran cop, having worked hard in the bureau for years. But the prospect of pursuing his death as a possible murder case could further complicate the Zhou situation. In the final analysis, any more speculation concerning the Zhou case wasn't seen as in the Party's interest.

"His wife is sick and jobless at home, and his son is still in middle school," Yu concluded on a somber note.

Chen got his point. If Wei had died in an accident, there wouldn't be any bureau compensation for his family.

Walking back into the room with the phone in his hand, Chen felt even more guilty. Had he attended the meeting, at least he could have tried to speak up for Wei, though he wondered whether that would have made any difference. Probably nothing would, unless it was proved that Wei was doing his duty, investigating around the corner near Wenhui Office Building, when he was killed.

But what was Wei doing there?

"I have to leave, Mother," he said. "Something has come up at the bureau. I'll come back soon."

THIRTEEN

THE NEXT MORNING, CHEN went to Pingliang Road in the Yangpu District.

According to the address he had, the Weis lived on an old lane. In the early sixties, a number of "worker apartments" were built there, which were undoubtedly an improvement over the pre-1949 slums, but each apartment unit had then been partitioned and partitioned again, resulting in an entire family inhabiting one room of the original three-bedroom design, and all of the families sharing the kitchen and toilet.

It wasn't a surprise that the lane showed all the wear and tear of the past decades, even more so now that the apartment buildings were in sharp contrast to the skyscrapers that surrounded them. As he stepped into the lane, Chen felt a weird sense of disorientation. He was walking under a network of bamboo poles stretched across the lane, filled with damp laundry, like an impressionist expanse obliterating the sky overhead. The lane was rendered even narrower by the bewildering jumble of stuff stacked along both sides—a locked bike with a large bamboo basket, another covered with a large plastic sheet, a broken coal stove, a ramshackle tool-and-junk shed, and all sorts of residential add-ons, legal or illegal, seeming almost to have sprouted magically from the original houses.

It was like another city in another time, and the people seemed baffled at his intrusion: an old man squatting sideways with his bare back stuck against the wall, looking up at him; another straddling a wooden stool with one foot outstretched, inadvertently blocking the lane; and several more farther down the lane, one holding a large bowl of rice, another stretched out on a tumbledown bamboo recliner, and still another vigorously scaling a beltfish in a moss-covered common sink. Chen had never been to the lane before, yet some of the details struck him as eerily intimate, virtually inviting, as if someone close to him was waiting for him in the depths of the lane.

He stopped and knocked on a peeling door, which had to have been repainted quite a few times, at least once in red. It wasn't a visit he was looking forward to, but he had no choice.

An emaciated woman with swollen eyes and silver-streaked hair opened the door. Behind her was a small room furnished with old, worn-out basic necessities and a new black frame containing a photo of Wei in his police uniform. The woman recognized Chen and seemed flustered.

"Oh, Chief—Party Secretary Chen."

"Please just call me Chen, Mrs. Wei."

"Call me Guizhen, then."

She stepped out of the doorway and invited Chen in.

She had a hard time finding a chair for Chen in the tightly packed room. Judging from the two beds squeezed into the less than fifteen square meters of space, Chen assumed one of the beds was for their son in middle school. Wei hadn't been able to buy a larger apartment for his family, and now it would be totally out of the question.

Chen knew that Guizhen used to do piecework sewing for a neighborhood production group at minimum pay but that the group went bankrupt several years ago. Since then, the family had been dependent on Wei's income alone. With his sudden death, they would have to apply for the minimum city resident allowance, which, if eventually approved, would be pathetically small.

Chen thought about the possibility of bureau compensation again. But regulations were regulations, and if Wei died in a traffic accident on his own time, then the only money available would be what his colleagues around the bureau chipped in for him.

"You might not know this, Guizhen, but I joined the police force about the same time as Wei did—though he was older, having come back from Jiangxi Province as an educated youth. I still remember that in our first year at the bureau, we were both assigned to traffic. He was transferred to homicide after that, and he's done a great job all these years." Chen paused briefly, then resumed. "Before he died, Wei was engaged in an important investigation, to which I was serving as a consultant. Since it was really a case for the homicide squad, we didn't meet every day, and not on the day of his accident. Consequently, I don't know exactly what he was doing that afternoon, nor why he was at that particular intersection."

"He left early that morning without telling me what he was planning to do. As a rule, he didn't talk to me about police matters."

"Did he say or do anything unusual that you can think of?"

"Er—he was dressed rather formally that morning. He's not the type of man who was particular about his clothes. But occasionally, he would choose to dress more formally because of his work."

Occasionally, Chen would do the same. And if Wei was going to the hotel surreptitiously, that would have made sense.

"About the location of the accident, did he say anything to you? Like, if there was something he wanted to do there, or somebody he wanted to visit in that particular neighborhood?"

"Not that I can recall. Not at all."

"Did he call during the day?"

"No. I called him toward evening, but I didn't get him. He could work late, though, even stay overnight at the bureau. But the next morning I still hadn't heard from him. I was worried, so I called the bureau."

"In the bureau, some of his colleagues are suggesting that he might have been planning to take an evening class. There's a night school in the area."

"I don't know, but I don't think so," she said, wiping her eyes. with the back of her hand. "He worked hard all those years but was still a detective of the second rank because he didn't have a college degree. We were both 'educated youths' with our best years wasted during the Cultural Revolution, and sometimes he grumbled about it. But what could he do? Already in his fifties, he didn't have the time or energy for night school. Besides, our son is in middle school, and we couldn't afford the expense of another student."

That made sense but left unanswered the question of why Wei had been where he was.

"Let me ask a different question, Guizhen. Did he bring his lunch with him that day?"

"No, not that day. He frequently brought his lunch but only on the days that he knew he'd be at his desk in the bureau."

So it was possible that Wei could have gone to the intersection for lunch, given those inexpensive food stalls on that corner. But that was a stretch. It was difficult to imagine that, after leaving the hotel, Wei would have climbed the overpass across the street just to get lunch.

In the short spell of silence that followed, Guizhen stood up to pour him a cup of tea.

"I'm sorry, but the water isn't that hot, Chief Inspector Chen," she said in apology.

For a poverty-stricken couple, so many things are sad.

"The thermos bottle no longer really works," she said desolately.

There was only one old-fashioned, bamboo-shelled hot-water thermos, which stood on the table like an inverted exclamation mark. There was no refrigerator or appliances like that visible in the small room.

He couldn't help remembering the home of another widow he'd recently visited. Mrs. Zhou was heartbroken, too, but at least her family would be well taken care of. Some of the money embezzled by Zhou might eventually be recovered, but some would never be found.

"The reason I'm asking these questions, Guizhen, is because I'm trying to look into the possibility of compensation. If we could establish that he died on duty, I'd be able to have him acknowledged as a martyr with the due arrangement for his family."

"I don't know how I could ever thank you enough, Chief Inspector Chen. You're sending a cart of charcoal over in the winter. Let me tell you something about Wei. You just mentioned that he entered the force at about the same time as you."

"Yes, that's what I remember."

"Sometimes I couldn't help nagging at him. He was nothing compared to you, even though it wasn't exactly his fault. Like most people of his generation, he remained at a low level."

"That was because of the cadre promotion policy with its overemphasis on higher education. I was just lucky, with an unfair advantage over some of my colleagues."

"Do you know what Wei said when he was assigned to work the case with you? He said that there were things about you he didn't like or agree with, despite your high-ranking position, but at the end of the day, he would rather work with you than with anybody else. Period. You were one of the few conscientious cops left in today's society."

"It means a lot to me to hear of his opinion. Thank you for telling me this, Guizhen."

Chen felt even more wretched about what happened to Wei and about his inability to do anything for Wei's family. He could tell

Guizhen all the things he planned to do, but it wouldn't make any difference unless he succeeded in doing something.

Suddenly inspired, like a magician he whisked out the envelope containing his mother's gift card and handed it to the widow.

"Something small for your family," he said.

She didn't open it. That wasn't the Chinese convention. Instead, she pushed it back.

"I can't take it from you. It would be a different story if it were from the bureau, since Wei gave his best years to the job."

"It's not from me," he said, believing that honesty would be the best approach. "It's from a Big Buck friend of mine. In fact, I had been debating whether or not to accept it. Now I can use it for a good cause, so you're actually helping me out."

She stared at him for several seconds, incredulously.

"I was with Wei just the day before his death, drinking coffee and reviewing the case," he went on, pulling out the Häagen-Dazs gift card from his wallet. "For our discussion, he picked an ice cream place, mentioning that it was his son's favorite. This one is from me. Please accept it for both of them."

"Chief Inspector Chen . . ."

He rose and took his leave without waiting to hear anything else she might want to say.

But he'd barely made it to the end of the lane when he heard footsteps rushing up behind him. It was Guizhen, still clutching the envelope.

"It's way too much."

"Let's not talk about it anymore. As I have said, you're actually helping me out. The Big Buck friend gave it to me because of my position. I wouldn't be able to live up to Wei's trust if I took it for myself."

"I shouldn't—" Once again, she didn't finish the sentence. "Oh, you asked me if there was anything unusual about Wei that morning."

"Yes?"

"Before he left home, he examined and reexamined the picture in *Wenhui Daily*. The picture of Zhou and the pack of 95 Supreme Majesty, you know. He went so far as to look at it through a magnifying glass. At home, he seldom talked about his work, but that morning he showed the picture to me, asking whether I could make out the words on the cigarette pack."

"Could you?"

"No, I couldn't. They were too small and blurred."

FOURTEEN

CHEN'S SATURDAY STARTED WITH something that had little to do with his responsibilities as a chief inspector.

Detective Yu had called the previous evening.

"It would be a great favor if you could come to Longhua Temple on Saturday—just for ten or fifteen minutes, no more than that. It's the Buddhist service for Peiqin's late parents—her father was born a hundred years ago. Peiqin says that I shouldn't tell you about it. We know it's not something appropriate for a Party cadre like you to attend. But one of her cousins recently held a similar service, spending money like water, and inviting as many big shots as possible. So I think—"

According to a popular Buddhist belief, the deceased, once they reached the age of one hundred, went on to another life. So on the hundredth anniversary of their birth, their children generally arranged a religious service, preferably in a temple. It was extremely important in the tradition of Buddhist reincarnation, since afterward, there were no further obligations to the dead on the part of those still living in the world of red dust.

Chen wondered whether Peiqin really held such beliefs, but that didn't matter as long as her relatives did. Since Detective Yu never asked him for any favors, the chief inspector wasn't in a position to say no.

Besides, it might be a nice change from the latest round of ever-depressing routine meetings. He'd had to spend most of Friday at a meeting of the Shanghai Party Committee. As a new member, he wasn't required to say much, but all the political speeches by the leading members of the committee were not only boring but also inexplicably exhausting.

Qiangyu, First Secretary of the Committee, had made a long speech, emphasizing the great achievements in the city under the correct leadership of the Shanghai Party Committee. There might be something significant in the speech, Chen had vaguely sensed, so he had tried to read between the lines, but he soon gave up, surrendering instead to a dull yet dogged headache.

By Friday evening, Chen was glad of the chance to do something different, and something for Peiqin's sake.

"Of course I'll be there. I'll stay for as long as the ceremony takes; you can count on me, Yu."

Saturday morning, Chen was sitting in the back of a Mercedes driven by the bureau chauffeur, Skinny Wang.

"The Yus will have a lot of face at the temple today," Skinny Wang said, "in front of their relatives."

In the final analysis, Chen reflected, people had to believe in something—anything—in this age of spiritual vacuum. With no concepts such as the heaven or hell of Western religions, Chinese people took vague comfort in doing something like the temple service to help the dead in the next life.

The newly materialistic society was shaping many aspects of life according to its own terms—even things like this temple service. *The more expense, the more face.* That was a type of competition the Yus couldn't afford, which was why Yu, a non-Buddhist, had to bring Chief Inspector Chen—supposedly a high-ranking Party official—into the scene. It was all for the sake of face. Face was an important issue to the Shanghainese.

"Here we are, Longhua Temple," Skinny Wang declared.

Because of the ever-expanding boundaries of the city, the temple, originally located near the outskirts, was no longer considered too far away. And because of that location, it was larger than other temples nearer to the city center.

The driver parked and followed Chen as he stepped into an enormous courtyard leading to an impressive front hall lined with the gilded Buddhist statues, all of which were wreathed in spiraling incense. The wings on both sides of the main hall were rented out as service rooms and fetched large fees for the temple.

"Chen Cao, Party Secretary of the Shanghai Police Bureau, and member of Shanghai Communist Party Committee," said Peiqin. Not exactly surprised, she introduced him loudly to people as soon as he entered. "The legendary Chief Inspector Chen, head of the Special Case Squad, you must have heard or read about him—he is Yu's boss."

Peiqin's introduction included all the new official titles Chen had acquired. Chen understood.

"It's from our Party Secretary," Skinny Wang chimed in, putting down in front of the service table a large flower wreath with a white silk banner bearing Chen's name and official positions.

On the table were black-framed pictures flanked by burning candles, surrounded by a variety of Shanghai snacks and fruit.

"Both Yu and Peiqin are my friends," Chen said to the others in the room, after bowing to the photos.

Yu and Peiqin bowed back to him as a token of their gratitude.

127

Chen then held a bunch of tall incense in his hand, bowing respectfully three more times.

As Chen did so, all the others in the room seemed to be staring, holding their breath.

There were several chestlike cardboard boxes stacked up against the table, Chen observed as he put the incense into a container. The boxes probably contained netherworld money for the dead. Years ago, money for the dead was simply placed in large red bags. The imitation boxes with padlocks vividly painted on them represented an "improvement with time," showing sophisticated consideration for the convenience of the dead in the other world. Chen couldn't help wondering whether his gift of the wreath, standing alone, was out of place. Then he noticed that the wreath bore several ribbons and bows folded to look just like silk ingots.

"I don't know how to thank you, Party Secretary Chen," Yu said.

"There's no need for that, Yu. It's an opportunity for me to pay tribute to my uncle and auntie."

Like the use of "Party Secretary Chen" by Yu, "uncle and auntie" by Chen was for the benefit of others. Chen was becoming increasingly self-conscious, so he walked over to a monk arranging large envelopes on a side table. He tried to engage the monk in a conversation about Buddhism, but the latter simply stared at him blankly, without responding, as if Chen was an alien.

Peiqin moved over and whispered, "The service might lessen my guilt a little."

So that was one of the reasons she wanted to have the service. Her father had gotten into political trouble in her elementary school years and had died in a far-away labor camp. During the Cultural Revolution, her mother also passed away. Peiqin hardly ever talked to others about her parents. Only once did she tell Chen that as a little kid, she had been secretly resentful of her parents because her family background had shaped and determined her life in those years.

A line of monks started to file into the room. Like the others, Chen began kowtowing again. To his surprise, the head monk pronounced his name and position solemnly at the head of the list of the service participants, as if it would mean a great deal to the dead.

It caused another whispered stir in the room. Some of Peiqin's relatives began talking to one another, and her second aunt, a fashionable old lady with silver hair and gold-rimmed glasses, wobbled over using a bamboo stick.

She said to Chen, in earnest, "Thank you so much, Chief Inspector Chen. You have made the day for Peiqin, and for all of us as well. I've seen your picture in the newspapers. Perhaps we'll also see a picture of you in the newspapers here at the temple . . ."

She didn't have to finish the sentence: she knew the request was preposterous. Any pictures of him in the newspapers were in conjunction with articles about his work. They were never about him, a Party member police officer, being at a Buddhist service in a temple.

But Chen simply nodded, pulled out his cell phone, and punched in a number.

"Are you free this afternoon, Lianping?"

"Yes. Why, Chief Inspector Chen?"

"I'm at Longhua Temple. My partner, Detective Yu, and his wife, Peiqin, are going to have a meal as part of a service here. Some of their relatives were talking about the possibility of there being some pictures of the event in the newspaper . . ."

"All for the sake of face—in this world or the other. I understand," she said, but then added in a louder voice, "It's a free lunch, right? Actually, I want to thank you for thinking of me. I'll be there in twenty minutes, Party Secretary Chen."

Both Yu and Peiqin appeared flabbergasted, catching only fragments of the phone conversation during the monks' chanting.

In less than twenty minutes, Lianping walked in, her arrival heralded by a quick succession of flashes from the camera in her hands.

She came over to give Chen a hug, her cheek touching his. She was wearing a low-cut black dress, black heels, and a white silk scarf around her neck—along with a red-stringed *Wenhui* name tag.

"If Chief Inspector Chen wants me to come, how could I not?" she said with a sweet smile, shaking hands with Peiqin and Yu before she turned to the others. "I've been working on a profile of Chief Inspector Chen for *Wenhui Daily*, and these pictures will appear with the article. Chen is not just a hard-working policeman but a multifaceted person. The picture might well be captioned, 'Chen kowtows with his partner at the temple—the genuine human side of a Party official.'"

It sounded almost plausible, but he doubted that she would really run such a picture in the Party newspaper.

With the service gradually reaching the climax, he managed to withdraw into a corner, where Lianping soon joined him. They were left alone for the moment. Others knew better than to bother them, except when some latecomers had to be introduced to the distinguished guest, Chief Inspector Chen.

"Guess how much the service costs?" she whispered.

"A thousand yuan?"

"No. Far more than that. I've checked out a brochure at the entrance. The hall rental alone costs more than two thousand—and that doesn't include the fee for the service or the red envelopes for the monks."

"Red envelopes for the monks?"

"Have you heard the proverb, *An old monk chants the scripture without putting his heart into it*? That's easy for a monk to do, chanting, as they do, 365 days a year. According to folk wisdom, that would make the Buddhist service less effective. To make sure that the monks perform the service wholeheartedly, red envelopes are absolutely necessary."

In spite of her youth, she was perceptive, as well as cynical and opinionated, about the absurdities of contemporary social reality.

"Because of your high official position, your presence adds to their collective face," she went on, with a teasing smile. "So you are doing them a great favor. For that matter, Zhou would have been as passionately welcomed here, before his fall, of course. Ours is a society of connections—connections that are established through the exchange of favors."

He was taken aback.

"Detective Yu is my partner, and a good friend too," he said. "Don't read too much into it. We're not 'exchanging favors.'"

"I know things are different between you two. You're his boss, and you don't have to come. That's why I'm here taking pictures. But the service is beyond me. Philosophically, Buddhism is about the vanity of human passions, but this service is the very embodiment of vanity in the world of red dust, more relevant to the living than to the dead."

"That's true. I tried to talk to a monk about the difference between Mahayana and Hinayana. He simply stared at me as if I were an alien from another planet, gibbering in an indecipherable language."

Their conversation was interrupted by Peiqin's summoning all of them to a lunch at a restaurant across the street. According to a red notice on the gate of the restaurant, the meal was being held in a large room with three round tables. Yu and Peiqin were there, busily leading people to their respective tables.

Lianping was seated next to Chen at the main table. It was possibly a well-meant trick arranged by Peiqin, who was as eager for Chen to "settle down" as his own mother was. He had no objection to the seating arrangement, and Lianping smiled, playing along with whatever interpretation the host might have of her.

"The shrimp is fresh," Lianping said, peeling a large one with her slender fingers and placing it on his saucer—almost like a little girlfriend—before whispering in his ear. "I wonder why it's not a vegetarian meal."

Peiqin, leaning over to pour wine into Chen's cup, overheard her comment and responded with an approving nod.

"We checked out the menu of the vegetarian restaurant attached to the temple. It was two hundred fifty per person for the so-called vegetarian buffet, including Häagen-Dazs, as much as you can eat."

"What's the point of featuring Häagen-Dazs with a vegetarian meal?" Chen exclaimed.

"The meal following a service has to be expensive, or else the host—as well as the guests—will all lose face. Not to mention the ghosts of the dead. It's difficult for a vegetarian meal to be that expensive, hence the Häagen-Dazs."

"I think you made the right choice here, Peiqin," he said, helping himself to a chunk of sea cucumber braised with oyster sauce and shrimp roe.

A cell phone chirped. Several people immediately checked theirs, but it was Lianping's. She took out her phone and glanced at it without trying to answer it.

"Somebody has just forwarded me a microblog," she said.

"Microblog?" he said, the slippery sea cucumber falling from his chopsticks into the small saucer.

"It's just like a blog, except it's limited to no more than 140 characters. The government hoped such a short piece wouldn't stir up big trouble. But it's like a small Web forum, and people can read, comment on it, or forward it on their cell phones instantaneously. As a result, it's turning into another big headache for the 'stability-maintaining' officials. They're talking about requiring that people who access this sort of microblog register with their real names."

"So the Internet cops can easily track them down," he said, shaking his head. "Do you write microblogs as well?"

"No, but I read those of others." She leaned over and said in a low voice, "I've made some inquiries about Melong. The Web forum of his was one of the most popular in the city, appealing to a large group of readers. Because of its popularity, it attracted a lot of ads, which more than supported its operations. Melong is quite a character.

He keeps his forum popular, controversial, and from time to time comes perilously close to the last 'red line' drawn by the authorities, but never really crosses that line that would prompt the government to take action and shut the forum down. He's an old hand at avoiding any direct confrontation with the authorities while running the forum his way."

"So he's sort of independent."

"Sort of. You could say that. At least, he doesn't have to work another job. But he's also an occasional hacker. There are stories that he makes real money as a hacker, but one can't tell whether there's any truth to those stories. He's a cautious one. Anyway, I've never heard of him getting into trouble because of hacking. Within the circle, he's known for doing things in a way that is characteristic of jianghu."

"Jianghu—you mean he views his circle as an imagined world with its own ethical code, like those martial arts novels?"

"Yes. He's known for one particular attribute: he holds fast to his own rules. There are things he will do, and things he won't do. For instance, it's said that he makes a point of protecting his sources— which in turn adds to the popularity of his site. Then again, one never really knows: according to some sources, Melong also has connections in the government, and that's why he's been able to run it his way all along."

"What else?"

"What else?" she repeated, smiling, picking up a piece of beef in oyster sauce. "Like you, he's a filial son."

How did she know that about him?

An unexpected toast made by that aunt of Peiqin's provided an excuse for Chen not to respond to Lianping's comment.

"I want to thank you, Party Secretary Chen, and your beautiful journalist girlfriend. When the pictures appear in *Wenhui*, Peiqin's parents will be so happy in the netherworld."

He stood up in a hurry, cup in hand, but he didn't know what to say in response, or whether it was even appropriate to make a toast back.

Peiqin smiled across the table apologetically. Yu scratched his head.

Lianping pulled out her cell phone again, looked something up, then picked up a pink napkin and scribbled something on it. She pushed it over to him as he sat down again awkwardly.

"Here's Melong's phone number. You may as well call him. You can tell him you're my friend."

"Thank you."

The lunch came to an end, fortunately before someone else tried to make another toast.

Everyone walked across the street and back to the temple. Some carried boxes of food, and they didn't forget to put the boxes in their cars before reentering the temple.

Instead of going back into the room where the service was held, they now gathered around a huge bronze burner in the courtyard. It was time for people to burn the sacrifices for the dead. They started putting into the fire the boxes of netherworld money, along with some other imitation sacrifices, including a vividly detailed paper mansion.

"Look at the address," Lianping said, standing beside him.

"123 Binjiang Garden."

"The most expensive subdivision in the city of Shanghai."

"So the dead can enjoy the top luxuries in the netherworld, if not in this world. I don't think that has a lot to do with Buddhism, the burning of symbolic sacrifices for the dead. Perhaps it has more to do with Confucianism."

"There is something I don't understand about Confucianism. Confucius said, 'A gentleman doesn't talk about ghosts or spirits,' but at the same time, he urges people to offer sacrifices to their ancestors."

"These days, we're in an age of spiritual and ideological vacuum, and ours is a society with no religion to fall back on. For most people, nothing exists or matters but this present world. So this service, influenced as it is by the materialistic considerations of the here and now, provides a sort of cold comfort."

So saying, he leaned toward the burner. Among the sacrifices being consumed in the roaring flame, he was astonished to see a carton of imitation cigarettes.

"What? 95 Supreme Majesty!"

"You know, there's a new picture of cigarettes online," she said, her face flushed with the heat.

"Another photo related to Zhou?"

"No. Not directly. It's of some other Party officials in a conference room. For a conference, drinks and cigarettes on the dais are a given. The expensive ones are provided for free as a necessary government expense. In this new picture, however, the cigarettes have been taken out of the pack and placed on a small saucer. Why? So that people can't recognize the top brands. The conference organizers must have been nervous about causing another scandal. But they were foolish. No smoker ever dumps their cigarettes out of the pack like that, so the cover-up effort only drew more attention to it. It resulted in another avalanche of sarcastic comments from netizens about the picture."

She had a point. He himself would never have dumped the cigarettes out into a saucer, and he was no stranger to such things being provided at the government's expense. Fortunately, she was changing the topic.

"By the way, I've just heard that there will be a new bronze Confucius statue erected soon in Tiananmen Square. I wonder whether people will burn incense there as well."

"That's impossible," Chen said. "Think about the May Fourth movement, and Mao's denunciation of Confucianism."

"Nothing is impossible in today's miraculous China. Remember the old saying? When one is seriously sick, one can't afford to choose a doctor. But do you think resurrecting such an ancient idol will really solve the ideological crisis in our country?"

Her brows were arched. She was sharp. He saw the cynical humor in her eyes, and he liked that.

Whatever sacrifice was still burning in the containers in the temple courtyard, it was dying out.

FIFTEEN

MONDAY MORNING CAME, AND it was back to the office routine for Chief Inspector Chen. His work was interrupted by a number of expected and unexpected calls, making his day more fragmented than usual. In the midst of all that, he managed to spend some time working on various theories about the Zhou case. However, none of them seemed to be leading anywhere.

Party Secretary Li returned Chen's call regarding Wei's death.

"I have no objection to you looking into the cause of Detective Wei's death. Wei was a good comrade. But policy is policy. Unless you can prove that he was pursuing his investigation at that particular intersection, there's nothing we can do about providing compensation."

Chen could guess why the Party boss was so adamant. There was no use arguing with Li.

Later, an unexpected call came from Shan Xing, a *Wenhui* journalist who covered the crime beat. He, too, had heard of something about Wei's death and was trying to establish a possible connection to Zhou's death. Chen didn't say anything in response. Shan Xing went so far as to speculate about the timing of the arrival of the Beijing team in Moller Hotel. Again, Chen refused to make any comment.

Hanging up, Chen turned on his computer. Among the incoming e-mails was one from Lianping with a number of pictures of the temple service. Her message was a short one: "I've not yet decided which one to use for the profile. My boss approved the idea."

Instead of going through the pictures, however, Chen decided to compose an e-mail to Comrade Zhao in Beijing. The tone he intended to take was that of a very respectful long-time-no-report letter to the ex-secretary of the Party Central Discipline Committee. In fact, there was very little Chen could really report. He didn't mention the Zhou case in any detail, but he did express his concern about absolute corruption coming out of the absolute power of the one-party system. In passing, he touched upon the Beijing team now at the Moller Hotel. He hoped that Comrade Zhao would write back, throwing him some hints about what was going on at the top or the true reason for the Beijing team's having been sent.

To his surprise, Lieutenant Sheng of Internal Security gave Chen a call just as he was about to send the e-mail. Sheng was some sort of computer expert dispatched from Beijing, but he seemed to have bogged down in his assignment in Shanghai. Sheng didn't discuss his work in any detail; it was just a polite, base-touching phone call. Could Sheng's work or the call have something to do with the Zhou case? Chen didn't push for clarification. He hadn't been on too-friendly terms with Internal Security.

Shortly after noon, Detective Yu popped into his office with a brown paper bag containing some of the sacrifice cakes from the previous day.

"According to Peiqin, it's a time-honored convention that anyone present at the service must have some of the cakes from the sacrifice table. It's called heart-comforting cake. In our hurry, we forgot all about it. If it's convenient, Peiqin also wants you to take some to your journalist girlfriend."

"Peiqin never gives up, does she?" Chen said. "I only met Lianping a week ago—as an author meeting his editor."

"I simply repeat what Peiqin told me to say, Chief," Yu said, "but the cake isn't too bad. It's made of sticky rice. According to her, you can eat it as it is, but if you prefer, you can also steam or warm it first, and it will taste better."

After Yu left, Chen took out a cake shaped like a silver ingot with a red imprint in the center. He might as well have it for lunch.

He had hardly taken one bite of the slightly sweet cake when he got a call from Lianping. It turned out to be an invitation to a concert at the new Oriental Art Center in Pudong.

"A ticket for a concert there costs more than a thousand yuan, but they gave me two for free. It would be too much of a waste if I were to go by myself."

It was a tempting invitation. A trip to the concert hall would be an acceptable excuse for him to take a break. He'd worn himself out thinking and speculating about all the possibilities, but to no avail. A change of scene might help to clear his mind.

Besides, considering her willingness to come over to the temple last Saturday and her promptness in delivering the pictures to him and Peiqin, he wasn't in a position to say no.

"That's nice. I'll be there."

When he put down the phone, he noticed that it had started raining outside, a slow drizzle. He wondered at the promptness with which he had accepted her invitation. A siren was sounding in the distance.

He went back to the unfinished e-mail. It took longer than he expected to compose one to Comrade Zhao. He experienced a sense of relief when he finally sent it out.

Then he settled back to concentrate on the paperwork on his desk.

It was near four o'clock when he looked up again. The drizzle seemed to have continued off and on.

It could be a headache getting hold of a taxi on a rainy day, especially during rush hour. The Oriental Concert Hall was in Pudong, an area relatively new to him. He wasn't sure if he could get there by subway or how bad the traffic would be. It would be better to leave early, he concluded, putting a paperback and a paper-wrapped heart-comforting cake into his shoulder bag.

He decided not to take the bureau car. It would be too much to have the driver wait there until the end of the concert, and he might also tell stories afterward. It took Chen more than forty minutes to get there by the subway, but it was still faster than he'd expected. When he emerged from the subway, the rain was finally easing off, with a suggestion of a rainbow stretching out against the dismal horizon.

To Chen, Pudong was almost like another city. The map he brought with him didn't help much. Some of the streets and street names hadn't existed when the map was printed about two years ago. The surrounding high-rises jostled together into an overwhelming oppression. At least, it felt that way to him. He looked up at the gray clouds sailing precariously among the concrete and steel skyscrapers.

He thought he might as well wander about a little, just like Granny Liu lost in the Grand View Garden in the *Dream of the Red Chamber*. But he soon got weary of bumping around aimlessly. He glanced at his watch again. There was still more than an hour before the concert.

He saw a small Internet café tucked in behind a construction site. Originally, it might have been a temporary place for the workers to take a short break. It would probably be pulled down once the high-rise was finished. It might not be a bad idea for him to check his e-mail here, he thought, before going on to the concert hall.

When he stepped up to the front desk, a young man asked him to show his ID.

"I just want to check my e-mail," Chen said.

"It's a new regulation just put into effect this month. It was under the strict orders of the city government, and there's nothing we can do about it."

"Really!"

He produced his ID, and the young man recorded the ID number on a worn-out register before giving Chen another number.

"Fifty-one."

That must refer to the computer assigned to him. He walked over to number 51, toward the end of a row of desks.

Chen recalled what he'd heard from others during the investigation. Apparently this new effort on the part of the government was another step in the ever-tightening control of the Internet. It was no surprise that such a regulation had gone into effect without his knowledge. Internet control, too, was beyond the domain of the police bureau.

He sat down at the computer and pressed the power button. A boy sitting next to him was noisily wolfing down a steaming bowl of instant beef noodles, his eyes still locked onto a game in a crisis as it played out across his screen.

Signing on to his account, Chen found among his incoming mail a reminder from Lianping about this evening's concert. She was also still pushing him to write something for her from the point of view of an ordinary cop.

He then decided to check his Hotmail account, which he had acquired while visiting the United States as part of a delegation. Some of his friends in the States kept complaining about difficulties reaching him through his usual Sina e-mail account. He didn't check the Hotmail regularly, but it was still early, and he had some time to kill.

But he had problems gaining access to the Hotmail account. An assistant came over, tried several times, but with no more success than Chen. Chen was ready to give up when the assistant pointed him to another computer.

"Try that one."

Chen moved to the new one, which seemed to work better but was still mysteriously slow. After three or four minutes, he conceded defeat. He decided to do some research through Google instead but was again informed that he couldn't have access to it.

Shaking his head, he switched back to his Sina account and retrieved a draft he'd saved.

Crumpling a rejection slip, I step back into my role / shadowed by the surrounding skyscrapers. / I try in vain to make the case reports yield / a clue to the bell tolling over the city. / For all I know, what makes a cop makes me. / And I investigate through the small lanes / and side streets, the scenes once familiar / in my memories: a couple snuggling like / paper-cutouts on the door, a loner connecting / cigarettes into an antenna for the future, a granny / bending over a chamber pot in her bound feet / like a broken twig, a peddler hawking out of debris, / almost like a suspect . . . A sign DEMOLITION / deconstructs me. Nothing can avert the coming / of a bulldozer. It is not an easy task to push, / amidst the disappearing scene, the round to an end.

He wondered whether the poem had been inspired by Lianping's insistence. The images weren't new, but the idea of an ordinary cop's persona provided a framework, in which he found it easier to put what he wanted to say. He still wasn't satisfied with it, but he thought that was about all he could afford to do with it for the moment. After reading it one more time, he sent it out as an attachment.

He then noticed a new e-mail from Peiqin, who had also received the pictures Lianping had taken of the Buddhist service.

Thank you so much, Chief, for coming to the service, and for bringing along your pretty, talented girlfriend. The digital pictures she took are high-resolution. They can be enlarged as much as you like. On one of the pictures I discovered something I didn't even see at the temple—the address on the paper villa.

Chen turned to click Lianping's photo file. The picture Peiqin talked about was that of the paper villa burned as sacrifice in the temple courtyard. He enlarged the picture and, sure enough, could see the address clearly on the door—123 Binjiang Garden. It was the same thing Lianping had pointed out to him at the time. It was one of the most expensive subdivisions in Shanghai, a symbol of wealth and status in the city.

Once again, an elusive idea flashed through his mind like a spark. He stared hard at the screen. Possibly there was something he'd overlooked. However, the idea vanished before he could really get hold of it. The screen stared back at him.

Finally, he stood up from the computer.

At the front desk, the clerk checked the time he spent on "Computer 51" and another clerk charged him accordingly. They didn't bother to record that he'd moved to a different computer, he observed. After all, the employees weren't netcops. For them, the regulation was only an inconvenience, so it wasn't realistic to expect them to observe it conscientiously. He pushed over a five-yuan bill, and the clerk handed him the change.

He stepped out and made his way back to the concert hall. He was still about twenty minutes early. The concert hall was an ultramodern construction with a huge glass façade that incorporated metal sheeting of variable density. From where he stood near the entrance, he caught a glimpse of the interior partially covered with enamel ceramic, which alone must have cost an obscene amount of money.

He was startled out of his observation by a car pulling up alongside him, a slender hand waving out of the window.

"Have I kept you waiting long, Chief Inspector Chen?"

"Oh, no."

"Sorry, the traffic was terrible," Lianping said. "I'll park the car in the back and join you in one minute."

In four or five minutes, she emerged from the crowd with two tickets in her hand. She was wearing a light beige cashmere cardigan over a white strapless satin dress, and she had on silver high-heeled slippers, as if she was walking around in her living room.

She belonged to a different generation: "born in the eighties," as it was sometimes called. The term wasn't just about the time but about the ideas and values imbued by that time.

The lights in the concert hall were dimming as they entered and took their seats.

Tonight it was Mahler's Symphony No. 5 by the Singaporean Youth Orchestra. He had read and heard about Mahler, but he didn't usually have time to go to concerts in the city.

Somewhere backstage, a musician was erratically tuning his instrument. Lianping opened the program and studied it. In the semi-darkness, Chen found himself beginning to miss, somehow, the career he'd once designed for himself. It was during his college years, when he went to concerts and museums quite regularly. Like the rest of his generation, he had a lot to catch up on because of the ten years lost to the Cultural Revolution. But then he was assigned to the police bureau. Half closing his eyes, he tried in vain to recover the dream of his youthful days . . .

Turning to Lianping, he saw the rapture on her face as the symphony began, developing swiftly into emotional intensity. She was so enthralled she leaned back, slipped off her shoes, and, dangling her bare feet, subconsciously kept time with the melody.

He, too, was losing himself in trancelike impressions from the transformative performance, in the midst of which some fragmented lines came surging to his mind, carrying him to a transcendental understanding of the music, a vision breaking out in the splendid notes.

During the intermission, they chose to step outside.

In the magnificently lit lobby, Chen bought two cups of white wine. They stood drinking and talking while people were milling around.

"So you can get complimentary tickets?"

"Not for the most sought-after performances, but frequently, yes. In this new concert hall, the ticket prices are so high that there's no possibility that all concerts will sell out, so why not give a couple of free tickets to a journalist? A mention in *Wenhui* could be worth much more."

"You have to write a review of it?"

"A short piece will be enough. One paragraph. Nothing but clichés. All I have to do is say something about the excellent performance, something about the enthusiastic audience. Occasionally all I have to do is change the name and date. It will be nothing like the poem you sent to me."

"Oh, you've received it."

"Yes, I like it very much. It'll come out next week," she said, then pointed at a poster. "Oh, look; a red song concert—also next week."

"What a comeback," he said.

Of late, people were being urged to sing revolutionary songs again, particularly those that were popular during the Cultural Revolution, as if singing them could once again make people loyal to the Party.

"It's like black magic," she said. "Remember the Boxer Rebellion? Those peasant soldiers chanted, 'No weapons can hurt us,' as they rushed toward the bullets. Of course, they bit the dust."

It was a scathing comment, an echo from a scene in an old movie. For the moment, however, he found himself standing so close to her that the perfume from her body made his mind digress.

"I have a question for you, Chen," she said. "In classical Chinese poetry, the music comes from subtle tone patterns for each character in a line. With no such tone pattern in free verse, how can you come even close to music?"

"That's a good question." It was a question he'd thought about, but he didn't have a ready answer that could meet the expectation in her gaze. "Modern Chinese is a relatively new language. Its musicality is still experimental. So *rhythm* may be a better word for it. For instance, the varying length of the lines. It is called free verse, but nothing is really free. None of it is totally with or without rhythm or rhyme."

She was becoming something of an enigma. At one moment, she seemed so young and fashionable, but in the next moment, sophisticated and perceptive. That didn't keep him from appreciating her; if anything, it made him appreciate her even more than before.

A ringing bell announced that the second half of the concert would soon start.

"By the way, I almost forgot," she said, seemingly as an afterthought. "Here."

She held out a small card, on which was written Melong's name and phone number.

"Thank you. It's so thoughtful of you, Lianping. But you gave the number to me back at the restaurant."

"He changes his number every two or three months. Only those who are really close to him can keep track. I just got it from someone else," she said, draining the glass.

In the fading light, she took his arm, as if lost in thought.

They made their way back to their seats. Then the second half of the concert began, which they enjoyed all the way to the end. He was aware of her holding her breath, leaning toward him during the fantastic finale.

When the curtain fell, she still seemed enthralled by the music, clapping her hands longer than most people.

They walked out with the rest of the crowd. It felt suddenly noisy out in the open. Yet there was a pleasant breeze to greet them, ruffling a wisp of hair off her forehead.

"Thank you so much. I had a great evening," he said.

"The pleasure was mine. I'm so glad you enjoyed it."

He started looking for a taxi, which he knew might be difficult to find, with all the people still pouring out of the concert hall.

"You didn't drive?"

146

"No, I don't have a car."

"Surely there is a bureau car you could use."

"Yes, but not for a concert, and not when I'm in the company of an attractive young journalist."

"Come on, Comrade Chief Inspector Chen," she said. "Look at the line of people waiting for a taxi over there. It'll take you at least half an hour to get one. Let me give you a ride. Wait right here for me."

She came back around in her car, a silver Volvo. The model had a clever Chinese transliteration—*Fuhao*, which could also mean "rich and successful." She opened the door for him. The car was brand new and had a GPS system, which was particularly helpful in still-expanding Pudong.

Her hands on the wheel, she looked confident as she maneuvered the car dexterously in and out of traffic, like a fish in water. The shimmering neon lights outlined and re-outlined the night outside. He enjoyed the play of the lights on her face as she turned toward him, pressed a button. The moon roof pulled back luxuriously. She flashed a starlit smile. He couldn't help but feel that this city belonged to young, energetic girls like her.

She started to tell him bits and pieces about herself. She was born in Anhui, where her father had a small factory. Like a lot of non-Shanghainese, her father held on to a dream that his daughter, if not he himself, would be able to live and work in the city of Shanghai. To his great gratification, she obtained a job at *Wenhui Daily* after graduating from Fudan University. In spite of majoring in English, or perhaps because of it, she did well covering the financial news.

"You're the number-one finance journalist. It says so on your business card, as I remember," he commented as she took a sip from a water bottle.

"Come on. It simply means that you're the one trusted by the Party boss, the top journalist in the section. It does come with a bonus of one thousand yuan per month."

"That's fantastic."

"But it also means that to keep it, you have to write every piece with the interest of the Party in mind." The car took an abrupt turn, and she went on, "Oh, look at the new restaurant on your right. That is the number-one-restaurant choice for lovers, according to the *Mass Recommendation Web Forum*. It is totally dark inside, like a cocoon. The young people can't even see the food—instead, they are touching and feeling and groping the whole time."

She had a way of talking about things, jumping from one topic to another, like a sparrow flitting among the boughs, but she surely knew more than he did about the young, glamorous parts of the city.

"I grow old—"

"What do you mean, Chief Inspector Chen?"

"Oh, it just reminds me of a line."

"Come on. You're still the youngest chief inspector in the country," she said, patting his hand lightly. "I've researched it on the Internet."

When the car slowed down in the jam-packed tunnel to Puxi, he asked her where she lived.

"It's close to Great World. My father is a businessman, so he was able to make the down payment for me on an apartment there. It's been a good investment, having quadrupled in value in less than three years."

"Oh, so it's close to my mother's place."

"Really! Drop by my place next time you visit her. I've got the latest coffeemaker."

The car was already pulling up, however, by his subdivision near Wuxing Road.

She got out of the car at the same time as he did and was now standing opposite him, her clear eyes sparkling under the starry sky. It was an intoxicating night with a balmy breeze.

"Thank you so much. I've really enjoyed the evening. Not just the music, but also the conversation." He awkwardly added, "It's late, and my place is a mess. Perhaps next time—"

"So that's a rain check," she said, smiling and sliding back into her car.

He stood watching as her car disappeared into the distance. It was a wasted evening in terms of the investigation, but as he hastened to reassure himself, not entirely so. There was his visit to the Internet café prior to the concert, the mail from Peiqin with the pictures, and then the latest information about Melong. Perhaps some dots were beginning to form into possible lines, though nothing was yet clear . . .

Alone, in the stillness of the night, he might be able to figure something out.

Lianping reminded him, he realized, of a character from a French book he read long ago—*Rameau's Nephew.*

And again, he was getting confused.

SIXTEEN

MELONG WAS SITTING ALONE in his home office, brewing his third cup of Pu'er tea that morning, and restlessly alternating between putting his feet on the desk and then putting them back down on the floor.

He felt like a trapped animal.

The Confucian maxim that one should "pay respects to ghosts and spirits, yet keep yourself at a distance from them" had been working out so far—at least in his dealings with the cops, the net-cops, and with Internal Security and the city government as well. But this time, "paying his respects" didn't appear to be enough. The human-flesh search initiated by the photo of the pack of 95 Supreme Majesty appearing on his Web forum had resulted in an avalanche of questions from the authorities. The initial reaction to the picture wasn't totally unexpected, but the subsequent developments astonished him. Still, Melong didn't think he could be blamed for the results.

What he did wasn't that different from what others in his position had done, and controversy adds to the traffic of a Web forum. What he hadn't told the netcops was the sense of satisfaction he felt over the downfall of another corrupt official, and in seeing the embarrassment of the "ever-correct-and-glorious" Party authorities.

Still, what he *did* tell them was true. He had no idea who'd sent the original picture. Using all his expertise, he'd traced the IP address of the sender to a particular computer, but it turned out to be at an Internet café. The netcops must have made the same effort and come up with the same results. So that was the end of it. Or it should have been.

But it wasn't. The netcops concocted a conspiracy theory that somehow Melong had gained access to Zhou's computer, got hold of that picture, posted it online, and then invented the story of an anonymous user having sent the picture from an Internet café. They based their scenario on his hacker credentials. After all, they claimed, an ordinary person wouldn't have been able to read the cigarette brand from a newspaper photo.

They were bent on punishing him, not because they really believed their theory or because they were worried about his occasional computer hacking, but because the Web forum was becoming a chronic headache for the Party authorities. This was an opportunity to shut it down for a seemingly legitimate reason.

For the moment, the netcops might still be looking for evidence, but with or without it, they were going to "harmonize" the Web forum out of business. It was just a matter of time.

A loud coughing from the room in the back reminded him that the Web forum wasn't the only thing worrying him. He'd never felt so helpless.

He was preparing another cup of strong tea—black enough to dye his gray hair—when the silver-gray cell phone started to ring. Strange. It was a "private phone," for which he'd just bought a prepaid SIM card only a couple of days ago. Only a few knew the number, which he would change again in a month. He picked up the call.

"Hi, I'd like to speak to Melong."

"Speaking. Who is this?"

"Chen Dao."

It was an unfamiliar voice, and an unknown name.

"Chen Dao," Melong repeated the name, still unable to recall anything about it from his memory.

"Your friend Lianping recommended you to me."

"Lianping?" He knew her, but it wasn't like her to recommend him to someone, and he didn't remember having given her the new phone number. "What can I do for you?"

"I'd like to talk with you. How about over a cup of good tea at Tang Flavor on Hengsan Road?"

He had heard that Tang Flavor served excellent tea. It also wasn't a good idea to meet with a stranger at his home office, which might well be bugged, or over a phone that might be tapped.

"Okay, I'll meet you there. How about half an hour, depending on the traffic."

Half an hour later, Melong arrived at Tang Flavor. Located close to a subway, the teahouse enjoyed a loyal customer base and was particularly popular for the Chinese snacks that were served for free with the tea.

Melong's private phone rang again. This time it was a text message.

"Welcome. I'm on the third floor. A6."

He went over to the stairs, where a waitress in a scarlet Tang dress led him to a private room. She held the door for him with an engaging smile.

Upon his entrance, a middle-aged stranger stood up and reached out his hand. He was wearing a white shirt, and there was a dark blue blazer draped over the back of a mahogany chair.

"So you're Chen Dao?"

"Chen Cao," he corrected, "of the Shanghai Police Bureau."

Now the name rang a bell. Melong must have heard it wrong over the phone.

"I was afraid to say more on the phone," Chen said with a wry smile, "since some people might not want to show up after learning I'm a cop. Thank you for coming over at such short notice."

"It's an honor to meet you, Chief Inspector Chen. I've heard a lot about you," Melong said, then added, "You're investigating the Zhou case, correct?"

"I've heard about you too," Chen said, without responding to his question. "Lianping suggested that I consult with you. She tells me that you're a computer genius."

He was a regular cop, not a netcop involved with overseeing the Internet, so what could Chen possibly want to consult him about? As is stated in the old proverb, people don't come to a temple without having something specific to pray for.

"So do you know Lianping well?" Melong asked. "She's an excellent journalist, but I haven't seen her in a while."

"We had lunch yesterday."

"That's great," Melong said, pulling out a pack of cigarettes. "Smoke?"

"Take one of mine." Chen produced a pack of Panda. "But first, a disclaimer. An old friend gave them to me. It's not something I could afford myself."

"Don't worry about it, Chief Inspector Chen. Let me be frank with you. You're not the first cop who has come to me, but you're the first real one."

"What do you mean?"

"Well, all the people who've come to me before are 'netcops'—

wang guan. They started showing up long before the scandal of Zhou and the pack of 95 Supreme Majesty. They have been no strangers to me from the day I launched my Web forum."

"Yes, I've heard of these so-called netcops. Let me reassure you that I'm not one of them."

The waitress came into the room carrying a thick tea menu and a long-billed bronze kettle.

Chen ordered ginseng oolong, and Melong chose Pu'er, the Yunnan tea.

"Enjoy your tea," the waitress said, bringing out the tea leaves from drawers in the table, putting each into a teapot, then pouring hot water from the kettle into their respective pots. "Snacks, which are on the house, are also listed on the menu."

"We'll have tea first," Chen said. "When we are ready for anything else, we'll let you know."

When they were again alone in the room, Chen resumed. "You were talking about your Web forum, Melong."

"Yes, for a Web forum like ours to survive, two things are necessary," Melong said. He was guessing that was the purpose of this meeting with Chen. Chen was supposed to be almost at the top of the city police bureau, so he had to concern himself with the Zhou case and its cyber background. Disgruntled as Melong was with the netcops, there was no point in making another formidable enemy of a regular cop who was inquiring into the Internet scene. "Those two necessary things are the permission of the government and the popularity of the content. There's no need to say much about the first part. For that, social harmony is the bottom line. On the other hand, if only a few people visit the forum, it won't last. The number of hits determines the amount of ad revenue. Enough ad revenue is required for a forum to meet its bills."

"I understand. Now, let's be a bit more specific, Melong. Why such a big fuss about that picture of 95 Supreme Majesty? Why start one of those searches over that?"

"Let me first say that a human-flesh search isn't necessarily started by a Web forum. Any photo or article can be posted online, but if no one pays attention, nothing will happen."

"That's true."

"So when I posted the photo, I didn't know what kind of response it would get."

Which was exactly what he'd told the netcops. There was no point in talking about his efforts to urge the forum users to respond and react, which then turned into the frenzied crowd-sourced search for incriminating information on Zhou. There was no visible change in Chen's facial expression, Melong observed. Allegedly, Chen was one of the few cops who still adhered to some principles. That had to be true, or Lianping wouldn't have given Chen his number.

"Is this kind of human-flesh search ideal?" Melong started up again. "Surely not—at least, not for an ideal society. But in a society like ours, what else can people possibly do? There isn't a real independent legal system, despite all the talk—"

Melong cut himself short. The police officer sitting opposite him, however unorthodox, was still a representative of the system.

"Nor are there any independent newspapers," Chen responded, nodding. "So the Internet has emerged as a necessary alternative, and an outlet for the people."

"You've got it, Chief Inspector Chen. One of the netcops said something similar to me, except that he emphasized that the Internet is a controlled outlet, and that netcops function as the necessary control. No one should think that they're anonymous or invisible in cyberspace and that they can say whatever they want without worrying about the consequences. That's absolutely not true. Thanks to technology, not only are sensitive words detected and deleted—'harmonized,' all for the sake of a harmonious society—the Web site itself can be blocked and banned, and the government can also trace the comments all the way back to the user."

"I'm well aware of that," Chen said slowly, sipping at his tea.

"About these Internet human-flesh searches, I hear some claim that these people are simply trying to do the job of journalists. But could you imagine something like that being published in *Wenhui Daily*? Others claim that these netizens are just unruly mobs, lacking moral and social responsibility. But who has the power to define social responsibility? Whatever else may be said, these Internet feeding frenzies are an undeniable indication that people don't have any other way to seek justice or voice their opinion."

Melong was confounded by the thrust of Chen's statement. He decided not to say anything, at least no more than was absolutely necessary, in case Chen was setting up a trap.

"There are so many people now joining forces, or taking part in one search or another, that it reminds me of an old Chinese saying— the law cannot punish when too many people are involved." After a pause, Chen went on, "But can you tell me more—any details at all—about how you got the photo you posted online?"

Here it came. Melong wasn't unprepared.

"I've already told the netcops everything. But for you, I'll go over this one more time. I got an e-mail with that photo attached. The e-mail message was simple. 'This picture appeared in *Liberation*, *Wenhui*, and other official newspapers last Friday. Look at the pack of cigarettes in front of Zhou, the director of the Shanghai Housing Development Committee. What's the brand? 95 Supreme Majesty. Do you believe an incorruptible Party cadre working wholeheartedly in the interests of the people could afford it?'

"Officials smoking the top, most expensive brands is nothing new. But out of curiosity, I looked at that day's newspaper, which threw new light on the picture. As a rule, we don't post anything without knowing the identity of the contributor. This time, however, it was a picture that had already been published in the official media, so we didn't have to worry about its authenticity. I simply posted the photo online and put the e-mail message underneath it. What happened then, you must already know."

"The netcops came to you after that, right?"

"It wasn't just the ordinary netcops. Before they showed up, some people from the city government hurried over, a group headed by somebody named Jiang. Then Internal Security showed up too. At their insistence, I dug out the original e-mail. They looked into it, and according to the IP address, it was sent from an Internet café not too far from here. That's it." Melong paused and took a big sip of tea before he continued on. "They want me to help them ferret out the anonymous sender, but what's the use of dragging me in? They have far more resources at their disposal than I do."

Melong chose not to go into what netcops might do to him. There was no point. The chief inspector couldn't side with him.

"Yes, that is really up to them to do. They're the netcops, after all."

The sarcasm in Chen's statement was unmistakable. It was difficult, however, for Melong to play along in the dark. He thought he'd better wait until the cop showed all his cards.

"You think so too?" Melong asked.

"It's not easy to run a Web forum like yours. You're doing something meaningful, an alternate way for people to find out what's happening in our society, our socialist society with Chinese characteristics. On your Web forum, they're allowed to speak their mind despite the difficult circumstances and stringent regulations."

"Thank you, Chief Inspector Chen. Things must not be easy for you, either, what with all those complicated responsibilities on your shoulders."

"You're right." Chen lit a cigarette for him, and then one for himself. They spent the next minute wrapped up in the silent, spiraling smoke. "The case I'm working on is another difficult one. For me, the one and only focus is determining the cause of Zhou's death. But before we could get anywhere near to a conclusion, my colleague Detective Wei died in a suspicious accident. I hold myself more or less responsible for the accident that killed him. He might have discovered a clue while investigating, but I was too busy to discuss the case with him that morning, and I failed to warn him of the risk involved in taking the case in that direction."

Melong began to see why Chen set up this meeting at the teahouse. The chief inspector was intent on revenge, and in desperation, he was seeking Melong's help. But if he thought it involved something like hacking into Zhou's computer, the way the netcops did, then Chen was making the same mistake.

"It's difficult for me," Chen continued, "because there are so many different people working on the same case, and some of them were involved before we were brought to it. The shuanggui of Zhou began a week earlier, and they already had his computers and files taken away. All the information made available to me looks like it was secondhand or preselected."

"According to one of the netcops who spoke to me," Melong said tentatively, "the hard drive of Zhou's computer was destroyed before they got to it. But who do you think are the likely suspects?"

"For the moment, I'm working on one possible direction, though it's only one among many. The picture in the newspaper is too small and the resolution too low for anyone to be able to see the cigarette brand. So whoever sent the picture in must have had access to the original one on Zhou's computer—one that was high enough resolution that it could be enlarged so that the details would be readable. This occurred to me when I was looking at some other pictures that were sent to me electronically."

"That makes sense," Melong said, without adding that it was the same theory that the netcops were working on.

"Now, who could have access to the original photo? The people close to Zhou, who would be able to sneak into his office and check his computer or his camera," Chen said. "As Detective Wei said to me, one approach would be to focus on who might have benefited from making Zhou's problems public."

"That would narrow down the list."

It was like a tai chi performance. Each of the players made a show of striking out in a direction, without really hitting the opponent. The true intention was to understand each other. Melong got it. While Chen seemed to be moving in the same direction as the netcops, he wasn't after Melong.

Whether a target or not, Melong didn't want to have anything to do with the police.

"But it's just a list. That's why we have to help each other, Melong. Once the case is solved and everything comes out, I don't think the netcops or any of the others will waste their time on you."

The hint was unmistakable. Given Chen's position and connections, it wasn't impossible for the chief inspector to help. At least this time. Melong started debating with himself.

A cell phone rang. It was Chen's. He pulled out a white phone.

Melong moved to step out of the room, but Chen gestured for him to stay.

"Sorry, it's just from my mother, but I have to take it."

Chen spoke like a filial son. Melong couldn't help noticing the change of expression on Chen's face. It looked like one of immediate relief. The next few fragmented words and sentences that were Chen's side of the conversation didn't make much sense. They were, of course, out of context.

"I did . . . my colleague's widow . . . to Mr. Gu about it . . . Yes, I'll thank Dr. Hou properly . . . come around either tomorrow or the day after that . . . Yes, I will . . . East China . . . Take good care. See you."

Chen put the phone back into his pants pocket and said, "My mother had a minor stroke, and she's just checked out of East China Hospital. I keep the phone on at all times. She's old and all alone, so I'm concerned."

"She doesn't live with you?"

"No, she insisted on not moving in, saying that she prefers to stay in the old neighborhood. But she won't stay in the hospital too long, worrying about the cost."

"Which hospital did you say it was?"

"East China Hospital."

"No surprise, for a high-ranking cadre like you."

"No, that wasn't it. She was admitted because of a doctor I know there. He's also the head of the hospital. It was due to connections, you might say, but I have to do whatever I can for my mother. Anyway, he's been taking good care of my mother, whether it has anything to do with my position or not."

"In today's society, no one is capable of doing anything without connections, and connections come from one's position," Melong said, then added in spite of himself, "Not everybody is as lucky as you are."

"What do you mean, Melong?"

"My mother has been diagnosed with lung cancer, second stage, but before any hospital in the city will admit her, she has to wait at least two months. She has no chance of getting into a top one such as East China. I feel so helpless," he said, with a slight sob in his voice. He drained the last of the tea from his cup. "I'm a total unworthy son."

"I understand. I feel exactly the same about myself," Chen said; then he pulled out another phone and punched in a number.

Melong watched Chen, puzzled.

"Dr. Hou, I have to ask you for a favor," Chen said emphatically. "A friend's mother needs to get into the hospital as soon as possible. She has advanced lung cancer. I know how difficult it is for you to arrange an admission at East China, but I still want to beg you for it this time."

Melong couldn't hear Dr. Hou's response, but it wasn't long before Chen spoke again.

"Thank you so much, Dr. Hou. I owe you a big one."

Apparently Dr. Hou was saying something on his end, but Chen cut him short. "We can call it even now. Don't mention that again."

The last part was intriguing. It sounded like an exchange of favors, but Chen was already turning back to him. "Dr. Hou will admit your mother first thing tomorrow morning. Don't worry. He'll take care of everything."

"Such a huge favor," Melong said as he stood up and bowed low. "I have to say, as in a martial arts novel, 'If I cannot pay you back in this life, in the next I will be a horse or an ox working for you.'"

"You don't have to say that, Melong. But in those martial arts novels, people also say, 'The green mountains and the blue water will always be there, and our paths will cross again.'"

That quote was to the point, Melong knew.

"Now I have to go and prepare for her admission tomorrow. As a son yourself, you must understand," Melong said. "But I'll call you, I give you my word, as soon as I have something."

SEVENTEEN

ON THE EVENING OF the next day, Chief Inspector Chen left the bureau and walked out into the gathering dusk, still lost in thought.

Walking sometimes helped him think, especially when he was confronted by many possible directions. It was like an English poem that he'd read back in college. The poet could afford to speculate about the consequences of a road not taken in the yellow wood; a cop could not.

That afternoon, after the routine bureau meeting, he'd once again tried to shift his investigation in a new direction.

First, he tried to look into what Zhou had done during the last days of his life. But soon Chen gave up. What if the pack of 95 Supreme Majesty was just a trigger? Zhou might have been involved in something long before that. The presence of the city government team at the hotel pointed to such a possibility. Then Chen tried to figure out what Detective Wei had been doing on the last day of his life. Chen made several phone calls, reaching out to every possible contact, but it would be days before he learned anything useful.

Finally, Chen tried to find out the reason the Beijing team had been dispatched to the hotel. Comrade Zhao hadn't written back yet, and there were all sorts of whispered stories, but none of them proved to be substantial.

Ultimately, he was exhausted, with nothing really accomplished. He decided to call it a day and go pay a visit to his mother. She was back home and living alone, where only an hourly maid who could hardly speak Shanghainese came by occasionally.

He kept walking, absentmindedly, until he found himself at Yunnan Road, a street he'd known well back in the days when he still lived with his mother. It was a street known for its ramshackle eateries with a variety of cheap, delicious specialties. Smelling the familiar scents, he thought it would be a good idea to buy some cooked food for his mother.

Nowadays, it was called a "gourmet street," with a number of new, tall buildings and splendid restaurants in place of the old shacks. He walked over to Shenjiamen, a recently opened restaurant that sported an impressive array of basins near the entrance, plastic and wooden containers of various colors and sizes and shapes, each containing sea and river delicacies. He came to a stop at the sight of crowding squid, squirting clams, squirming trout, jumping frogs, and crawling crabs, as if they were still scuttling along the silent floors of rivers and oceans. A snakelike hose dipped in and out of the basins, pumping air into them in a bubbling appearance of life. There were several people lingering, likely or unlikely customers, squatting or standing around. A young mother looked down at the little boy tugging at her hand, her face radiant under the neon light that flashed: *Private Room, Elegant Seat.*

His phone rang and interrupted his reverie. It was Jiang of the city government.

"Fang has disappeared, Chief Inspector Chen."

"Fang?"

"Zhou's secretary. Nobody knows where she is. Not even her parents."

"I've not met or interviewed her. Detective Wei told me that you didn't see her as a potential suspect."

"Not a suspect in Zhou's death, no, but she might have been privy to his corruption. We talked to her quite a few times, and she denied any knowledge of his criminal activities."

"She's just a secretary. On the list of people privy to Zhou's problems, she might not be at the top."

"She wasn't just a secretary—she was *a little secretary*, Comrade Chief Inspector Chen."

"I didn't know, Jiang," Chen said, though he recalled both Wei and Zhou's colleague Dang using the term. He ignored Jiang's sarcastic tone. Trying to find out more, Chen said, "In fact, you didn't tell me anything about her."

"It was Zhou who brought her into the office. She studied in England a couple of years ago, and she still has a valid passport, as well as a valid visa that would allow her to travel to England and Europe. We have to prevent her from slipping out of the country. I've already informed customs and provided them with her picture."

"I see." But something didn't add up. She might know something about the details of Zhou's shady schemes, but that wouldn't be a "state secret." It was certainly nothing for Jiang to panic over.

"You have to find her as soon as possible, Chief Inspector Chen. I've discussed it with your Party Secretary Li, and you're the one with experience in searching for a missing person."

"Please fax or e-mail me all the information you have about her immediately. Send the photos you have of her as well. At the same time, inform Liao of the homicide squad that I'll do my best," Chen added before hanging up.

This was another twist, although Chen didn't see anything particularly surprising about Fang's disappearance. Jiang had, by his own admission, talked to her quite a few times, undoubtedly bringing a lot of pressure to bear on the secretary—or *little secretary*—so much so that it was very possible that she couldn't take it anymore and ran away. An understandable reaction on her part, and she might come back before the police even started looking for her. It was very apparent that Jiang wasn't telling him everything. Why would Jiang have bothered notifying customs?

He decided not to visit his mother right now. Instead, he stepped into a small Internet café across the street. Like in the one near the concert hall in Pudong, it had a plastic sign marked *Registration* on the front desk. This time, he produced his ID without being asked.

Perching on the chair in front of his assigned computer, he had a free cup of tea, which tasted like it had been rebrewed, and then started looking through his e-mail. The first batch of material had already come in from Jiang, including several photos. The photos were of Fang when she was still in her twenties. They showed a handsome, spirited girl, and there was nothing that suggested she was or would become a *little secretary*. He glanced through some of the background information, but there was nothing really new or useful, either. It might take him hours to sort through everything.

His cell phone rang. Caller ID showed that it was Lianping, so he picked up. After exchanging greetings, Chen asked, "What's up?"

"I'm going to the Shaoxing Literature Festival tomorrow. "

"That's nice—have you ever been there?"

"No, this will be my first time. It's only one hour outside of Shanghai, and the sponsor is providing me a 'journalist's package.' It includes a ticket to tour Lu Xun's residence, meal coupons, and if I stay over, accommodations at a four-star hotel."

"What a nice package!"

"I mentioned your name to the sponsor and they would love to invite you to come and speak. Everything would be covered, and it would also include a handsome speaker's fee."

"Thank you, Lianping. I might not have the time to attend the festival or to give a speech, but I'll think about it."

"Please do. If you decide you can come, I'll put you in touch with the organizers. I'll be there, you know."

After hanging up, he thought about it. For a brief moment, he felt drawn to the city of Shaoxing, if only for the chance to take a short vacation there. *Oh, a "vacation" is the draw, is it?* he joked with himself—surely not *the one who invited you?* He tried to mock himself out of thinking about a possibly romantic vacation. Shaoxing was a city with a long cultural history, he reflected. It was known for its association with many celebrated men of letters, and particularly with Lu Xun, a modern Chinese writer whom Chen passionately admired.

With the investigation in the state it was, however, he didn't think he could spare the time for the trip. So he started to settle back into the various files about Fang when another call came in, this time from Melong.

"I have something for you, Chief Inspector Chen. Where are you?"

"I'm on Yunnan Road."

"Ah, you're on the gourmet street. It's quite close to me. How about I meet you there in ten minutes? I have something to show you."

"That's good. I'll wait here for you," he said, looking across the street at a restaurant on the corner near Ninghai Road. "I'll be at the Four Seas Cross-Bridge Rice Noodles."

Chen left the Internet café and walked over to the noodle restaurant. To his surprise, it wasn't crowded. He sat down at a corner table. He had hardly finished looking through the menu when Melong stepped in with a large envelope in his hand.

"This is one of the few places around here that hasn't really changed," Melong said, sitting down opposite. "An excellent choice."

But even this noodle place had changed some, the service fancier and the menu more varied than Chen remembered. The waiter put down on the table more than a dozen tiny saucers of fresh toppings, including thin-sliced pork, beef, lamb, fish, shrimp, and vegetables, before bringing over two large bowls of noodles immersed in steaming hot soup covered with a thin layer of oil. They were supposed to immerse the toppings in the soup, then wait for a minute or two before eating. They were the same cross-bridge noodles Zhou had had for his last meal.

The moment the waiter stepped away Melong pushed the envelope across the table to Chen.

It contained a bunch of pictures of Zhou and Fang in the office, the two touching and kissing each other there. One picture showed Zhou sitting on the desk with his trousers half removed, and her kneeling in front of him on the carpet, naked to her waist, her hair cascading down over her bare back. Then there were several more explicit ones showing the two of them in bed, totally naked, engaged in the entangling ecstasy of rolling cloud and rain. The pictures were of low quality, and most of them were rather blurry.

"Where did you get these?"

"You know a thing or two about my work, don't you? These photos were found on Dang's computer."

"Dang's computer—how?"

But Chen didn't have to wait for the answer. One of the angles he'd discussed with Detective Wei was who would benefit from Zhou's murder, an approach he had mentioned when talking with Melong. While the relationship between Zhou and Fang was not unanticipated, the source of the pictures put Dang in a new light. Figuring out why Dang had taken them was a no-brainer. They were evidence he could use against Zhou, having secretly installed a video camera in Zhou's office.

The pictures would have been enough to bring down Zhou and for Dang, the second in command, to succeed to Zhou's position. Dang might have simply been biding his time until the 95 Supreme

Majesty scandal broke out, making it no longer necessary for him to release those photos.

Alternatively, he could have been blackmailing Zhou with these pictures.

"The other day you mentioned that people in Zhou's office were on your radar," Melong said. "I checked into each of them, and this is what has come up so far."

He didn't have to explain further. Chen nodded.

But that led Chen back to a question that had occurred to him earlier in the day.

He wasn't interested so much in Fang's appearance in these pictures as he was in Jiang's panic about her sudden disappearance. A clandestine relationship between a boss and his little secretary wasn't really surprising in China. Jiang must have known something about it before Fang disappeared: but was he now worried about these graphic photos coming to light? Was Jiang just irrationally panicky?

Or was it something else?

When Chen pulled himself back into the present moment after being so lost in thought, he realized that Melong was looking at him with a wry smile.

"What is it?"

"The noodles are now cold and taste like glue with all the soup soaked in."

"I'm sorry. It's my fault entirely."

"No, it's my fault. I should have shown you the pictures after we'd finished eating."

"Let's order something else."

"No thanks. I'm not really hungry. "

"I owe you one, Melong. I'll treat you to a better meal another day." He added belatedly, "How is your mother?"

"She's already in the hospital. The doctor is taking special care of her. I should go over there now. The hospital won't admit visitors after eight."

Watching Melong get into a taxi, Chen felt a twinge of guilt about not visiting his mother. In a somber mood, he pursued his plan to have some cooked food delivered to her. He walked over to Little Shaoxing Chicken Restaurant and settled on the Shanghai-style smoked carp and half a three-yellow chicken.

Even though it was getting late, Chen contemplated, perhaps it wasn't too late for him to go and interview Fang's parents.

So he walked back over to the Internet café. The attendant recognized him and led him to a computer without asking to see his ID again. He logged on and retrieved the file Jiang sent, then copied Fang's address.

He couldn't shake the feeling, however, that there was something else, something dancing just on the edge of his thoughts. Was it in Lianping's call about the festival in Shaoxing, something possibly connected to the investigation, that slipped away when he was distracted by Melong's call?

Then he got an idea.

He took a folder out of his briefcase and looked through it. It turned out to be just as he remembered.

Last year, Zhou had made two trips to Shaoxing. Born and raised there until he was seven, he left for Shanghai when his father's job was transferred. Zhou hadn't been back there even once until last year. The information gathered by Detective Wei was quite detailed, including all of the trips Zhou had taken in the last several years and their purpose, as well as the people, especially the local officials, he met with. But that wasn't the case with his trips to Shaoxing. Wei had no details on them. So Zhou had gone to Shaoxing for some unrevealed personal reason.

There was a note in the folder stating that Zhou had no property under his own name in Shaoxing. Wei had done a thorough job, taking into consideration Zhou's position and connections.

Of course, a man could suddenly be so nostalgic as to decide to visit his old home, even going there twice in one year. But that wasn't likely, particularly not for a busy official like Zhou.

Chen took out his phone and made a call to Party Secretary Li, saying that he might have to make a speech at a literary festival outside of Shanghai but that he'd be back in a day.

"Of course you need to go, Chief Inspector Chen."

Li didn't even ask where the festival was, or about the ongoing investigation.

"If there's anything urgent, just call me, and I can be back in an hour or two."

"Don't worry about it. Just go. After all, you're a celebrated poet."

After hanging up, Chen checked the Shanghai-Shaoxing train schedule online. There were several fast trains going there the next morning. He'd take one, even though this trip was nothing more than a long shot.

He stood up and left the Internet café.

Outside, there was a lone black bat flittering about in the evening that was spread out against the somber sky.

EIGHTEEN

THE NEXT MORNING, CHEN took the new fast train to Shaoxing station.

Once on the train, Chen called Detective Tang, one of his connections in the local police bureau. A few years ago he'd helped Tang break a tough case, one which, if Chen hadn't intervened, would have taken months longer before it got any official attention from the city of Shanghai.

"What good wind brings you to Shaoxing today, Chief Inspector Chen?"

"Well, somebody told me there was a literature festival here, and I just happened to have something else to do in town."

"What can I do for the Shanghai Police Bureau?" Tang said, coming directly to the point.

"No, I'm not here in an official capacity, so I didn't make contact through official channels. However, I do need to ask a favor."

"I'm glad you thought of me. Of course I'll do whatever I can to help. I could never forget your assistance back in Shanghai when that pig-headed Party Secretary Li—"

"Let's not talk about him right now. You might have heard of the Zhou case—the pack of 95 Supreme Majesty and all that. It's not exactly my case, but it's a case that's special to the bureau, and one of my colleagues died in an incident possibly connected to the investigation."

"One of your colleagues died. I'm sorry to hear that. So now the investigation is on your radar."

"Yes. I've learned that Zhou was born in Shaoxing, but he left for Shanghai when he was six or seven years old. He hadn't returned to Shaoxing until about a year ago. And he came back more than once. It would be a great help if you could assemble any information about Zhou's two visits to Shaoxing and about any relatives he might have contacted here—perhaps you could bring the information to the train station? Let me give you my cell phone number," Chen said, rattling off the number of a cell phone he'd just purchased. "Of course, please, not a single word about my visit to your colleagues."

Two hours later, as he walked out of the Shaoxing railway station, Chen was surprised to find himself facing a large modern square thronged with people and beyond it, an impressive six-lane thoroughfare filled with noisy traffic. There was also a line of taxis waiting along the curb.

Chen's assumptions about Shaoxing had come mainly from the writings of Lu Xun, a "revolutionary writer" endorsed by Mao and the Party authorities during the Cultural Revolution. Lu Xun's books were the only literature he could read during those years without having to disguise them by wrapping them in the red plastic covers of *Quotations from Chairman Mao*. In his stories, Shaoxing was more a rustic town than a city, with villagers, boats, a market fair, farmers like Ah Q, and country kids like Runtu. But Shaoxing, like anywhere else in China, had changed dramatically.

He caught sight of Tang pushing his way through the crowd,

carrying a map in one hand, looking like one of the tourists. A stoutly built man in his late forties, Tang had deeply set eyes and a square jawline, an interesting mixture of supposedly southern and northern characteristics. He was wearing a light gray jacket, a blue shirt, and jeans.

Instead of asking any questions, Tang simply shook hands with Chen and handed over the map of Shaoxing. "Sorry, I can't park here. It's just across the street. I'll be back to pick you up in one minute."

Chen watched him as he pulled up in a shiny black Buick. It wasn't a bureau car, as Tang had promised not to tell his colleagues.

After Chen got into the car, Tang handed him a large manila envelope.

"Zhou's visits here weren't about official business. He contacted only some of his relatives and friends. I put together a list of them—names, addresses, and numbers. That's about all I could come up with on such short notice."

"You've done an extraordinary job. So where are we going?"

"His cousin's place. They saw each other last year."

The car was already turning into a quiet residential area, with narrower streets and shabbier lanes, where some of the old houses were in disrepair.

"I've also included some information about his counterparts in Shaoxing," Tang said with an apologetic smile. "But I have a meeting I have to attend."

"Don't worry about me. You've already done so much."

"When the meeting is over, I'll see what else I can dig up, and I'll contact you as soon as I have anything. In the meantime, after going through this list, you might as well do some sightseeing here, or participate in the festival if you prefer. By the way, where is the festival?"

"Lu Xun's old home."

"A good choice."

"A politically correct choice. But I may go to Lanting Park instead."

"As you like, but let me buy you a Shaoxing dinner at the end of the day. It's nothing fancy when compared to the food of Shanghai, but I guarantee the flavor is authentic."

"Thank you, I'd like that. Did you find any property listed under Zhou's name here?"

"No, but I'll check into that too."

The car pulled up near an old apartment complex, which looked pretty much the same as those built in the late seventies in Shanghai. Most of them were four-story concrete buildings that had become discolored with the passage of time. Chen guessed that they weren't too far from the center of the city.

"Here we are, Zhou's cousin's home. Her name is Mingxia."

"Thanks, Tang. Call me if you learn anything new."

"I'll do that," Tang said, and then pulled away.

Chen walked over to a relatively new building and knocked on a door decorated with a red paper-cut character for happiness that was posted upside down in accordance with the superstition, as "upside down" is pronounced in Chinese exactly the same as "arrival."

The woman who answered the door was plump, in her midfifties with streaks of gray in her hair, deep lines on her forehead, and a single shining gold tooth. She was dressed in a baggy, dark blue short-sleeve blouse and pants.

"Are you Mingxia?"

After examining the ID he held out, she nodded and let Chen in without saying another word. It was a one-room efficiency apartment packed with old furniture and other mysterious stuff. She pulled over a shaky rattan chair, from which she removed a pile of old magazines, and motioned for him to sit.

Chen wasted no time in explaining the purpose of his visit.

"Zhou left Shaoxing when he was still a kid," she said. "For years, he didn't come back to visit. At least, not that I was aware of. But he finally did return last year and treated us to a meal at a hotel restaurant, a five-star one. Then he did it again, a couple of months later, in a new restaurant named after a character in a Lu Xun story."

"Did he tell you why he came back?"

"No, not exactly. I assumed that, as in the old proverb, it's important for a successful man to return to his old home wrapped in glory. A generous treat for us folks who live here is naturally a part of that."

"Do you remember anything unusual that he said or did during his visits?"

"No, I spoke only two or three words to him each time. We were seated at a big banquet table, more than ten of us, each of us thanking and toasting him across the table. I wondered whether he even noticed me."

"But he must have talked to the others. For instance, about family back in Shanghai or his work?"

"He mentioned that the housing prices were still quite cheap here. I remember because we all took him as someone with reliable inside information. A free-standing villa in the best location here in Shaoxing would cost less than one million yuan, and he told us that it's a steal."

"So he encouraged you to buy?"

"A bargain or not, it's still way beyond me. He mentioned one particular high-end subdivision, I think."

"Was he going to buy something for himself?"

"No, he didn't say anything about it."

"What's the name of the subdivision?"

"It's near East Lake, but I can't recall the name."

"Was there anything else, Mingxia?"

"Well, I don't know. He didn't come back with his family. Instead, there was a secretary sitting with him, waiting on him. She deboned the Dong Lake fish for him during one of the banquets. But then that's not that unusual for someone in his position, is it?"

"You mean having a little secretary?"

"I couldn't tell. But she wasn't that little, and not that young. Much younger than Zhou, of course."

After talking for another forty-five minutes, Chen took his leave, practically empty-handed. All he'd learned was that Zhou had traveled with Fang, which, given their relationship, probably didn't mean anything.

He began wondering if it was worthwhile to keep pursuing this angle.

Next, he decided to visit Chang Lihua, the director of the Shaoxing Housing Development.

Chang appeared genuinely surprised by Chen's unannounced visit.

"You should have told us earlier about your visit, Chief Inspector Chen."

"I haven't told anybody about my visit. There's no point beating around the bush with you, Director Chang. You must have heard what was going on with Zhou. It's a very complicated and sensitive case. The less people know about it, the better. Your help would be most valuable to us."

"Thank you for telling me this," Chang said, producing a pack of cigarettes. He was about to offer one to Chen, when his hand jerked back as if he'd been bitten by a poisonous snake.

They were Panda. Since they had once been made exclusively for Comrade Deng Xiaoping in the Forbidden City, the memories of its imperial uniqueness lingered. That was what made them so expensive.

"Don't worry about it, Chang. What really got Zhou into trouble wasn't a pack of 95 Supreme Majesty, as we both know only too well."

"I know. And the housing prices are much lower in Shaoxing, with no housing market bubble to worry about. It's not at all comparable to the situation in Shanghai."

"Shanghai's bubble economy is not what concerns me," Chen said. "Since Zhou worked in the same sector as you, Director Chang, I suppose he talked to you about the housing market during his visits to Shaoxing last year."

"Of course we had met and talked in the past, but last year he wasn't here on business. He just called me from the station, a few minutes before his train was leaving," Chang said, trying to recall. "He did touch on some of the changes in the housing market, specifically the new regulation against the construction of independent villas in the city of Shanghai."

"Why did he bring that up?"

"With the new high-speed train next year, Shaoxing will be only an hour away from Shanghai. A villa here could become a real bargain."

"So he wanted to buy one?

"That I don't know. It was only a short conversation before he boarded his train. Perhaps the call was just out of courtesy."

As he left Chang's office, Chen couldn't help feeling that the Shaoxing trip would turn out to be another waste of time. So far, it hadn't yielded anything helpful to his investigation.

Still, he did not want to give up so quickly. There might be some details he hadn't examined closely enough.

The proverb cited by Mingxia—that it's important for a successful man to return to his old home wrapped in glory—came from the story about Xiang Yu, the king of Chu, in the third century BC. Xiang Yu, at the peak of his military power, was swayed by an ancient saying, "If one is rich and successful without going back to his old home in all his glory, it's like walking in one's best clothes in the dark." So he had led his troops back to his old home, a strategically disastrous move that eventually led to the demise of his kingdom. Despite the results, the concept had become rooted in China's collective unconscious. It was almost unimaginable for a successful Party official not to show off for the people back home. But to do so after many years, to do so twice in one year, and to do it in the company of Fang . . . it didn't add up. What if the stories of him traveling to Shaoxing with a younger woman—not his wife—made it back to Shanghai?

Chen's cell phone rang, interrupting his thoughts. It was Detective Tang.

"Anything new, Tang?"

"Sorry, I haven't found any property listed under his name."

"Could you check another name?"

"Another name?"

"Fang Fang—possibly a villa near the East Lake. It's a long shot. If it helps at all, the transaction was probably done last year."

"That narrows it down. I'll check into it right now."

It would take a while, however, before Chen would hear back. In the meantime, he had some time to kill.

Cutting across the side street, he noticed an arrow-shaped sign pointing the way to Lu Xun's residence. It looked like it was only a ten-minute walk away. The festival was being held there, but he should be able to maneuver around without being seen by the participants. He found himself heading in that direction.

Among modern Chinese writers, Chen admired no one more than Lu Xun, who fought against the injustices of society in the early decades of the twentieth century. For years after 1949, Lu Xun was endorsed by the Party government as the one and only proletarian writer because of his criticism of the Nationalist government.

Beyond a stone bridge, Chen saw a group of tourists getting off a bus near the entrance to an old street, most of them holding maps and brochures in their hands. An elderly man wearing a fake pigtail over a gray cotton gown shuffled up to the tourists, as if he had just emerged out of an illustration of a story by Lu Xun, selling souvenirs from his bamboo basket.

The original Lu residence must have been large, presumably housing the whole clan. Apart from a considerable number of halls and rooms, Chen saw the Hundred-Flower Garden at one side of the street and the Three-Flavor Study on the other, both of them mentioned in Lu Xun's writings. Chen managed to curb the temptation to walk over to them.

About half a block away, in front of a quadrangle house, was a vertical wooden sign reading *Young Writers' Base of Lu Xun Academy*. The door stood ajar, through which could be seen a corner of the tranquil flagstone courtyard. It was probably something like a writers' colony. If so, he might try to come and stay here for a week, basking in the feng shui of Lu Xun's old home, though he was no longer a young writer. Hearing voices coming from within, he hurried away.

"Buy a scroll of Shaoxing brush pen calligraphy—Lu Xun's poem." A scholarlike peddler with a flowing silver beard intercepted him on the street. "The calligrapher is an undiscovered master: in a few years, the scroll could be worth a fortune."

The scroll showed a quatrain in bold Wei style.

How can I afford to be passionate as of yore? | Let flower bloom or fall, I care no more. | Who could have thought that in the southern rain, | I'm weeping for a son of the country again?

It was a poem Lu Xun composed for Yang Xingfu, an intellectual who was killed in the fight for democracy. Unexpectedly, memories of Detective Wei came back, overwhelming Chen in the guilty realization that he was not a poet like Lu Xun, not having written a single line for the dead.

"Two hundred yuan," the peddler declared. "You are a man of letters, and you know the true value."

"One hundred," he bargained without thinking.

"Deal."

Back in Shanghai, the scroll could hang in his office, he mused, as a souvenir of the trip, and in memory of Detective Wei.

Like everywhere else in China, Shaoxing was inundated by wave upon wave of consumerism. Along the street, except for the houses marked as part of Lu Xun's residence, all the houses had been

181

turned into shops or restaurants named in connection to the great writer. One salesman held a brown urn of Shaoxing rice wine on top of his head while jumping in and out a ring of wine bottles like an acrobat. Chen couldn't recall any such scene in the stories.

He wished he could find a small tea room, but at least he was relieved not to see a Starbucks. He stepped into a small tavern instead, where he ordered a bowl of yellow wine. At this time of the day, he was the only customer, so a waiter also brought him a tiny dish of peas flavored with aniseed. Picking up a pea, he debated with himself whether he should go to the festival, perhaps make only a quick appearance. But once he was there, it might not be easy to get away quickly.

He couldn't see any real point in going, just to join in the chorus singing the praises of "socialism with Chinese characteristics." Lu Xun, for one, would never have done that.

Chen thought about an article he'd read recently. It was about a surprising comment Chairman Mao had made regarding Lu Xun in the fifties, during the heat of the antirightist movement. When asked what Lu Xun would have been doing if he was still around, Mao said simply that Lu would be locked up and rotting in prison.

As he sat there lost in thought, Chen got another call from Tang.

"Yes, there is a property registered in the name of Fang, Chief Inspector Chen. It's a villa near Lu Xun's old home."

"What's the address?"

"I'll text it to you in a minute. There used to be a phone line under her name, but it was canceled about half a year ago. Which isn't too surprising, since more and more people use only mobile phones. Also, the property seems to be unoccupied most of the time. According to the subdivision security, a woman moved in just a couple of days ago. Possibly she's none other than Fang. The security guard is pretty sure she's there now."

"Good, I'm on my way."

There was nothing surprising about the property being registered under her name. Either Zhou was cautious, having purchased it for himself but put it under her name, or he was really smitten and bought it for her.

The subdivision was about two blocks behind Lu Xun's home. From a distance, he glimpsed a stretch of new roofs shining in the sunlight.

There was no ruling out the possibility that she was kept under surveillance in that subdivision. If he was able to track her down there, so could others. Still, he had to approach her. He turned a corner on the street, looking over his shoulder one more time.

NINETEEN

TURNING AROUND, CHEN CAUGHT sight of Kong Yiji Restaurant.

Kong Yiji was the protagonist in one of Lu Xun's stories. He was a scholar, totally down and out because of his having failed the civil service examination, his quixotic insistence on the old ways at the end of the Qing dynasty, and his inability to adjust to the changing society. Consequently a helpless drunkard, Kong spent his money— whenever he had any—in a small tavern, where he postured and lectured in an impossibly bookish way.

In that story, the tavern was shabby. It was frequented by short-coated, poor customers who could only afford to drink standing at the counter with just a one-copper plate of aniseed-flavored peas. The relatively better-off, long-gowned customers would sit sipping their wine and relaxing in an adjacent room.

The new restaurant was huge, even though its façade sported some decorations depicted in the story, such as a hot water container for wine warming; a row of dented, ancient-looking bowls and saucers; and a signboard on the wall with a chalk inscription declaring, "Kong Yiji still owes nineteen coppers." Chen walked over and stepped inside.

"Give me a private room," Chen said to the young waitress who came up to greet him, "a small one."

"Just for two?"

"Yes, just for two. You know what I want."

"Sure, we have one for you."

The waitress led him to a cozy room lined with pink floral wallpaper. It was furnished with a dining table and chair, a long couch, and a coffee table sporting a statuette of a naked Venus, none of which had anything to do with the original story or its protagonist. That bookish archetype would have never dreamed of a romantic rendezvous in a room like this. The waitress handed Chen a pink-covered menu.

"These are specialties of your restaurant?" Chen asked.

"Yes. There is a minimum charge of seven hundred yuan for the private room. I can recommend some—"

"That's fine. Bring me whatever you recommend, but make sure to include the local specials."

He then took out his notebook and scribbled on a page:

Don't worry about who I am. I know you're in trouble, and I want to help. Come to the restaurant. Private room 101. I'll be waiting for you.

He tore out the page, put it into an envelope, and addressed it before handing it to the waitress.

"Deliver it to the address on the envelope. Make sure she herself gets it. Here's ten yuan for delivering it. When she comes over, I'll have another twenty for you."

The waitress eyed him up and down slowly before she nodded, like one waking from a dream. Her face lit up with an arch smile.

"I see, sir. She'll be here."

He wondered what the waitress saw, but that hardly mattered.

A middle-aged man wearing a long, worn-out blue gown appeared in the doorway, gesticulating, mumbling literary quotations that ended invariably with the refrain, "forsooth, little left, indeed, little left." Originally, it referred to the peas in the impoverished character's hand, Chen recalled. He waved "Kong Yiji" away, closed the door, and wondered what Lu Xun would have thought of that.

Twenty minutes later, there was a light knock on the door.

"Come in, Fang."

A woman in a plain white blouse and black pants stepped in, a suggestion of hesitation in her timid movements. She appeared to be in her early or mid thirties. Thin, slender, she had a slightly long face, almond-shaped eyes, and a black mole on her forehead.

He stood up and signaled her to a seat, raising his finger to his lips like an old friend. The two sat in silence, waiting, as the waitress came in to serve the cold dishes and then pour the rice wine in two bowls in front of them.

Chen took a slow sip from the bowl. The wine was surprisingly sweet and mellow. The dishes of food in front of them appeared interesting. Smoked duck, white fish fried with green onions, stinking tofu, salt-water-boiled river shrimp, fermented winter melon, and dried bamboo shoots. Thanks to Lu Xun, the special dishes all appeared to reflect the traditional local flavor, even though it was done for a strictly commercial purpose.

"Don't hurry with the hot dishes. We'd like to talk first," he said to the waitress. "And please make sure to knock before entering."

"Of course."

The moment the waitress stepped out, Chen produced his business card and placed it on the table before Fang.

"Thank you for coming on such short notice, Fang. I'm Chief Inspector Chen Cao, Deputy Party Secretary of the Shanghai Police Bureau, and also a member of Shanghai Party Committee."

He didn't like to use the titles printed on his business card, but they might help in the present situation.

"Oh, I've heard of you, Chief Inspector Chen, but—"

"Let's open the door to the view of the mountains. I told others that I'm here for the literary festival, but that's only a smokescreen."

"A smokescreen? For somebody like you?" She gave him an incredulous look and said nothing else.

"I'm here because of the Zhou case."

"That's what I guessed."

"Do you believe Zhou committed suicide?"

"Does it matter what I believe?"

"It matters to me. You might remember Detective Wei, a close colleague of mine."

"Yes."

"Did you hear that he died? The day before he died, he interviewed you."

"Died? How?" she said, her face blanching.

"Killed by a car. I don't believe he died in a simple traffic accident—not while he was in the middle of investigating Zhou's death. I'm here because of that investigation but also because of Detective Wei's death."

She made no response.

"Detective Wei wasn't in charge of the shuanggui investigation—the Party investigation into Zhou's corruption—but I believe that his investigation into the cause of Zhou's death led to his fatal accident. I want justice for Wei. And I believe you want justice for Zhou, if Zhou was murdered."

She nodded, her fingers touching the wine cup without lifting it.

"Thank you for telling me all this," she said, making a visible effort to pull herself together. "Yes, I want justice done if he was murdered, but I'm only the office secretary. People have put a lot of pressure on me, trying to force me to say things I don't know. I couldn't do that, so I wanted to get away from it all for a few days. That's all I can tell you."

"If you were really just enjoying a vacation here, I don't think people would be frantically looking for you everywhere. You've only worked in that office for two years. How did you come to have a luxurious villa bought for you? I've already talked to your parents. They've told me what happened after you returned from overseas. We may go over all this, and, if need be, the transaction records for the property will prove everything."

She kept her head hanging low, her lips sealed tight.

"Let me assure you that you're not a suspect in my investigation, and I will do nothing to harm you. But I can't say the same about the others who are looking for you." Taking another sip of the deceptively sweet wine, Chen went on, adopting a different tone, "I'm not just a cop; I'm also a poet. As the proverb says, even my heart goes out to beauty—like you. If anything, I'm trying to get you out of trouble."

"But how?" she said. "How can you help me?"

"Tell me what you know about Zhou—and then, only then, will I be able to find a way."

"He's dead because of a pack of cigarettes. How can anything I tell you about him help?"

"What you tell me may help us get the real criminal. The one who was behind all of this. Only by pushing this investigation through to the end will I be able to get everyone else off your back. We have to help each other," he said, then added gently, "If it would make it a little easier for you, tell me something about yourself, how you started to work for him."

"My parents have already told you everything, I suppose," she said. Still, she started telling Chen her version.

About seven years ago, after she graduated from a college in Shanghai, she had gone to England to further her studies. She studied hard and got an MA degree in communications. People believed that she would have a great future, but she couldn't find a job in England. In the meantime, she used up all the money saved by her not-that-well-off parents. She couldn't stay in England any longer, so she had no choice but to go back to Shanghai. Once back, she found herself a "haigui"—a derogative term for a returnee from overseas, which was pronounced the same as the word for "sea turtle"—and soon turned into a "haidai," a derogative term for the jobless from overseas, pronounced the same as the word for "seaweed."

Then she happened to read about Zhou in the newspapers. He had once lived in the same neighborhood as she, had moved away when she was still very young, and was now an important Party official. In desperation, she contacted him, wondering whether he would remember a little girl from the old neighborhood. He did, and to her surprise, he went out of his way to help her get the job as the secretary in the housing development office. At first, she thought he'd simply taken pity on her, but nothing was simple and pure in the world of red dust. It didn't take long for her to grasp the true meaning of being a little secretary. She was unwilling, then reluctant, but ultimately resigned. *Spring is gone, no one knows where.* She was no longer young, and she thought she should feel flattered that a powerful man like Zhou wanted her as a little secretary. Zhou was considerate enough to keep their relations a secret in the office, though possibly more because of his own position, since he had to think about the political consequences. Still, he seemed to care for her in his way, even though he chose not to divorce his wife. He arranged for them to go to England on vacation, where they were able to spend a week like a real couple, staying in the sort of five-star hotels that she had never dreamed of being able to stay at when she was there as a student. It was all at the government's expense, of course. Then he took her to Shaoxing to buy her a villa. When she asked him why, he told her that there was no telling what might happen to him in the future and that now at least she would have something to fall back on—and wasn't she glad to own her own home?

Ever since the 95 Supreme Majesty scandal had broken, she'd been living in unceasing trepidation. Though he might not have confided in her about all his dirty business deals, she knew enough to realize that he was finished. As for herself, while she might not end up like him, it was only a matter of time before she was fired. Dang wouldn't let her keep that crucial position in the department. What's more, Jiang and his team were putting a lot of pressure on her to speak out against Zhou. She didn't know what to do, so she called in sick and fled. She needed a break and a place she could quietly think about her options.

"I didn't think anyone knew about this place," she concluded.

Her account focused on her own experience, Chen noticed, and it didn't have much to do with Zhou, though she didn't try to conceal their relationship.

What could Jiang have wanted from her, considering how anxious he was to have Zhou's death declared a suicide?

And why had she really fled here, all of a sudden? Presumably there was much pressure put on her, as she claimed, but she should have known that running away only made matters worse.

"What do you intend to do now, Fang?"

"Perhaps I can go back to England. That is, if I'm able to sell the property here."

"Do you think you could get out of the country? As far as I know, your name and passport picture have been sent to the customs authorities throughout the country."

She didn't respond.

"Let's talk a bit more about Zhou," Chen said.

"What more can I tell you? Jiang believes I know 'secrets' about Zhou, but Zhou always told me that it wouldn't do me any good to know about his business. I really believe he was trying to keep my interests in mind," she said, with a catch in her voice. "He told me one day that everything he did for me was because I had been so nice to him in the old neighborhood. Allegedly, as a little girl, I'd flashed a sweet smile at him one day when he was utterly down and out. That was when he was working at a neighborhood production group for seventy cents a day and not seeing any light at the end of the dark tunnel."

"It's just like Jia Yucun at the beginning of *Dream of the Red Chamber*," Chen commented without elaborating on it. It was possible that the archetype of an appreciation for beauty overwhelmed Zhou.

"I just did what I was supposed to do as the department secretary, never inquisitively or intrusively."

"Did he have any other secretaries?"

"You mean little secretaries? Not in the office. Some people said that he kept me simply as a cover for other ones. I suppose that's possible, but I don't think he had the time for that."

"But as his secretary, you surely know some of the confidential details about his work."

"He worked hard and was under a lot of pressure," she said, discernibly hesitant. "It was not an easy job for him. Nominally, he was the one in charge of land and housing development for the city, but there were so many other officials anxious to have a finger in the pie. He had to walk a tightrope all the time. For instance, there was the scandal of the West Eight Blocks. The head of the Jing'an District practically gave the land away, selling it at an incredibly low price to the developer. The developer got a loan on it for five times the amount he'd paid. Zhou knew about that, but the district head had already gotten approval for the deal from Zhou's superior. What could Zhou do with those higher-ups who were far more powerful? He didn't really talk to me about those things, but they weren't really secrets, not in today's China."

"Yes, I have heard of the West Eight Blocks. The head of Jing'an District was shuangguied because of it, but the scandal didn't touch Zhou. Not at the time."

"Whatever sort of official Zhou might have been, he was good to me," she said, her head hanging low. "It's not fair that Zhou alone was to be punished when it's really like a chain of crabs bound together on a straw rope—all connected."

She then went on, repeating what she'd already said, adding nothing new or substantial.

But Chen didn't believe she was telling him everything. He had to break down her resistance.

"I don't know how I can help you if you don't tell me everything," Chen said, interrupting. He brought out the envelope from Melong and handed it to her. "Take a look."

Her hand was trembling as she took out the pictures.

"So it was you, Chief Inspector Chen?"

"What do you mean?"

"I was sent copies of these pictures a couple of days ago."

"Really! I didn't send those. Do you know who else might have sent them?"

"No, I don't. It looks like everybody is trying to blackmail or threaten me."

"Everybody? Tell me about it."

"The day I got these pictures, Jiang and his people came to talk to me, saying that the consequences would be too much for me if I didn't cooperate. And then, that evening, Dang also called, telling me I would have to give up."

"Give what up?"

"I don't know what he meant. Tell Jiang's people everything? Give them something that they believed Zhou had given to me? But the message I got was that if I didn't do what they told me to do, then the pictures would come to light. That's why I ran away."

"Can you guess where I found the pictures?" Chen asked deliberately. "On Dang's computer."

"What?!"

"He's after something, but what it is, I don't know."

"Zhou had already had his name dragged through the mud. I

didn't want that to happen again, not because of me. He told me he'd kept this property a secret, so I came here."

"But you can't hide out for long. What then?"

"I don't know. I'll be able to eke out an existence, I think, for two or three months on my savings. The storm may have blown over by then, and I'll be able to turn a page somewhere else."

So the pressure Dang and Jiang were putting on her wasn't to get her to speak out against Zhou but for her to give them something they thought Zhou had entrusted to her.

Her story was so unlikely that Chen believed it was actually true, whether or not she was innocent. But what could Dang be after? For that matter, what could Jiang and his team want so desperately? This opened up totally new possibilities.

"Hidden treasure?" he murmured, almost to himself.

Zhou was said to have amassed a huge fortune, and what had been exposed on the Internet was merely the tip of the iceberg. Dang must believe that Fang knew about it.

Was that what Jiang was after, too? It wasn't likely. It could be a huge amount but not so much that it would be worth such an effort on the part of the city government. If any more details about such corruption were to leak out, it wouldn't do the city government any good.

"Those people are capable of anything," she muttered, though not in response to Chen.

Jiang's continuous presence at Moller Villa could possibly backfire on him now, with the Beijing team stationed at the same hotel. Even though Fang might not have told him everything, hemming and hawing as she had about details, her fear was genuine. If Zhou had been murdered for something—whatever that might be, Chen had no clue and too little knowledge to speculate—that something was still out there, and Fang wasn't an unlikely next target on the list. That was the real reason she'd run away.

She hadn't said that in so many words, but she didn't have to.

Zhou might have hidden the something away—this crucially important "something"—but could it possibly be in her possession? From what Chen could see, while it might have been a matter of life and death to Zhou, it wasn't to Fang. There was no point in her holding on to it, particularly at the expense of becoming a fugitive.

At the same time, it had to be something that was a fatal threat to Jiang and his people, and something Zhou believed would provide him protection. Nothing like that had come to the surface yet—not as far as Chen could see.

Then how could he help Fang? With others watching and plotting for reasons unknown—to him, and perhaps to one another—it'd be better not to reveal her whereabouts to any of them. Otherwise, before he was capable of making a move, she'd be snatched out of his hands.

He dipped a piece of stinking tofu in the hot sauce. It was slightly cold yet still crispy, but the hot sauce wasn't spicy enough, just as Lu Xun had deplored in a story. It was probably titled "In the Tavern."

Fang's staying here wouldn't harm anybody, he decided. Nor would it obstruct the investigation of Zhou's death. Turning to Fang, he said, "Things are complicated. Because of Zhou's position and because of his connections, you might as well stay here for a while, for your own safety. You'll have to avoid contacting others. Do your parents have any idea where you are?"

"No, they don't. They're old-fashioned people. They would be upset that I have a villa given to me by Zhou, so I've never told them anything about it."

"That's good. Don't contact them, either—not until I tell you it's okay. It won't be too long. Soon there may be a drastic change in the situation," he said, not saying more than was necessary. "In the meantime, if you can think of anything that might have caused

Zhou's death, or about things he might have left behind—anything at all—let me know immediately. You have my cell number. But make sure that you call from a public pay phone, one that's not near here. You're right about one thing. Those people are capable of anything."

TWENTY

IT NEVER RAINS BUT it pours.

Lianping thought this as she sat in a Shaoxing taxi, toying with the cell phone in her hand.

While on the way to Lanting Park, where she was going to meet Chief Inspector Chen, she'd received an unexpected call from Xiang.

Xiang offered no explanation about why he had left Shanghai so abruptly and had neglected to call her for almost two weeks, except to say that he'd been extremely busy. Not just during the day but also late into the night. It was no secret that a lot of business deals were done at the dinner table, by the karaoke machine, or in the massage room at the baths. These were all characteristic of China's socialism, and she knew better than to probe or protest. For a young man of the so-called "wealthy second generation," his devotion to business was commonly seen as a plus.

The reason he finally called her was that, according to him, he'd just signed a major deal crucial to the future of his company and he wanted to celebrate with her. He also said that he would have a huge surprise for her when he returned early next week.

She was reminded of a Tang dynasty poem from the collection translated by Chen.

How many times / I have been let down / by the busy merchant of Qutang / since I married him! / The tide always keeps its word / to come, alas. / Had I known that, / I would have married the tide rider.

She hadn't expected the call from Chen, either. For that matter, Chen was just as busy, if not more. She'd invited him to the Shaoxing festival in an impulsive moment. He promised he'd think about it, but that usually meant no, especially considering how overwhelmed he was by the investigation.

Still, she was amazed at how many times he'd seen her the past week. That could be because of his work, she told herself. His visit to the *Wenhui* office might have been mainly because of the cop killed on a nearby street, and his last-minute request that she join him at the temple because Detective Yu was a close friend and coworker. But to her surprise, Chen had come to Shaoxing, even though he'd missed the major event of the festival—the meeting at Lu Xun's residence.

Could that have been deliberate? She had to be at that meeting for her article, but there would be no point in his wasting his time with those empty political talks. Unlike her, he didn't have to worry about the expense involved in coming to Shaoxing. So it was possible he'd come there because of her.

The taxi was pulling up along a quaint street. Looking out, she saw Chen standing near the park entrance and waving to her, tickets in hand. However she might interpret the motives for his trip to Shaoxing, he was here, waiting for her, and that was what really mattered.

He came over and opened the taxi door for her.

"I wanted to surprise you, Lianping."

"You certainly did that. I thought you'd abandoned me. But you must have already had plans for the day." She waited, her brows tilting when he failed to respond immediately.

"We have the afternoon to ourselves," he said. "Later, we could rent a black-awning boat, like in Lu Xun's stories, and sail into the eventide."

At the moment, she couldn't recall any stories about a black-awning boat sailing into the dusk, but it was enough to be walking in the park with him.

"Sorry I missed the morning event," he said.

"No big loss for you. You know how boring conference speeches can be," she said.

The elderly gateman of the park didn't even look up from the local newspaper he was reading with intense absorption. He just waved them in after Chen dropped the tickets into the green plastic box. They were just another tourist couple wandering around looking for something interesting to do on a rainy afternoon.

The park matched the description in the brochure Lianping had glanced through. There were pavilions with tilted eaves, white stone bridges arching over green water, and verdant bamboo groves scattered here and there, with memories of the area's history whispering through it all.

Wang Xizi, a celebrated calligrapher, spent most of his life in Shaoxing during the Jin dynasty in the fourth century. He was commonly called the sage of calligraphy, unrivaled in caoshu, the semicursive script. His most renowned work was the "Preface to the Poems Composed at the Lanting Orchid Pavilion," an introduction to the poems composed by a group of writers during a gathering at Lanting. The original calligraphy was long lost, but some finely traced copies and rubbings remained.

"Look at these statuettes of white geese in the green meadow. There are so many stories about them in classical Chinese literature," Chen said in high spirits. Perhaps his mood was due to the change of scenery, Lianping thought. She didn't think he was trying to impress her. There was no need for him to do so. "According to one legend, Wang learned how to turn the brush from watching the geese parading around here."

She wasn't that intrigued by these stories, which were from so long ago and far away. Chen was walking close to her, though, and that made all the difference. But Xiang was coming back, something she decided not to think about at the moment.

Despite the many legends about the park, they were the only tourists there. They sauntered over to a stream embosomed in trees and bamboos, where a fitful breeze brought down a flutter of glistening raindrops from the green boughs above.

"It's here. This is Lanting," he exclaimed. "Wang and the other poets gathered at this stream, engaged in a wine-poem game."

"A wine-poem game?"

"They let wine cups flow down from the head of the stream. If a cup came to a stop in front of someone, he had to write a poem. If he failed to do so, he had to drink three cups as punishment. The poems were then collected, and Wang composed a preface to the collection. He must have been very drunk, flourishing his brush pen inspired by the exquisite scene. That preface marks the very peak of his calligraphy."

"That's incredible."

"Many years later, in the Tang dynasty, Du Mu wrote a poem about the scene. '*Regretfully we cannot stop time from flowing away. / Why not, then, enjoy ourselves in a wine game by the stream? / A blaze of blossom appears, indifferent, year after year. / Lament not at its withering, but at its burgeoning.*'"

"I've never read it, Poet Chen. That's a marvelous poem, but the last line is a little beyond me."

"When I first read the poem, probably at your age, I didn't understand the ending, either. Now I think I do. When it first blooms, it's still full of dreams and hope, but there's nothing you can do to

200

slow the journey from blooming to withering. That's something to lament."

She was intrigued by his interpretation. She tried to conjure up the ancient scene of the poets reading and writing here, but she failed.

"The times have changed," he said, as if reading her thoughts.

It was engaging to have him talking like an experienced guide, she thought as they strolled in sight of a yellow silk banner streaming in the breeze over an antique-looking hall. The banner read, "Calligraphy and Painting—Free to People Who Really Appreciate Chinese Art."

"Free?" she said. "Perhaps people here at Lanting still practice art for art's sake, like in ancient days. We might find a scroll of the poem you just recited to me."

They entered the hall. The front part of it had been turned into an exhibition room, with scrolls hanging from the walls. To their puzzlement, each of the scrolls was marked with a price, not exorbitant but not cheap, either. Behind a glass counter near the entrance, a man wearing an umber-colored Chinese gown stood up, grinning. He read the question in their eyes and said, "They're free. We just charge for the cost of making them into scrolls."

"Exactly. Writers and artists cannot live on the northwest wind," Chen commented. "If you add up all the paintings and calligraphies in this hall, you couldn't buy one square meter in the subdivision of Binjiang Garden."

"Ah yes, the Binjiang Garden in Pudong. The paper mansion that the Yus burned at the temple was in that subdivision," Lianping said.

Another peddler emerged from the back room of the hall, gesticulating, swearing, and pushing on them a brocade-covered box containing brush pens, an ink stick, an ink stone, and a jadelike seal.

"There are four treasures of our ancient civilization. They are instilled with the feng shui of the culture city. An absolute must for the 'scholar and beauty' romance," the peddler said, making his unrelenting sales pitch.

They left quickly, like a fleeing army.

"It's more commercial than I thought," she said with a touch of regret. She was intrigued by the peddler's reference to the "scholar and beauty romance," which was a popular genre in classical Chinese literature.

"It's too close to Shanghai to be any different, and day trippers like us don't help. *Here, there, everywhere, green grass spread out to the horizon.*"

The line probably referred to commercial activities, Lianping thought. But he didn't have to cite a Tang dynasty line for that. He was extraordinarily exuberant, coming across not unlike one of those scholars in a classical romance, eager to sweep a young girl off her feet with allusions and quotations.

"Let's go to Shen Garden," he suggested. "It might be quiet there, without the commercial hustle and bustle."

"The other garden shouldn't be too far away," she said as they walked out of the park, "but I don't know how to get there."

Outside, they couldn't find a taxi. A rickshaw—or, rather, a rickshaw-like tricycle with a man pedaling in the front—pulled up to the curb. They got in, even though the seat in the back was hardly wide enough for the two of them. They were sitting close.

It started drizzling. Chen pulled up the all-around awning, as if wrapping them in a cocoon. Still, they were able to watch the shifting scene outside through a transparent curtain, shimmering in the light haze of rain.

"This is the best vehicle for sightseeing in the old city," the tricyclist said, winding his way through side streets lined with rustic houses with white walls and black tile roofs. "If you reserve for half a day, I can give you a huge discount, taking you to East Lake and Dayu Temple, all for one hundred yuan."

"Dayu Temple?"

"Dayu was one of the great emperors in Chinese history. He succeeded in controlling the flooding that was ravaging the country. A huge temple was recently built in his honor in Shaoxing. In fact, it's a splendid palace."

Lianping knew who Dayu was—he was a legendary figure in ancient Chinese history. She knew nothing, however, about the connection between Dayu and Shaoxing. In recent years, a number of cities built temples or palaces to attract tourists, making far-fetched claims of connections to legendary figures.

"I don't think we'll have the time," Chen said, making the decision for both of them.

The vehicle pulled up next to Shen Garden, and they got down. They purchased entrance tickets and noticed, through the open gate, that the garden appeared to be rather deserted.

It turned out to be smaller than Lianping had expected, though it was probably just like other gardens designed in the tradition of southern landscaping. It had vermilion-painted pavilions, stone bridges, and fantastically shaped grottos in groves maintained in a style of cultivated nature that had appealed to the literati in the Ming and Qing dynasties. Not far from the entrance, she saw a billboard with a history of the garden focusing on the romance between Lu You and Tang Wan during the Song dynasty.

The garden appealed to tourists because of the romantic poems composed by Lu You that were connected to the garden. There was also a Shaoxing opera based on the classic love story, which she had heard about from her mother, a Shaoxing opera fan, though Lianping herself hadn't seen it.

After several turns along the moth-covered path, they passed a solitary stall selling local rice wine and then came to a pavilion with a large, oblong rock beside it, the flat surface of which had two poems engraved on it and highlighted in red paint.

I

The sun is sinking behind the city wall
to the sad notes of a shining bugle.
Here in Shen Garden,
the pond and the pavilion appear
no longer to be the same,
except the heartbreaking spring ripples
still so green under the bridge,
the ripples that once reflected her arrival
light-footed, in such a beauty
as to shame wild geese into fleeing.

II

It's forty years since we last met,
the dream broken, the scent vanished,
in Shen Garden, the withered willows
produce no more fluffy catkins.
An old man about to turn into the dust
of Mount Ji, I still burst into tears
at this old scene.

"The poems are autobiographical," Chen said, starting in again. "In his youth, Lu You married his cousin, Tang Wan, whom he deeply loved. Because of opposition from his mother, however, they were forced to divorce, though they still cared for each other, even after each of them remarried."

"They both remarried? Didn't the institution of arranged marriage forbid women from remarrying?"

"Not exactly, at least in their case. Neo-Confucianism didn't gain momentum until after Chen and Zhu in the Ming dynasty. In Lu You's time, it was still permissible for a woman like Tang Wan to remarry.

"In 1555, they met in the garden by chance. They were both remarried by then, and they had to observe the etiquette of the time. Still, she served him a cup of yellow rice wine in her delicate hand, all that was unsaid between them rippling in the cup. Lu You wrote a ci poem, lamenting a 'spring still so green,' to which Tang Wan composed one in response, and died of a broken heart not long afterward. Many years later, at the age of seventy-five, he revisited the garden and wrote the lines carved in the rocks here. Their ill-starred romance added to the popularity of the poems."

"It's a sad story."

"Oh, I forgot," he said abruptly, before turning back to the path along which they had come. "Wait in the pavilion for me," he said, as he walked away.

She stepped into the pavilion, wondering what he was up to.

Then she saw him hurrying back, carrying two cups.

"Huang Teng wine. The wine served by Tang Wan in Lu You's ci poem."

"What's Huang Teng?" She took one of the cups from his hand.

"It's possible it was the name of the place where the wine was brewed at the time."

They sat down in the pavilion, which didn't provide comfortable seating. The stone bench was narrow, cold, hard. Also a bit too high— Lianping sat with her feet dangling, barely touching the ground. She shifted and tucked her feet up under her, the cup still in her hand.

Once again she tried to conjure up the ancient scene between the lovers in the garden—the same pavilion, the same pine tree, the same stone bridge, thousands of years ago. Lu and Tang met on a day just like today, aware of a message, perhaps the same as today, drawing nearer to them in the late afternoon.

"The gardens have been rebuilt a couple of times," Chen said, as if reading her thoughts again. "*The pond and the pavilion appear / no longer to be the same.*"

The pavilion must have been rebuilt too. Relatively new graffiti, comments, and lines written by tourists decorated the posts and railings. Some wrote sentimental lines in imitation of Lu You's, and some simply left their names with a red heart beneath.

"It's nothing but clichés," he said with a cynical note in his voice.

"You translated the love poems into English, didn't you?"

"No, not me. They were translated by Yang, a talented poet and translator like Xinghua. I happened to get his manuscript while working on a murder investigation. He died during the Cultural Revolution, and the manuscript had been kept by his ex–Red Guard lover, who was murdered several years ago. That in itself was a touching story. I made some changes to the manuscript, added a few poems, and then sent the collection to the publisher. The editor insisted on adding my name to the book as a political cushion, since Yang's name could be too much of a reminder of the atrocities committed during the Cultural Revolution." He resumed after a short pause, "By the way, you should see the Shaoxing opera version of the love story. My mother is a loyal fan. I'll have to buy a bunch of postcards for her."

"That's a good idea. I'll buy some for my mother too. But I have a question for you. When Lu You and Tang Wan met again, she not only had remarried but also was no longer that young. Why was he still smitten?"

"Good question. In his mind, she was still what she was when he first saw her, just like that little . . ." he said, trailing off at the end.

"Just like who?" she pushed, in spite of herself, wondering whether he was thinking, *Just like Wang Feng,* the ex-*Wenhui* journalist whom Chen was said to have dated. Wang Feng had recently come back to Shanghai for a short visit. They could have met up again.

"Oh, somebody I met here this morning," he said, and then added, "whom I didn't meet until this morning."

In the short silence that ensued, the light drizzling rain was letting up. A bird started chirping somewhere among the glistening foliage. So it wasn't someone from his past, she reflected. But who was it, then? Possibly someone involved in the investigation.

Did he come to Shaoxing just for her company? Or did he have other motives?

Quickly, she let the thought pass, saying to herself that if he wanted to tell her about it, he would.

"I interviewed someone here for the investigation I'm working on."

She felt a wave of disappointment rippling through her, which was followed by a wave of relief. He didn't come because of her or because of her suggestion after all.

Looking over at him, she saw he was hurriedly taking out his cell phone.

"Sorry, I have to take this call. It's from the doctor at East China Hospital. It could be urgent—"

"Oh, go ahead."

He pushed the button, then stood up and walked two or three steps out of the pavilion. A short distance away, he started talking, his brows knitted.

It was difficult for her to guess the content of the phone conversation from the fragmented words she occasionally overheard. He seemed to be saying little except "yes," "no," and other terse, disjointed words.

While he talked to the doctor, she turned to look at the distant hills wrapped in light mist. The mist came rolling off the hills like a scroll of traditional Chinese landscape painting, as if what wasn't painted in the space was telling more than what was.

Finally, he came back, putting his hand on her shoulder absent-mindedly as he joined in and gazed at the same view.

"Is everything fine with your mother?"

"She's fine. The doctor had something else to discuss with me." He then changed the subject abruptly, "Oh, we'd better go to the festival for the dinner party. Otherwise, people will start complaining about Inspector Chen."

"Whatever you say, Chief Inspector Chen."

"I had a cup of Shaoxing rice wine during lunch. It was extraordinarily mellow and sweet. I had it with a small dish of peas flavored with aniseed, just like Kong Yiji in a Lu Xun story. It makes me think that the dinner won't be too bad here."

"Of course, you are first and foremost a cop," she said, barely concealing the satirical edge in her voice, "always covering yourself meticulously, while at the same time, an epicurean enjoying yourself at every opportunity."

Whether he took that as a compliment or something else, she didn't know, but it put a period to their moment in the secluded garden.

He helped her to her feet.

The trail ahead of them appeared slippery, treacherous, and moss-covered here and there.

An indistinct sound came from behind them, hardly audible, perhaps bubbles from the fish bursting on the surface of the pool.

TWENTY-ONE

CHEN RETURNED TO SHANGHAI the next morning. Once there, one of the first things he did was check his e-mail. In his in-box was a response to his e-mail to Comrade Zhao, the retired secretary of the Central Party Discipline Committee in Beijing.

Thank you for your note. For a retired Party cadre of my age, I've been doing fine. I don't want to get involved in too many things, and of late, I've been reading Wang Yangming. Your father was a neo-Confucianist, so you must be familiar with Wang Yangming. I particularly like a poem he wrote in his youth. "The mountains nearby make the moon appear small, / so you think the mountains larger than the moon. / If you have a view stretching out to the horizon, / you'll see the mountains against the magnificent moon." *While reading the poem, I thought of you. You, too, should have a view reaching all the way to the horizon.*

As for the team you mentioned, there's nothing I can tell you. You're an experienced police officer and you know better. At your age, Wang Yangming was already playing an important role in maintaining the well-being of his country.

It was an enigmatic e-mail. There was nothing surprising about Comrade Zhao being tight-lipped about the Beijing team. It wasn't like the retired Party leader, however, to quote a poem in his e-mail.

Despite the fact that his father was a neo-Confucianist, Chen didn't know much about Wang Yangming. What he did know was that he was an influential Ming dynasty Confucian philosopher who advocated the concept of innate knowing, arguing that every person knows from birth, intuitively but not rationally, the difference between good and evil.

Chen decided to spend some time researching Wang Yangming on the Internet. It turned out that Wang Yangming embodied the Confucianist ideal of a learned person who is both a scholar and an official. In 1519 AD, while serving the governor of Jiangxi province, he suppressed the uprising of Prince Zhu Chenhao, saving the dynasty from a huge disaster.

It was gratifying that Comrade Zhao expected Chen to have a career as prominent as Wang Yangming's, but why express this now, all of a sudden?

The poem itself didn't impress Chen. Wang Yangming wasn't known as a poet, but the context in which Zhao quoted the poem made Chen think. Chen was sure that it meant something.

Writing Zhao for an explanation, however, would be useless.

With the sun obscured by the floating clouds, / I'm worried for not seeing Chang'an.

Chen picked up the phone, thinking for a minute, and then dialed Young Bao at the Writers' Association.

"I need to ask you a favor, Young Bao."

"Whatever I can do, Master Chen."

"You've got a friend who works at the Moller Villa Hotel."

"Yes, a good friend. In fact, I'm going to meet him at the hotel canteen for lunch today."

"Can you copy a couple of pages from the visitor registry for building B? Specifically, last Monday and Tuesday."

"That'll be a piece of cake. He works in building B, and from time to time, he works at the front desk, keeping the register. I'll call you as soon as I get it."

That afternoon Chen went to meet with Lieutenant Sheng of Internal Security. The meeting had been requested by Sheng, and the meeting place was the hotel where he was staying. It was the City Hotel, located on Shanxi Road, only a two or three minutes' walk from the Moller Villa Hotel. Perhaps it was just a coincidence— something that Chen, as a cop, didn't believe in.

The request was a surprise. Chen had crossed paths with Internal Security on previous occasions, but rarely had it been on friendly terms. In the last analysis, Chen was a cop before all else.

Internal Security had different priorities. For them, the Party's interests were first and foremost. In the name of the Party, they were capable of doing anything and everything.

So, Chen wondered, what was the purpose of the meeting?

Chen arrived at the hotel and was promptly ushered in to see Lieutenant Sheng. Sheng was a tall man in his late thirties or early forties. His receding hairline highlighted a broad forehead covered with lines. His accent revealed his origins—it was unmistakably from Beijing.

"I'm so glad to meet you, Chief Inspector Chen. I've heard a lot about you."

"I'm glad to meet you, too, Lieutenant Sheng. You're here on special detachment from Beijing, I hear."

"Oh, there's nothing special about it. If anything, I think I was sent because of the computer science classes I took at night school."

"That can be important these days."

"You're a capable and experienced police officer, so there's no point in beating around the bush," Sheng said. "I was sent here because of the Zhou case, but I'm to focus on a different aspect. You know how all this trouble started. It was that search—the human-flesh search engine—which started on that Web forum. These witch hunts have become an Internet mass movement, and they are getting out of control. They are tearing the image of our Party and government to shreds. The bloggers and forum users—those so-called netizens—will use any and every excuse, no matter how flimsy, including a pack of high-priced cigarettes, to vent their frustration and fury against the Party authorities. If it keeps on like this, the stability of our socialist country will be destroyed."

Chen listened without responding immediately. It was always easy to talk about motives, no matter what sort of investigation it was, and as far as Internal Security was concerned, the motive behind the Internet pile-on in the Zhou case was obvious.

Jiang, who was in charge of the team from the city government, seemed to be inclined toward the same conclusion. Sheng should have talked to Jiang instead.

"So what are you going to do?" Chen said, choosing to avoid a confrontation for the moment.

"We are going to nail the troublemaker who first sent the picture of the pack of 95 Supreme Majesty to the Web forum. As for Zhou, whatever he might have done, he has already been punished to the fullest."

"Tracing the photo shouldn't be too difficult for you. There are many Internet experts working for the government, and they should be able to trace it back to the source."

"It's not that easy. We've traced it only as far as the Web forum on which it was originally posted. The moderator claims that he received the picture from an anonymous sender."

"I'm not a computer expert," Chen said, determined to play

dumb, "but isn't it possible to trace the IP address back to the computer that sent it?"

"Well, it was sent from a computer at an Internet café—a place called Flying Horse—and done in such a devious way that despite the new regulations, we've hit a dead end. We have reason to believe it was a premeditated attack."

Chen didn't know what new regulations Sheng was talking about, other than the new requirement to show ID at the cafés. It wasn't news that the government was continually tightening its control over the Internet. That was one of the jobs of Internal Security.

"I see. So, the sender took precautions. I suppose that's not surprising, since the controversy about governmental controls of the Internet has been going on a while," Chen said cautiously.

"But think about what happened after the original photo was posted. There were so many pictures and posts that popped up almost immediately. That was like a blitz. Everything had been orchestrated."

There was no arguing with Internal Security, so Chen didn't try.

"So let's help each other, Chief Inspector Chen. If I find anything useful in your investigation, I'll let you know immediately."

"And vice versa, of course," Chen said, though he wasn't so sure about that. He couldn't shake the feeling that Sheng was trying to sound him out. But that was a game two could play.

For the moment, the meeting was unfolding with no tangible animosity between them, even though it was by no means a meeting between allies. Each had his own agenda—one that was undisclosed and unknown to the other.

From the tall window of the hotel room, which had a balcony overlooking Shanxi Road, Chen thought he glimpsed a corner of the other hotel across the street. The traffic appeared once again to be stuck in a terrible snarl.

"Have there been any new developments in your investigation, Chief Inspector Chen?" Sheng said, finally coming to the point.

"Well, it's much like the proverb, 'A blind man is riding a blind horse toward a fathomless lake in a dark night,'" Chen said vaguely.

"Come on. You're a celebrated poet, always full of poetic hyperbole."

But he wasn't. The metaphor he recited wasn't applicable just to him but to the others involved in the case as well. The proverb had come to him last night as he lay sleepless in a Shaoxing hotel room, staring at the shifting patterns of shadows across the ceiling.

He had thought of it again in the morning, after reading the e-mail from Comrade Zhao.

Sheng lit a cigarette for Chen, and then one for himself. Waving the match out casually, he changed the topic. "How was your trip to Shaoxing?"

"Oh, it was for a literature festival. Shaoxing is the hometown of Lu Xun," Chen said, immediately on high alert. "Internal Security truly is well informed."

"Please don't take that the wrong way. I just happened to be talking to your Party Secretary Li yesterday and he mentioned your trip."

That was possible. Still, it came as no relief to Chen. Li had been informing Internal Security of every move he'd been making.

"The festival is simply an excuse for a group of writers to go sightseeing and feasting. The Shaoxing wine there is really superb. I finished off a small urn of it and got so drunk that Bi Liangpei, the chairman of Shaoxing Writers' Association, had to help me all the way back to the hotel."

That was mostly true. Bi had walked him back to the hotel, but Chen hadn't been that drunk. He remembered trying to find Lianping amidst the chirping of small insects in the hotel garden in the dark, which somehow reminded him of the earlier scene in Shen Garden. She wasn't registered at the hotel. He wondered whether she'd taken the night train back to Shanghai.

"I wish I could have been there," Sheng said, setting a cup of instant coffee down on the coffee table. "I was here, doing nothing but working through a list of the people who posted about Zhou online and posted evidence of his corruption. However, the pictures they posted of Zhou's cars and houses were all real. There's no way to accuse them of slandering him, and I have to admit it's understandable why they targeted him. Since such a large number of people were posting and protesting about Zhou, it's out of the question for the government to punish them all. Some of them were simply following the crowd."

Sheng abruptly seemed to be singing a different tune.

"So . . ." Chen echoed noncommittally, waiting for Sheng to continue.

"The sender of the first e-mail, however, is a devious troublemaker. There's no question about it. The human-flesh search was coordinated with the subsequent barrage of online posts, which were too sudden and overwhelming for Zhou or anybody to properly respond. It was devastating to the image of our Party."

"With corruption rampant among our officials," Chen said, "that kind of Internet attack probably won't stop anytime soon."

"You're right about that. A brand-new Internet star specializing in human-flesh searches popped up recently, though I don't think he'll be a real problem."

"An Internet-search star?"

"Yes. And such stars have fans of their own. Once they have developed a huge following, they may demand Web sites pay them to post their blogs," Sheng said, shaking his head. "As for this new star, he's surnamed Ouyang. His special skill is determining the brand of watch an official is wearing in news photos, and then posting the photos online with the brand and price of the watch listed underneath."

"Expensive watches, I bet."

"Rolex, Cartier, Omega, Tudor, Tissot . . . you name it," Sheng said with unconcealed irritation. "He recently caused a huge uproar with a post containing more than twenty pictures of Party cadres wearing those luxury brands. He didn't even have to comment on it. In a single day, it was posted and reposted on numerous Web sites, triggering another wave of crowd-sourced searches with more than a hundred thousand responses."

"Yes, those expensive watches blatantly belie the image of hard-working, plain-living Party cadres."

"But posting about it can lead to disillusionment with our Party and the socialist system. We have to do something about it."

"Ouyang didn't do anything wrong by reposting some news-paper pictures. Openly punishing him for that could backfire."

"We didn't have to punish him overtly. We just asked him out for a cup of tea, and Ouyang agreed to cooperate. He won't be post-ing anything like that again."

Chen had heard of asking someone out for "a cup of tea," which meant government officials like Sheng warning a troublemaker over tea. Sometimes they didn't just use a stick. Sometimes they offered a carrot as well.

"But with regard to the Zhou case, do you have any idea who might have sent the photo?" Chen asked.

"According to Jiang, the sender must have had access to the origi-nal electronic file—not just the version published in the newspaper. He wouldn't have been able to pick out the brand name off a pack of cigarettes from the low-resolution reproduction."

"That occurred to me as well," Chen said, "so it might be an in-side job."

"Or someone with access to inside information. A computer hacker, for example, could have accessed the original without anyone knowing. The moderator of the original Web forum is a hacker, and we're doing a thorough background check at the moment." Sheng then went on with a serious air. "As for it being an inside job, the sud-den disappearance of Fang, Zhou's secretary, speaks for itself."

"But wait—I'm confused. What could she have possibly gained?

Zhou helped her when she was in need. Because of Zhou she obtained a secure, well paid job."

"You must have heard something about the secret relationship between the two."

"According to Detective Wei's files, which included several pictures of her, she's not a knockout, and already in her early or mid thirties. One could easily imagine younger and much prettier girls flocking around Zhou."

"Zhou was a cautious man in his way," Sheng said, the lines on his face knitting deeper. "As a high-ranking Party cadre, he had to be conscious of his public image. With a middle-aged secretary, he didn't have to worry about gossip. As for what might have happened between a boss and his little secretary, one never really knows. True, Fang is no longer that young, but she still could have been able to demand something of Zhou. Her status in the office, for instance. And through that position, she might have amassed a lot of inside information. That wouldn't be a new story in the sordid dramas of these corrupt officials."

That was an unusual analysis from an Internal Security officer. Chen thought; then he nodded and said, "But she's disappeared."

"She might be off in hiding, preparing to sell her inside information for a good price."

"I see your point." Of course, that was a possibility. But was Sheng moving in the same direction as Jiang, as far as Fang was concerned? Chen couldn't tell.

"In the meantime, we'll focus on that Internet café as well as on the Web forum. The Internet regulations are new, so there might be some loopholes. We are going to request reinforcements and put more manpower on the task. By checking the movements of every one of them during that period, we'll be able to find the culprit."

Sheng was apparently under a lot of pressure to find the person who sent the photo and mete out a severe punishment as a serious warning to other potential troublemakers. Those would-be trouble-makers would think twice before trying to "harm China's stability."

"By the way," Sheng went on, changing topics, "have you heard anything from the Central Party Discipline Committee in Beijing?"

Chen had anticipated the question. It was whispered among people in the know that Comrade Zhao, the ex-secretary of the Central Party Discipline Committee, had taken on Chen as a sort of protégé. Chen, because of his connection to Comrade Zhao, might have been assumed to be able to tell Sheng something about what was really going on at the top, possibly the true purpose of this meeting.

For an instant, Chen was filled with the same frustration as those netizens. The one and only focus of Internal Security was politics, on the necessity of "maintaining stability" at the expense of these so-called "troublemakers." Zhou's death, and for that matter Wei's death, were totally irrelevant to them. On the spur of the moment, Chen decided to respond cryptically, instead of answering Sheng's question.

"I appreciate your telling me all this, Sheng. Now between you and me, let me say something. If I were you, I wouldn't rush into action."

"Yes?"

"Across the street, you can see the Moller Villa Hotel. It's a special hotel, in which are currently stationed two special teams—Jiang's team from the Shanghai city government, and another team from the Central Party Discipline Committee in Beijing. A week earlier there were three. The Shanghai Party Discipline Committee Team, which was also there, has already decamped. It's all rather unusual, isn't it?"

"Very unusual—"

"And you were sent from Beijing as well, right?" Chen asked, then paused deliberately. "Usually, a case like Zhou's would have been concluded long ago. It's in the Party's interest to wrap up cases like this quickly, isn't it? Why has it been dragging on?"

It was Sheng's turn not to respond. Silence hung heavily over the room.

Chen continued. "The water may be too deep for us to jump in headfirst. Like pieces on a chessboard, we're positioned there by others. Our respective roles might not be known to us, that is, in the larger picture. As long as we do our jobs conscientiously, that's about all that is asked of us. But we also have to make sure that our work doesn't get in the way of the larger picture."

"Yes, I think I'm beginning to catch your point, Chief Inspector Chen."

"That's why I quoted the metaphor about the blind man and the blind horse. To be frank, some of your Internal Security officers and I may have had misunderstandings in the past. But I hope not this time. You're different, Lieutenant Sheng. You invited me over to talk about our common goals, even though we have different priorities."

"I'm glad to hear that, Chief Inspector Chen."

"But do you think the Central Party Discipline Committee team would come from Beijing and stay here for a small potato like Zhou?"

"No, I don't . . ." Sheng added hesitantly, "I think I've heard of something between Beijing and Shanghai."

"As the song goes, 'I don't know which direction the wind is blowing,'" Chen said, then added in a whisper, "I've just received an e-mail from Beijing."

"From Beijing?"

"He quoted a poem to me by Wang Yangming. From what I can tell, the basic message is: you can't afford to lose sight of the big things in the distance because of the small things close at hand."

"There's no point in his stating things too explicitly," Sheng said, without even having to ask who "he" was.

It was then that Sheng's phone rang.

As Sheng picked up his phone, Chen stood up and started walking toward the balcony for a cigarette. Then he came to a dead stop. He heard the name of Fang repeated by Sheng into the phone. Chen slowed down, pretending to look for matches, walking back two or three steps to retrieve some from the coffee table. He overheard several more fragmented words.

"Shaoxing, or near Shaoxing . . . a public phone . . . her parents don't know anything . . ."

He lit a cigarette, stepped out to the balcony, and inhaled deeply. The city was looming all around him, with old and new skyscrapers, impersonal and oppressive.

When he went back inside, Sheng had finished his call and had made another coffee for the chief inspector.

Sheng didn't say anything about the call, probably thinking that the chief inspector wouldn't be able to make anything out of one or two out-of-context words.

But Chen knew what he'd heard, and what he was going to do.

TWENTY-TWO

TWENTY MINUTES LATER, CHEN stepped into a public phone booth on Yan'an Road, took a quick look around, and then dialed the number of the cell phone he'd given Fang.

When she picked up, Chen blurted out, without pausing to greet her, "I warned you not to call your parents."

Despite his warning, she'd called her parents in Shanghai from a pay phone near Dayu Temple, like a lonely, lost tourist.

"I'm all alone here, in the house he bought me, surrounded by nothing but memories of him, and the echoes of my own footsteps. I really can't stand it anymore."

"But their phone in Shanghai was tapped," he said. "Now they've been able to narrow down your location to Shaoxing. It's only a matter of time before they track you down to that villa. You have to move—as soon as possible."

"Where?"

"Anywhere. Away from Shaoxing. I know things are hard for

you, but you have to stay out of their hands. What happened to Zhou shouldn't happen to you."

"But how long do I have to hide and wait?" She went on without waiting for an answer: "Is there anything new in Shanghai?"

"We're making some progress, but—"

"The other day," she said, interrupting, "you asked me to recall anything unusual—anything at all—about Zhou before he was shuangguied. I thought this through several times, and I think there might be something, but I'm not sure."

"Yes?"

"There's a small bedroom attached to his office. He usually worked late, so occasionally he stayed overnight. One evening, after more pictures were posted on the Internet, he looked very upset. He wanted me to join him in that bedroom to, among other things, dance for him."

"What? In a parody of the Mighty King of Chu?" Chen asked. Zhou must have known of the impending disaster and had reacted like the King of Chu, who requested that his favorite imperial concubine dance for him before he went off to fight his last-ditch battle.

"I've seen the movie based on that story. I think it's called *Farewell My Concubine*. I'm no dancer, but he was so insistent that I did a loyal character dance for him. He hummed a Mao-quotation song, lighting one cigarette after another like there was no tomorrow . . .

"The next morning, when I first got to the office, he wanted me to take out a large plastic trash bag. That was odd because, as a rule, that was the cleaning woman's job. He said he needed me to do it because he was going to have some important guests that morning. Sure enough, they showed up even before he got back from his breakfast at the bureau canteen."

"Who was it that showed up that morning?"

"It was Jiang and his team from the city government. As soon as they saw he wasn't in his office, they headed straight to the canteen and marched him away from there."

"So Jiang's team came before the city discipline committee team did?"

"Yes. It was all so sudden."

"But what about the trash bag?"

"Before I dumped it, I took a look inside. It was nothing but ashes."

"Perhaps he burned documents overnight. There was nothing else?"

"Well, it wasn't *just* ashes; there were also some small broken plastic pieces."

"Where did you dump it?"

"In a large trash bin outside the office."

"Did the team from the city know anything about it?"

"No. The whole office was thrown into turmoil and no one paid attention to the trash bin outside. I went back and looked in the next day and everything was gone. The trash bin was empty."

"Now," Chen said, glancing at his watch, "what can you tell me about those plastic pieces?"

"They looked like pieces from a plastic pen. Perhaps he crushed it in agitation. It was bright red. I don't remember having ever seen such a pen in the office before. It wasn't something that struck me as unusual at the time, though."

"Did you notice anything broken or missing from the office?"

"No, nothing."

"Did you ever go back into his office after he was put into shuanggui?"

"No. I used to work in a cubicle outside his office. That morning they conducted a very thorough search, and they took away a lot of things, including the computers and all the files. Then his office was sealed up. My cubicle was ransacked, too, and a group of people came back and searched again about a week later."

So the search on that first morning had been done by Jiang's city government team. There was nothing surprising about that. Whatever they had or hadn't found, Jiang hadn't shared with Chen.

"About a week later. That was after Zhou's death, right?"

"Yes."

What were they looking for? Chen wondered. Whatever it was, they were still looking for it. Fang had touched on that possibility back when they had talked in Shaoxing.

Chen noticed that the screen on the phone was showing a message about the calling card running out of time.

"Sorry, there's no time left on my calling card. I have to go, but I'll call you again, Fang."

Late that afternoon Chen arrived at the City Government Building. As a rule, he would show his ID, then breeze through the security checkpoint. The guard would merely nod at him, never bothering to ask him to declare the purpose of his visit. With his ID in hand, Chen simply signed his name in the register book.

Instead of taking the elevator directly to Zhou's office, Chen went to a small canteen on the first floor and sat down with a cup of coffee. He pulled out his notebook and started making notes on events and observations over the last few days.

It wasn't until five thirty that he stood up and went over to the elevator, taking it to the floor of the City Housing Development Committee. There was no one in the hallway. He hurried over to the director's office. The door still bore a broken police seal.

The director's position left vacant by Zhou's death hadn't yet been filled. The city government, it seemed, was being extraordinarily cautious, taking their time in making a decision about the crucial position.

Chen took another look around, then inserted a key, entered, and closed the door after him.

It wasn't a really large office, but with the computer gone and the desk and chairs dust-covered, it looked rather desolate.

It would be unrealistic to think that he'd be able to find something critical in just one short visit, after the office had already been thoroughly searched. Still, he had to come and try.

Instead of digging into every nook and cranny, Chen opened the door to the attached bedroom, sat down in the leather swivel chair, and tried to imagine himself as Zhou on that night.

In spite of his efforts, a mental image of Fang dancing kept cropping up. Perhaps it was too dramatic to ignore the echo of the ancient story of an imperial concubine dancing for her lord, knowing that it would be her last before she committed suicide. It was a scene much celebrated in classical Chinese literature.

Making a beauty willing to die for you, / the King of Chu was after all a hero. These were two sympathetic lines by Wu Weiye, a Qing dynasty poet.

Like the King of Chu, Zhou had refused to give up, though he was aware of the approaching doom.

The parallels were eerie, but the details confounded Chen.

In the case of the King of Chu, his favorite concubine danced and then killed herself so that she wouldn't be a burden to her lord in his last battle. Fang didn't do so, nor did Zhou want her to.

The King of Chu still wanted to fight, clinging to the belief that he could break through the opposing army, that he had enough forces left at the camp east of the river to back him up. Zhou must have believed the same.

Chen again started to go over the sequence of events that fateful night, this time more closely. While she was dancing, Zhou hummed a Mao-quotation song and lit a cigarette—

Chen wondered whether there could be something in Zhou's choice of the Mao-quotation song, but he quickly brushed aside that idea. It could be simply that the melody was familiar to Zhou from his youth, or because Fang was dancing the loyal character dance . . .

The chief inspector again lost the thread of his thoughts.

He, too, wanted to light a cigarette. He took out his pack before he realized that he must have left his lighter back at the security checkpoint. That might be just as well. Theoretically, the office should be left intact and undisturbed. Still, his glance swept the office, falling involuntarily upon a lighter next to the mini marble bookstand on the desk.

He wasn't sure if that was the lighter Zhou had used that night. After all, a heavy smoker might have kept several of them around. Chen went over and picked it up. It wasn't a fancy, expensive lighter, but it was intriguing due to its torchlike shape, bright red color, and a Mao quote engraved in gold: "A spark can set the whole prairie ablaze."

He struck the tiny wheel atop the lighter. No spark. He tried harder. Still no luck.

It was probably another sign that he shouldn't smoke in the office. He shrugged his shoulders and slumped back down in the swivel chair with a thump.

He stroked the lighter again distractedly.

Why would Zhou have kept a useless lighter in his office?

A hunch gripped him.

Chen jumped up and started pacing around, and then sat back down again with the lighter clasped in his hand.

Setting the lighter down on the desk, he took out his Swiss knife, and with the screwdriver blade, he managed to open up the bottom part of the red lighter.

As the bottom fell off, Chen glimpsed an object inside.

Not a butane reservoir but a flash drive, with part of the plastic shell cut off to fit it in.

Finally, one of the crucial missing pieces had appeared.

That night Zhou had still wanted to fight—like the King of Chu—with something in hand that might save him from total destruction. Something that could ensure that people above him, far more powerful, would provide enough help to enable him to survive the engulfing storm.

"A chain of crabs bound together on a straw rope—" What Fang had said to him in Shaoxing came back to him.

What she said was an idiomatic expression that referred to a common sight in the food market. A peddler would bind live crabs together with a thick straw rope, making it easier for customers to carry without worrying about any of them escaping. As a figure of speech, however, it meant something quite different. "Crabs" usually meant evildoers. What bound them together wasn't a straw rope but their common interest—the schemes or secrets they shared. They had to protect or shield each other; no one could betray another, or one fallen would bring everybody else down.

Zhou must have threatened the people above him by telling them that the bell wouldn't toll for him alone. Zhou had in his hands evidence, which he hid in a place known to no one else, in the lighter in his office. However, Jiang came earlier than expected, surprising him in the canteen and taking him into custody there. In all the confusion, the lighter had been left behind in his office.

Eventually, the threat he posed led to his death in the hotel. He might have said something, and his coconspirators had had to silence him once and for all. But they still had to find the evidence he'd left behind, or they'd never be able to sleep in peace.

The arrival of the Beijing team at the hotel, with the possible showdown looming in the Forbidden City, only served to make them more desperate.

What Fang saw in the trash bag that morning, the tiny pieces of broken plastic, could have either been parts of the broken butane reservoir, or parts of the shell of the flash drive.

Chen didn't think he had to read the flash drive there and then. He had to get out of the office immediately.

Luckily, there was still no one in the hallway. He made it to the elevator and then to the lobby without anyone seeing him. He walked by the security guard with barely a nod.

Outside, it was surprisingly warm in the People's Square. Chen again began sweating profusely.

The square was swarming with people, as always. Several groups of people in their fifties or sixties were dancing or exercising to music blaring from CD players on the ground. They were enjoying the moment, with the sun setting and the City Government Building still shining in the fading light.

Behind the people filling the square, there was a line of limousines waiting patiently along the driveway in front of the magnificent City Government Building.

Amidst them all, a lonely figure was standing in a corner, absentmindedly clicking a red lighter in vain.

TWENTY-THREE

CHIEF INSPECTOR CHEN KNEW that the investigation had reached a critical point and that he had to make a decision.

But, instead, he decided to visit his mother.

At least for the moment, he wanted to put aside all the confusing and conflicting thoughts that were plaguing him, no matter how urgent the situation was. He couldn't shake the feeling that this would be his last case. The people involved were far better connected and more powerful than a chief inspector could deal with. This was a feeling that was intensified by the bits and pieces he'd been picking up over the last few days including, paradoxically, the conversation he'd had with Sheng, the Internal Security officer he'd met with at the City Hotel. The scenario he'd spun out for Sheng turned out to be almost self-fulfilling.

Whatever the flash drive contained, the chief inspector could choose to do nothing. No one knew about his discovery in Zhou's office. Chen was only consulting on the case; he wasn't really expected to make any breakthroughs on it. He wasn't supposed to carry out any secret missions for Comrade Zhao, despite the poem he cited for Chen. The power struggle going on in the Forbidden City was way beyond his grasp and his interest. It might be just as well to be nothing more than an ordinary cop.

But would that work? He wasn't sure. Others might not even let him keep his position as chief inspector.

As an alternative, he could give the flash drive to his immediate superiors, like a loyal Party member who believed in the system. But he shuddered at the thought in spite of himself.

For the early summer, it was an extraordinarily warm day. He looked up to glimpse a spray of red apricot blossom stretching out over a white wall on Zuzhou Road, trembling in a fitful breeze.

With so many details unknown to him, he couldn't properly analyze the situation. He thought once more of the metaphor of a blind man riding a blind horse toward a deep lake during a dark night. Any move he might make felt risky, unguided. What's worse, any move could play right into a political situation beyond his control, and out of his depth.

Even if he did decide to do what was expected of him in his position as a chief inspector, taking all the risk on himself, what about the people close and dear to him—particularly his old, sick mother?

He found himself walking over to the old neighborhood. Like the rest of Shanghai, it had been changing as well, though not much beyond new food stalls, restaurants, and convenience stores appearing here and there. Near Jiujiang Road, he saw a new whiteboard newsletter standing at the corner of the side street, on which was written, "To build a harmonious society."

It was another reminder that, as a Party member police officer, his job was supposed to be nothing more than damage control. As repeatedly urged in the *People's Daily*, everything he did was supposed to be for the sake of a "harmonious society."

But how was he supposed to do that?

He took a shortcut through a lane once familiar to him. He wasn't particularly surprised to feel a drop of water splashing on his forehead. He tilted his head to see a line of colorful clothing, freshly washed and dripping from bamboo poles overhead. It was another ominous sign for this assignment. According to a folk superstition, it was bad luck to walk under women's underwear, let alone under ones dripping from above—

"Damn! What a shitty taste!"

Chen was startled by a curse echoing from a middle-aged man who was eating from a large rice bowl, shaking his head like a rattle drum over a shrimp that he'd spat out onto the ground.

An elderly woman bending over a common sink beside him cast an inquiring look at the shrimp. "Oh, it was dipped in formalin so that it would look like a Wuxie white shrimp."

"It fucking tastes like Chairman Mao."

"What?"

"Isn't he still preserved in formalin in that crystal coffin?" The man stood up, raging in high dudgeon, dumping the remaining portion forcefully into the lidless garbage can. "What retribution!"

"Come on. Under Chairman Mao, you wouldn't have had shrimp like this."

"That's true. Then there was no shrimp at all at the market."

Lately, there had been a fashionable "rediscovery" of shikumen houses and longtang alleyways, which was probably nothing but a nostalgic myth conjured by some of the "already rich," wistfully thinking that the traditional way of living was still viable.

With an increasing income and lifestyle gap between the rich and the poor, with blatant corruption and injustice everywhere, with hazardous chemicals in the everyday food, how could ordinary people sit outside contentedly in a scruffy, shabby lane, as if in some old photograph?

The people who lived here were anxious to move out of one of the city's forgotten corners into new apartment buildings, but they remained helplessly stranded.

Near his mother's residence, Chen saw a fruit stall. Next to it, a gray-haired man was sprawled out in a ramshackle chair, its original rattan replaced by plastic straw rope or whatever stray material was capable of keeping it in a recognizable shape. Spread out over his face was a newspaper with a partially legible headline: "Reading . . . Paradise of Intelligence," and his stockinged feet dangled just above the cigarette-butt-strewn sidewalk. He seemed totally oblivious of everything going on around him, but he nodded at Chen mechanically, like a windup toy soldier.

Chen recognized him as a middle school classmate. He'd been laid off from his factory job years earlier, now managing to eke out a meager living with this fruit stall at the corner. He sat out here every day, barely moving, as if slowly turning into an unmistakable street marker. Chen stopped at his stall and bought two small bamboo baskets, one of apples and one of oranges, then went on to his mother's.

With the baskets in his hand, he knocked on her door.

Thanks to the help of the neighborhood committee, she'd moved down from the attic room to a corner room on the first floor, which was about the same size. The neighborhood committee went out of their way to look out for her, not because she was a good, old resident of many years but because her son was now a "big shot" in the Party system. Since she was still unwilling to move in with him or to leave the old neighborhood, the influence his position carried was about all he could do for her.

After knocking on the door a couple of times, Chen pushed it open and stepped inside. He saw her dozing on a bamboo deck chair, a cup of green tea sitting on a tiny table beside her. She looked fairly relaxed but lonely in the sudden shaft of light streaming in through the door. She was hard of hearing and hadn't heard his knock. Awakened by the sun in her eyes, she looked up, surprised at the sight of him in the room.

"Oh, I'm so glad you could come over today, son. But you didn't have to buy me anything. I'm really doing fine," she said, trying to get up, leaning heavily on a dragon-head-carved bamboo cane. "You didn't call."

"I had something to do at the City Government Building, so I decided to drop in on my way back."

"What's up?"

"Nothing particular, but your birthday is coming up next month. We must do something to celebrate, Mother. So I wanted to discuss it with you."

"For an old woman like me, a birthday doesn't call for celebration. But times have really changed. Several of your friends have called to talk to me about their plans to throw a birthday party."

"You see, people all want to do something."

"Peiqin came over yesterday and cooked several special dishes for me. It's so nice of her; she doesn't have to come, since I have the hourly maid coming in to help. Peiqin insisted, however, that I should have a special diet. She suggested that she cook for the occasion. White Cloud dropped in the other day, too, and declared that she would buy a large cake for the birthday party."

"That was so kind of them," he said, feeling even guiltier at her mention of both Peiqin and White Cloud. The old woman's one regret in this world of red dust was that her son remained single. In her eyes, Peiqin had always been a model wife, and White Cloud had, at one time, been a possible candidate. He hadn't seen White Cloud for quite a while, though he still thought of her occasionally. He was the one to blame for their estrangement, recalling a song she'd once sung for him in a dimly lit karaoke room.

You like to say you are a grain of sand, / occasionally fallen into my eyes, in mischief. / You would rather have me weep by myself / than have me love you, / and then you disappear again in the wind / like a grain of sand . . .

It was a sentimental piece titled "Sobbing Sand," but he remembered the melody. People invariably get sentimental when it's too late.

Chen started peeling an apple for his mother. Putting it on a saucer on the small table, he nearly tipped over the teacup.

Visiting her was perhaps just an attempt to delay the crucial decision, which he nonetheless had to make.

"You have something on your mind, son," she said, picking up a piece of apple and pushing it over to him.

"No, I'm fine—just too busy. Things can be so complicated in today's society."

"This world is too new, too capriciously changing for an old woman. I've been reading the Buddhist scripture, you know. It says that things may be difficult for people to see through. It's simply because everything is only appearance, like a dream, like a bubble, like a dewdrop, like lightning. So are you yourself."

"You're so right, Mother."

"Perhaps it's also like a painting. When you are deeply involved in it, you never really have perspective on it. You never really see yourself in the painting. Once you gain some distance, you might become aware of something you never saw before. Enlightenment comes when you're no longer part of anything."

It reminded him of several lines by the Song dynasty poet Su Shi, but for her, it came from Buddhist scripture. He was grateful that she retained her perspective and remained clear-headed, in spite of her frail health. But there was also something disturbing in her remark.

"I remember a favorite quote of your father's: 'There are things a man will do, and things he will not do,'" she said. "It's that simple, and that's all there is to it."

That was a quote from Confucius. Chen's late father was a renowned neo-Confucian scholar, who drew such lines for himself, and consequently suffered a great deal during the Cultural Revolution.

Where would Chief Inspector Chen himself draw the line today?

It didn't take long for his mother to appear tired. She started yawning repeatedly, without even finishing the apple he'd peeled for her. It might not bode well for her recovery, and he didn't want to add to her discomfort by staying any longer. So he took his leave of her, gently pulling the door closed as he left.

He walked through the neighborhood, becoming aware of people's occasional curious glances. Some of them might have recognized him, so he kept walking, his head ducked down. Soon he reached Yun'nan Road, where he stopped and waited for the traffic light to change before crossing the street.

In existentialism, one makes a choice and accepts the consequences. That's where freedom comes from. But what if the choice brought about consequences to others?

His mother, for instance.

The traffic light turned green.

Looking up, he saw a relatively tall building with its gold-painted name, Ruikang, shining on the façade. It wasn't exactly a new, upscale building, but because of its excellent location, one square meter here cost no less than thirty thousand yuan in the present market.

Then he remembered that Lianping lived in this building. It was close to his mother's, as she'd told him, and was just one block behind Great World, an entertainment center built almost a century ago that was now closed for restoration. For a non-Shanghainese girl, she was doing quite well. She had an apartment at the center of the city, her own luxury car, both symbols of the Shanghai dream.

He glanced around the subdivision but didn't see her car. Perhaps it was parked in back. He wasn't in any mood to drop in on her, but he was surprised that his thoughts kept returning to her even though he was in the midst of a developing crisis.

That was probably because she'd been so helpful with the investigation. He was impressed by her cynical criticism of the unbridled corruption in the nation's socialism with Chinese characteristics, though he'd known her for only a couple of weeks and known her real name, Lili, for only a couple of days. He was aware of the gaps that separated them—between their backgrounds and their ways of looking at society, not to mention their age difference. Still, it wasn't too much to say that she already left a mark on his police work. Not only had she provided him a general grounding in the world of the Internet, she had also given him a sense of the ways people used it to resist and expose corruption. It was also her suggestion that he go to Shaoxing, and prior to that she had helped him set up the meeting with Melong, both of which affected the course of his investigation.

Again, he restrained himself from thinking of her other than in a professional capacity. He walked down Guangxi Road, stopping abruptly at the corner of Jinling Road.

There was an Internet café at the corner called Flying Horse. It was the one mentioned by Lieutenant Sheng, the one from which the e-mail with the photo had been sent to Melong. The evening when Chen met Melong, at the cross-bridge noodle place, Melong had told him that the Internet café was nearby.

Next to the Internet café there was a Chinese herbal medicine store. There was a line of people waiting outside the herbal medicine store, obscuring the entrance to the Internet café. Like most others, Flying Horse was open twenty-four hours a day, and through the line of people Chen could see that the door stood ajar.

Suddenly, he realized that there was something he might have overlooked. Transfixed at the idea of it, Chen shuddered in spite of himself. He crossed the street and stepped into the Internet café. A smallish girl at the front desk asked him for his ID with a sleepy yawn. As at the other Internet cafés, the new regulation requiring that users provide ID and sign the register was being observed.

Chen showed her his police badge and pointed at the register.

"I need to make a copy of all the entries for this month."

She blinked at him as if desperately trying to rouse herself out of a stupor.

"My manager won't be back until eight o'clock."

"Don't worry about him. Here's my business card. Tell him to call me if he wants to talk. Now give me the register. You must have a copy machine in the office, and it'll only take me about ten minutes to copy the pages I need. I'll pay you accordingly."

She hesitated and then pushed a button, which brought the owner to the front desk. He was a stout man with a large head and broad shoulders. He appeared to be flabbergasted, having recognized Chen and realized his position.

"What wind has brought you here today, Chief?"

"So it's you—Iron Head Diao. That's your nickname, right?"

"Wow, you still remember me. We went to the same elementary school, but you were my senior. You're really somebody now," Iron Head Diao said obsequiously. "What can I do for you?"

"Let me see the register."

"This one?" he said, handing it to Chen.

Chen glanced at the first two pages. The register was a new one, with the first entry in it being from just three days ago.

"Let me look at the two before this one."

"Sure," Iron Head Diao said, reaching below the counter and pulling out two more register books.

"Is there anywhere I can check through them in peace?" Chen asked.

"Come back to my office. It's up in the attic."

Without any further ado, Iron Head Diao led him to the back and up a shaky ladder. In the office there was a desk as well as a copy machine.

"It's all yours," Iron Head Diao said before climbing down the squeaky ladder. "Stay as long as you like."

It wasn't much more than a retrofitted attic: small, dimly lit, but with enough privacy for Chen's purpose. What's more, there was also a surveillance monitor, which commanded a view of the whole place. While he could watch what was going on downstairs, no one would be able to see up into the attic office.

He started looking through the entries. The second register

covered the period he wanted to check. It only took him five or six minutes before he came to the date, the time slot, and a name, even though it didn't correspond to the number of the computer from which the e-mail with the photo had been sent to Melong.

Another piece of the puzzle fell into place.

Gazing at the page, Chen heaved a long sigh.

He looked at the surveillance monitor, which showed Iron Head Diao pacing about, smoking and glancing up furtively. His enormous head hung low, as if weighed down with worries.

Chen then did something quite unusual for him. He tore out a couple of pages from the register and stuffed them into his pocket. It surprised even himself, as it was something he couldn't have envisioned doing even a minute before.

It was unprofessional and unjustifiable, particularly for a police officer.

There were things that took precedence over being a cop, however, he hastened to assure himself. And he might not have to worry too much about it. A couple of missing pages from an outdated register might not be noticed.

He closed the registers, climbed down the ladder, and handed them back to Iron Head Diao.

As he left the Internet café, with Iron Head Diao waving at him from the door, still grinning from ear to ear, Chen realized that he hadn't written his name in the register. That might be just as well. Like the other day, at the Internet café in Pudong, there were always loopholes in regulations.

On the street corner, he saw a white-haired man in rags shuffling out of a sordid lane across Yunnan Road, despite the superstition that people should avoid walking under wet clothing, which was hanging from bamboo poles that crisscrossed the alley overhead. But what could an old man do, moving slowly, leaning on a bamboo cane? Possibly born, raised, and then grown old in that same narrow lane, he would have had to enter and exit the lane here, day in and day out, likely to be down and out until the very end.

Chen was about to cross the street when a black BMW convertible sped along Jinling Road, splashing muddy rainwater on him.

"You're blind!" The young driver cursed at him with one hand on the wheel and the other on the shoulder of a slender girl sprawled beside him, her bare legs stretched out like fresh lotus roots.

That such a contrast had become a common sight in the city depressed him.

Perhaps he *was* blind. At the moment, he really had no idea where he was heading. Then he got a phone call from Young Bao at the Writers' Association.

"I've got it, Master Chen," Young Bao said breathlessly. "And something more—hopefully, something that will surprise you."

TWENTY-FOUR

LIANPING WAS WAITING FOR Chen in an elegant private room at a high-end restaurant he had suggested. It seemed to her to be quite new. It was near the front entrance of Bund Park, and the window of the second-floor room overlooked a panorama of ships coming and going along the distant Wusongkou, the East China Sea.

Her mind was in a turmoil. So much had happened the last few days, and it was as if it had happened to somebody else. She thought back on all of it in disbelief.

But one thing proved that it really had happened—the dazzling diamond ring on her finger. Xiang had proposed, and she had accepted. He'd put the ring on her finger without waiting for a response. She hadn't taken it off.

She didn't know what to say to Chen, but she had to tell him about her decision. She owed it to him, and for that matter, she owed it to Xiang too.

On a fitful May breeze, a melody came wafting over from the big clock atop the Shanghai Custom Building. Her left eyelid twitched again. She must be stressed out, or perhaps it was just another omen. She remembered a superstition from back home in Anhui about twitching eyes.

Agreeing to marry Xiang wasn't an easy decision for her. It was more like an opportunity she couldn't afford to miss than something she really wanted. After all, she lived in materialistic times, having read and heard all the tabloid stories about pretty young girls hooking up with Big Bucks and living "happily ever after."

Tapping her fingers on the table, she wished she could have lived in the world of the poems recited by Chen back in Shaoxing, but she had to face reality. Just the day before, her father had written to her about the problems his factory was facing with both a shrinking market and the rocketing price of commodities. She could no longer bring herself to ask him for help with her mortgage payments. The subdivision committee had just increased parking fees, but it was still difficult to find an open spot, so they suggested, as an alternative, that she buy a permanent spot for thirty thousand yuan. And gas prices kept going up too. The list went on and on.

Still, she had to achieve the Shanghai dream—not just for herself but for her family too. Xiang represented an opportunity she couldn't let slip by, as her colleague Yaqing had repeatedly pointed out. Even though he was always busy and business-oriented, this could also bode well for his future. He was just like Chen in that he was overwhelmed by his work.

Looking back on it, she realized that the flirtation with Chen was perhaps the result of a vain, vulnerable moment. A connection to a high-profile Party cadre like Chen would be helpful to her as a journalist, and publishing his work in her section would also be to her credit. Add to this the fact that Xiang had vanished without telling her first or contacting her for days.

Then it developed further than she anticipated.

But now Xiang was back with an explanation for his behavior—a reasonable one—and with the surprise proposal, accompanied by a passionate speech as he slipped the ring onto her finger: "In Hong Kong, after finally signing the business deal, I realized that all the success in the world meant nothing without you."

To be honest, she'd been waiting for Xiang to make a move. Xiang hadn't done so earlier because his father had wanted him to make a different choice, one that made more business sense. Specifically, he wanted an alliance with another rich family in the city. Xiang finally made his own move, though, when she least expected it. She couldn't afford not to accept.

So what explanation could she offer Chen?

It occurred to her that maybe neither of them had taken it too seriously, from the day they first met at the Writers' Association. If there was a moment when something came close to developing between the two of them, it would have to be that afternoon in Shaoxing, with memories of the romantic poems and stories echoing around them in Shen Garden. It was also that afternoon, however, that she realized that nothing would ever develop between them. It wasn't that he was first and foremost a policeman or that he was too much of an enigma for her; it was that he had disappointed her in the same way Xiang had, and he had done so even more dramatically than Xiang.

She reached into her bag and touched the book of translated poetry he'd given her. Somehow she'd brought it here with her. Looking out the window, she recalled some lines from the volume.

She leans against the window | looking out alone to the river, | to thousands of sails passing along— | none is the one she waits for. | The sun setting slant, | the water running silent into the distance, | her heart breaks at the sight | of the islet enclosed in white duckweed.

Except for the absence of white duckweed, it was the same scene, more than a thousand years later.

She couldn't shake off the feeling that Chen might have approached her with an ulterior motive, though in her high-strung state of mind, she could be imagining things.

A waiter approached her with a pot of tea and interrupted the train of her thought. The service here was excellent. She had researched the restaurant online. It was obscenely expensive, yet perhaps that fact appealed to upstarts eager for a taste of elite status. Sipping at the tea, she looked out the window at the park.

It wasn't much of a park, and it looked even more crowded with the recent additions, such as the concrete monument that looked like the logo of Three-Lance underwear, the fashionable new cafés and bars, and the array of other architectural add-ons along the bank. She had never understood why the Shanghainese made such a big deal of the park, but she'd heard it was a place special to Chen.

Beyond the park, petrels glided over the waves, their wings flashing in the gray light, as if flying out of a fast-fading dream. The dividing line between Huangpu River and Suzhou River became less visible.

It was then that Chen stepped into the room, smiling. To her surprise, he was wearing a light gray Mao jacket. He had never dressed so formally in her presence.

"Sorry I'm late. The meeting with the city government took longer than expected. I had no time to change."

"No wonder you're wearing a Mao jacket. That's very politically correct, but there's no need to change, Chen. Mao jackets are also fashionable now: even Hollywood stars vie to wear one at the Oscars. It fits well with this upscale, high-priced restaurant."

"The food is not bad here," he said, "and it's on the Bund. You're paying for the view."

"To be exact, you pay to have your elite status confirmed, and for the satisfaction of knowing you can afford it."

"Well said, Lianping. For me, it's really more for the view of the Bund in the background. My favorite place in the city."

"It's your feng shui corner," she said, still hesitant about broaching the subject of her decision, though it wasn't fair, she knew, to put it off any longer. "Tell me more about it."

"In the early seventies, I used to practice tai chi with some friends in the park. Then I switched my major to English studies. Because of that, I was able to enter the college after the end of the Cultural Revolution with a high score in English. But as the proverb states, in eight or nine times out of ten, things in this world don't work out as one plans. Upon graduation, I was assigned to the police bureau, as you know," he said, taking a sip of tea. "But I still come back here from time to time, to recharge myself with the memories of those years. You may laugh at me for being sentimental, but here, on the very site where this restaurant now stands, for no less than three years I used to sit on a green bench almost every morning."

"It's the special feng shui of Bund Park for a rising star, where the water is constantly slapping against the memories of a forever youthful dream."

"Now you're being sarcastic, Lianping. It's more like the fragments of the past that I've been using to shore up the present."

"Now you're being poetic," she said in spite of herself.

"In those years, I never dreamed of being a cop, but now it's too late for me to switch to another profession. It's not the same for you— for you the world is still so young and various," he said, changing the topic. "Well, let me tell you something about this restaurant. It doesn't really reflect the history of Bund Park, but Mr. Gu, the owner of the restaurant, insists on doing it his way."

"Mr. Gu of the New World Group?"

"Yes. Considering the history of the park, this should be a Western-style restaurant, one that is full of nostalgic flavor. However, Gu wouldn't think of it. He wanted to serve Chinese cuisine to Chinese customers. This may just be his way of showing his patriotism."

"It's also a gesture of political correctness. There was the legendary sign outside the park, back in the twenties, that read 'No Chinese or dogs.' Of course, some scholars claim that the sign never existed, that it was a story made up by the Party authorities after 1949."

"Well, the line between truth and fiction is always being constructed and deconstructed by the people in power. Whether or not Gu believes in the authenticity of the sign, I don't know, but the controversy about it has helped the business. The restaurant is very expensive, which is symbolic of China's new wealth. Of course, it is open to Westerners, too, as long as they are willing to pay the prices. In fact, I've heard that quite a number of Western businessmen make a point of inviting their Chinese partners to dine here."

She looked at the menu and the prices, which were shocking, even after Chen's warning.

"Don't worry about it," Chen said. "We don't have to order a lot, and Gu won't charge me those prices. I just wanted a quiet place to talk to you."

She had no idea what he wanted to talk to her about, and she was debating with herself whether she should say something first. She had rehearsed a speech, but she hadn't worked up the confidence to deliver it.

"So, do you know a lot of Big Bucks, Chen?"

"Not a lot, but in today's society, even a cop can hardly accomplish anything without connections."

"Do you know Xiang Buqun of Purple City Group?"

"Xiang Buqun—isn't he the head of a large property group? I think I met him at the opening ceremony of the New World Project. Maybe on some other occasions as well. Why do you ask?"

"I want to talk to you," she said with difficulty, "about something I might not have told you. I've been seeing Xiang Haiping, Xiang Buqun's son, for quite a while. Last month he went to Shenzhen on business, but now he's back, and he's proposed to me."

"Xiang Haiping, the successor to the group?"

"Possibly the successor," she said in a low voice. She couldn't look him in the eye, but she caught sight of something indecipherable in his expression. Whatever it was, it wasn't the reaction she'd anticipated.

Before either of them could say anything further, Gu burst into the room. He was wearing a pair of rimless glasses, a light-colored wool suit, and a scarlet silk tie. A dapper man, though short in stature, he looked expansive.

"It's the first time you've come here, Chief Inspector Chen. I'm honored to have you here," he said, his glance taking Lianping in with unconcealed approval. "And Lianping is here with you today. I'm really honored to have *both* of you here."

She'd met Gu at some business conferences, though they were barely nodding acquaintances. As the chairman of the New World Group, Gu kept a low profile and had declined her request for an interview.

"We needed a quiet place, so I thought of you," Chen said. "But you'll have to treat me as you would an ordinary customer, Mr. Gu."

"How can you say that, Chief Inspector Chen? You've finally accepted the invitation to my restaurant that I extended a long time ago. No, there's no way I can allow you to back out. Besides, you don't want me to lose face in front of a beauty like Lianping?"

"So you're buddies," she observed, not knowing what else to say.

"Let me tell you something about him, Lianping," Gu said with a serious air. "Do you know how New World became so successful?"

It was obvious that Gu was in no hurry to leave them alone, and she felt somehow relieved. It might be just as well that there was another person with them in the private room doing the talking. She had already said what she had to say.

"How?" she asked.

"It was all due to a crucial loan made at the very beginning of New World, which was possible only because of Chen's superb translation of the business plan for the project. That translation was so difficult. A lot of the business terms didn't even exist in the Chinese language then. The translation had to convey the meaning textually as well as contextually. When the American venture capitalist read the business plan in English and learned that it had been translated by a high-ranking Shanghai police officer, he was so impressed that he immediately approved the loan."

The American might not have been impressed by Chen's command of English so much as he was by Gu's connection to "a high-ranking Shanghai police officer." For this sort of shikumen redevelopment project, right in the center of the city, official connections might have been the most crucial factor for it to succeed. The American probably knew that as well as she did.

"I begged him to help with the translation," Gu went on. "I even mentioned a bonus in the event the loan was approved. Naturally, I had to keep my word, but he wouldn't listen. When New World went public, I had no choice but to invest the bonus I'd promised in the shares of the IPO for him. It wasn't a large bonus, just about ten thousand shares."

She did a quick calculation in her mind. As a finance journalist, she happened to be familiar with the stock. After repeated stock splits, at least four or five of them by now, and at the present share price of over eighty yuan, that could add up to a sizable fortune.

But why was Gu telling her all this? It seemed so unlike the shrewd businessman she'd known him to be. Then she realized what was happening. Gu must have assumed he knew what was going on: a prominent Party cadre had brought a young girl to a private room in a fancy restaurant. So what could Gu do to help Chen out in this imagined romantic scenario? He was trying to make Chen seem even more of a catch, if possible, in her eyes—not only a rising Party official with a great future, but a Big Buck too.

"Cut it out, Gu. Don't talk about business in the company of a finance journalist. Someday, she might write about my shady dealings with Big Bucks like you," Chen said with a laugh. "For the record, I never agreed to any such bonus. For that translation, which was only about twenty pages in all, you paid me more than I could have made for translating twenty books. That was more than enough."

"No. It was far from enough for such a successful project," Gu insisted, waving his hand emphatically. He turned his attention to Lianping. "In today's society, an incorruptible police officer is almost an endangered species. I admire him not for his position, but for all the things he's done for the country. An ordinary businessman like me has to consider himself extremely lucky to have a friend like Chief Inspector Chen."

"If I write a biography of Chen someday," she said with a smile, "I'll definitely include that part, Mr. Gu."

"Please do, Lianping. You would be a fantastic biographer, providing all the intimate details. So let me share one more thing I've just learned about our chief inspector. His mother was in the hospital last month."

"East China."

"Yes. It's a special yet expensive hospital. A number of the nutritional supplements necessary for her recovery are pricey and aren't covered by medical insurance. They cost way too much for a cop like him to afford, so I left a gift card for her at the hospital. For once, the gift card wasn't returned to me but instead it was cashed. The store manager contacted me to verify the name of the woman who cashed it in. It wasn't his mother, but the widow of Chen's colleague. So what could I say?"

"Come now. You're painting a portrait of me as some kind of selfless model Communist, like Comrade Lei Feng. It was a gift card of such a large sum, my mother wanted me to give it back to you," Chen said. "Detective Wei died in an accident last week, and his family needed help badly. So, on the spur of the moment, I gave your gift card to his inconsolable widow. It was your good deed, not mine. Good deeds will not go unrewarded, as my mother always says. "

Chen hadn't told Lianping anything about it, but once he mentioned Wei's widow, she remembered the incident.

"His mother is a wonderful woman," Gu said. "You've met her, haven't you?"

"No, I only met Chief Inspector Chen a couple of weeks ago."

"For a woman of her age, she embodies Buddhist enlightenment. She believes in karma, and so do I," Gu said, changing the subject unexpectedly. "Indeed, karma is seen everywhere in the world of red dust."

"Yes?" she asked. The abrupt turn in the conversation mystified her.

"This morning I ran into Old Xiang of the Purple City Group, which is teetering on the verge of bankruptcy. He was hitting me up for an emergency loan. Only a few people know anything about it right now, so don't write about it in your newspaper, Lianping. But did you know how the Purple City got its start? By selling fake medicine."

Then it dawned on her. As a well-connected businessman, Gu might have heard something about Xiang and her. It wasn't the sort of information she'd expect Gu to share, but with Chen hovering in the background, she understood what Gu was doing. Did Chen realize the purpose of Gu's revelation? Probably. It wasn't as if the chief inspector needed that kind of help, but Gu must have seen it as another opportunity to do a favor for Chen.

She was then seized by a sense of foreboding. Xiang might not have told her everything. His marriage proposal had come out of the blue. She now wondered about it. Could his family's troubled business be the reason why he rushed to propose? Once their company filed for bankruptcy, Xiang knew he'd never be able to win her hand.

If this was the case, she should try to learn more from Gu. Gu, however, was already bowing out of the room.

"Sorry, I'm always garrulous when I'm around Chen. I just let myself get carried away. I have to go to a business meeting now, so I'll leave the two of you alone. Would you like me to send up any special dishes?"

"I have only one request, Gu," Chen said. "Don't have a waitress hover outside or check on us frequently."

"Of course. How about I have some appetizers brought in first, along with a bottle of French champagne? Then, whenever you're ready, let the waitress know. She won't do anything until you signal her."

"That's fantastic. Thank you for everything."

TWENTY-FIVE

FINALLY, THE TWO OF them were left alone, and the silence hung in the room like bubbles in chilled champagne. Chen shifted slightly and looked out the window at the promenade of multicolored flagstones, a long curved walkway above the shimmering water. After a minute, he turned back to face Lianping and break the silence between them.

"I'm sorry about Gu's interruption. Sometimes he's impossible, talking up a storm like that. But this was one place where I could be sure we'd have privacy."

"You don't have to apologize. Gu is an important businessman. He's declined my requests for an interview in the past, so I appreciate the opportunity to meet him again." She added, "I don't think he'll decline when I ask again, seeing as I'm a friend of Chief Inspector Chen."

"It's ironic, isn't it? Chief Inspector Chen's close connections to Big Bucks," Chen said with a wry smile. "In case you write about it one day, let me make sure you have the real story. It's true that Gu asked me to translate the business plan for the company, New World, and he paid me generously for it. But other than that, don't listen to him."

"Still, he believes that he's obligated to you."

"That's possible, but at the same time that I helped him, he also helped me in my work. His help was particularly valuable in a serial killer investigation."

"So you're buddies, each helping the other."

"Whatever you say, Lianping," he said, raising his teacup. "Apart from Gu's interruption, I also want to apologize for not keeping my word."

"What do you mean?" She stared at him in confusion.

"In Shaoxing, I promised to take you on a black-awning boat excursion in the mist-enveloped canal, like Lu Xun described in one of his short stories. I'm sorry I failed to do so."

"That's not something you have to apologize for."

"When Gu burst into the room, you were mentioning Xiang's proposal to you. Congratulations! I wish you all the best, Lianping." He paused, eyeing the ring on her finger, and then went on, "That afternoon in Shaoxing, I thought I might have the opportunity to enjoy sitting under a black awning with you sometime in the future, but now it's no longer possible. I meant it when I invited you that afternoon, until we were interrupted by that unexpected phone call. Remember?"

"It was from a doctor at East China Hospital, as I recall. You told me that your mother had been admitted there."

"Yes, but at that time she had already been discharged. That phone call was about me."

"About you?" She added in haste, "It's nothing serious, is it, Chen?"

"No, I'm fine. It wasn't about my health. You know the kind of people who stay at that hospital, don't you? The patients are usually high-ranking cadres, with the occasional Big Bucks. There are special wards reserved exclusively for top Party cadres. My mother was a rare exception, due to my personal connection to a doctor—let's call him Dr. H—whom I happen to know from years ago."

"I know it's a high-cadre hospital. Several months ago, I tried to interview somebody there, but I wasn't even allowed to get a foot in the door. Why? A top Party leader from Beijing was staying there that day."

"Well, the morning of the phone call, Dr. H entered a special ward where Qiangyu was staying while the doctors were conducting a routine checkup—"

"Qiangyu—the first Party secretary of Shanghai?"

"Yes. Dr. H was about to start the procedure, when Qiangyu got a phone call and went out to the balcony to talk. While he was waiting, Dr. H couldn't help casting a curious glance around, and he noticed a page spread out by the fax machine. To his astonishment, Dr. H saw my name on the page and, believe it or not, he took a picture of that fax with his cell phone."

"What? The doctor took such a risk for you?"

"The chain of misplaced yin and yang causality can be long indeed. Dr. H believed he owed me a big favor, but that's another story. Anyway, the fax turned out to be a proposal made by Qiangyu to remove me from my position at the Shanghai Police Bureau and to reassign me to be the National People's Congress's spokesman in Beijing. It would be a drastic change, though I hear that the Congress's spokesman position carries with it the same Party cadre rank."

"But why reassign you?"

"According to the page, Qiangyu was recommending me because of my unorthodox image and my ability to speak English. At the same time, he considered my performance in the police bureau to be innovative, yet not always in step with the political emphasis of the Party authorities. Needless to say, the transfer could be only the first step. What might follow is anybody's guess.

"At least, that's what Dr. H told me on the phone that afternoon."

Lianping was at a loss for an appropriate response.

An ominous silence ensued. They could hear the water lapping against the bank outside, the screeching of white gulls hovering around the ships, and the blaring of a siren cutting through the dusk.

"In reality, this new position would be decorative at best," Chen finally went on. "No one will pay any real attention to it. As the saying goes, out of sight, out of mind. From there, it'll be easy for them to make me disappear completely. Such a scenario is nothing new. After getting the phone call from Dr. H that afternoon, I was reminded of a proverb: 'When a clay Buddha statue sails across the river, it can hardly protect itself.' So, I thought, what would be the point of dragging someone else into the muddy water with me?"

She looked up at him and said, "That's why you suddenly wanted to go to the festival dinner instead?"

"Yes, I thought I'd better put in an appearance there, as a way of showing that I was in Shaoxing for the festival."

"But you've been doing an excellent job, Chen. In fact, you were assigned to the case because of your extraordinary work—"

"It's all *because* of the case."

"How?"

"I haven't discussed the details of the case with you, Lianping, because it's so complicated. To begin with, the elements in the case lead off in too many possible directions. For that matter, there were too many investigators working on the case—Jiang for the city government, Liu for the city Party Discipline Committee, Sheng for Internal Security, and then the team of the Central Party Discipline Committee from Beijing, not to mention Detective Wei and me, representing the police bureau. Each of these investigators was approaching the case from his own perspective, and with his own agenda."

"You're right about that. Just this morning I heard stories about the possible mission of the Beijing team. But that's probably old news to you. Please go on."

"We can exchange notes about the Beijing team later. Regarding the Zhou case, when Wei and I first took over, I was reluctant. After all, it wasn't unimaginable for someone in Zhou's situation to commit suicide. Bringing me on as a special consultant might be nothing more than a political show or, as Detective Yu put it, an endorsement of the inevitable conclusion that it was suicide. For Jiang, Zhou's shuanggui and Zhou's death were clearly cause and effect. Detective Wei, however, didn't think so, and he undertook his investigation in all seriousness. Wei suggested various theories about Zhou's death as well as suspects who might have decided to bring Zhou down. It seemed to me, however, that none of them had sufficient motive to murder him in a well-guarded hotel like Moller. I have to emphasize one thing: while I was assigned to the case as a consultant, Wei did most of the work.

"Then, in the middle of his investigation, Wei died in a 'traffic accident.' This immediately raised the question whether or not Wei's death was related to Zhou's."

"So you came to visit me at *Wenhui*," she said quietly, "because of the investigation?"

"I'm a cop," he said, avoiding her question. "I came there to check out the scene, and I wanted to talk to someone familiar with the area. What you told me while we were at the *Wenhui* café really helped. At that intersection, according to your analysis, it's not likely that a parked car would go from a full stop to running him down at high speed by accident. It wouldn't be advisable, however, for me to discuss it with you at length. I hope you understand."

"I understand. What I said to you was only common sense. But accidents do happen. How could you prove that Wei's death was the result of his investigation?"

"Technically, the theory that Wei was murdered is as implausible as the accident theory. The SUV was parked on Weihai Road, about one hundred meters from the corner. Wei was walking in one of a few possible directions—he was either walking straight along Weihai to the west, or turning onto it from the south of Weihai, or had approached it from the north. Taking into consideration the time it takes for the traffic light to change, it would have taken Wei one or two minutes at the most to reach the spot at which he was run down. How could the SUV driver have spotted Wei from that distance, started the engine, raced to the spot, and run him down? Unless, of course, Detective Wei's plans were already known to others. The SUV could have been waiting for him to arrive, and someone else could have been following Wei all along, to give the SUV the signal."

"That's so complicated."

"That's why it was so alarming. And who could have known Wei's schedule? I talked to his wife, and she knew nothing about his schedule that day. According to his colleagues, Wei didn't even come into the office that morning. I asked Party Secretary Li about it, and he was vague, saying that he couldn't remember whether or not Wei had called him that morning—"

There was a light knock on the door, and through the door came a call, "Cold dishes."

A young waitress in a scarlet silk mandarin dress stepped into the room. She served six dainty dishes on the table and glibly started introducing them.

"Deep-fried crispy rice paddy eel, live river shrimp in salt water, homemade tofu mixed with green onion and sesame oil, sticky-rice-filled dates, sliced xiao pork, spicy transparent beef sinew. This is all genuine Shaoxing cuisine. It's all fashionable homestyle cooking, and the ingredients are all organic and fresh. Mr. Gu insists on it. There is also champagne in the ice bucket."

"Shaoxing cuisine?" Lianping asked, looking at Chen.

"It's what I asked for when I called Gu to reserve the room," Chen said.

"It's all very Chinese," Lianping said, "except for the champagne."

"I could bring some Shaoxing rice wine?" the waitress offered. "We have Maiden Red. Eighteen years."

"That would be good."

The waitress walked out light-footedly, carrying the champagne bucket.

"Why did you ask Gu to prepare Shaoxing cuisine?"

"Remember the festival dinner?"

"Yes—once you appeared at the festival, you were surrounded by well-known and not-that-well-known writers, as well as officials of the local writers' association. They seated you at the distinguished-guest table, and you were the most distinguished one there, toasted by everybody."

"That's not what I wanted. Not at all. I didn't insist that you be seated with me, Lianping, because I had no idea how much longer I'd be 'distinguished.' It might not have been good for you," he said in a somber voice. "But that afternoon, I was thinking about a black-awning boat meal of Shaoxing local dishes and wine, just you and me."

The waitress returned, carrying a small red-covered urn and cups.

"There was only one left." The moment she tore away the urn cover, an intoxicating fragrance permeated the room. She skillfully poured wine for each of them into dainty white porcelain cups.

"If you push the top button on the wall, a small red light will come on outside. That red light is just like a 'Do not disturb' sign at a hotel. Whenever you're ready for the hot dishes, push the button below," the waitress explained, then bowed gracefully and left, closing the door after her.

Gazing at the amber-colored wine in his cup, Chen said, "There's an old folk tradition that whenever a daughter is born, the family buries an urn of rice wine. On the day of her wedding, many years later, they dig up the urn. It's a very special wine."

"It is eighteen-years wine and very rare."

"So I drink a cup to apologize for missing the meal with you in the boat that day," he said, draining his cup.

"Don't say that," she said, embarrassed. "Now I understand; I should be the one to apologize—but let's go back to what you were talking about before the waitress arrived."

"I was talking about Wei's schedule that day. I didn't know it, but somebody must have known about it. I wanted to check his phone records, but his phone wasn't found at the scene. It took me days to recover a list and recording of the calls he'd made that morning. It turns out he actually did talk to Party Secretary Li about his plans for the day. He told Li that there was something not right in the interview with the hotel attendant and that he would follow up on that lead. So Wei told him he was going to the hotel, and then on to *Wenhui Daily*."

"He was going to *Wenhui*? Why?"

"According to his wife, Wei asked her to examine and reexamine the picture of Zhou that ran in the *Wenhui Daily*. The picture was too small and low-resolution for anyone to make out the brand of cigarettes. For all I know, he could have been coming to meet with anybody at the newspaper—even you."

"Me?"

"Well, he didn't say anything specific about it in the phone call. There's a possibility that he wanted to discuss something with your colleague who handles the crime beat."

"Yes, that's possible," she said contemplatively, "but do you mean that Party Secretary Li . . . ?"

"I'm more inclined to assume that Li wasn't directly involved in the conspiracy. But he must have revealed Wei's plans to somebody above him, even though he wasn't aware of the consequences at the time."

"Somebody above him? Who do you think that could be?"

"I don't know. Possibly Jiang or someone else in the city government. That would also explain Li's claim that Wei died in a traffic accident. If Wei's death was investigated, it might come around and incriminate Li," he said, breaking a deep-fried crispy rice paddy eel into two. "But anyway, Wei must have been pushing in a direction that made some people panic. They had to get him out of the way, which means that it's also a point of no return for me."

"How is that? You're just a consultant on this case, aren't you?"

"I feel responsible for his death. I'd wanted to give Wei a free hand, so I told him he was to move ahead without discussing everything with me first. Wei seems to have done just that, despite the fact that there are some untouchable figures in the background of this case. There was a gap in communication between us, and I was also sick that weekend. Then Monday, the next day, he died in the 'traffic accident.'

"Wei's death, following Zhou's as it did, gave me new avenues to investigate. If Zhou was murdered in a well-guarded hotel for reasons unknown, Wei must have been close to uncovering those reasons. Because of that, he, too, was killed. Setting up Wei's death to resemble an 'accident' required planning and resources, so it's reasonable to assume powerful people were involved.

"There are only two clues to be found in the phone call Detective Wei made to Party Secretary Li that morning. One is the interview with the hotel attendant. The other is the planned visit to *Wenhui*. Let's leave the latter aside for the time being because there is too wide a range of possibilities. But with regard to that interview, I got a tape of it. I listened and relistened to it, but without getting anything from it.

"As far as I can see, once shuangguied, Zhou was already a 'dead tiger.' What he'd done wasn't something the government wanted people to know the details of. But the exposure of another corrupt Party official isn't exactly news in our socialism with Chinese characteristics, and evidence of Zhou's corruption had already been revealed on the Internet. So there had to be something else, something that the people above Zhou were desperate about, something that threw them into a murderous panic when they suspected Detective Wei was getting close to it.

"What could it be?

"I thought about contacting the hotel attendant, but ever since the Party Discipline Committee team from Beijing arrived at the Moller Villa, the hotel has become too sensitive of a place for me to get close to. Wei's death was a lesson I had to keep in mind. They are out there in the dark, watching, so I had to make my move without attracting their attention.

"In the meantime, I had to pursue other avenues of investigation. This might not be the time to go into all the details. While Wei's death made it impossible for me to back away from the case, dogged persistence alone doesn't necessarily pay off. Sometimes breakthroughs are the result of pure luck. So I'm truly grateful to you, Lianping, for your help with this difficult investigation."

"What are you saying, Chen?"

"You provided me with a general introduction to the sordid scenes and secrets of the housing market. Your perspective and comments about resistance and revelations in the world of cyberspace were also helpful. But it was your introduction to Melong that really helped."

"Melong?"

"Yes. His computer expertise led to me to a crucial link that I'd overlooked, and from there, to an unexpected breakthrough in Shaoxing. The subsequent developments came as a real surprise to me."

"I'm lost again, Chen," she said. "You went to Shaoxing for the festival, didn't you?"

"As a matter of fact, your suggestion that I go there reminded me of something I'd read but almost skipped over in Zhou's file. Zhou was born in Shaoxing, and left for Shanghai when he was only seven. For many years, he didn't go back to Shaoxing—not even once. Last year, however, he made two trips in quick succession, which seemed strange for a busy official like Zhou. So I decided to play the long shot and go to Shaoxing. Again I want to thank you, because without your suggestion that I attend the festival, and without your company in Shaoxing, I might not have made the trip.

"In Shaoxing, I was lucky enough to find someone close to him, and with help from Melong, she yielded an important clue."

"What's that—who's that?" She then added, "You mentioned some little—I remember—you met her there in the morning."

"I am afraid I have to skip some details here, but I think you'll understand why," Chen said, adding some wine to her cup. "With regard to the case, have you ever wondered about the fact that both the team from the city government and the Shanghai Party Discipline Committee officials—both originally at the hotel for the corruption investigation—remained at the hotel even after Zhou's death? Particularly Jiang, who has remained there despite all the work waiting for him back at the city government office as the right-hand man to Qiangyu. What's more, Jiang hasn't been that anxious to close the case, even though it's in the interest of the Party authorities to officially conclude that Zhou's death was a suicide.

"At the same time, Jiang repeatedly inquired after the police bureau's ongoing investigations. It occurred to me that he might be at the hotel for a reason unknown to me but crucial to him and his people. Particularly since he remained there even after the the Beijing team arrived.

"Unfortunately, I didn't come to see the light until after that trip to Shaoxing and after I guessed the purpose of the presence of the Central Party Discipline Committee's team in Shanghai."

"I've heard something about it," Lianping said. "Last week, Qiangyu sat down with the chief editor of *Wenhui*, telling him it was a difficult time and that he appreciates the support of the people loyal to him."

"So perhaps you understand," Chen said. He paused to take a sip of wine. "Now let's go back to the fax page that was on Qiangyu's nightstand at the hospital. Dr. H called me about the fax when we were at Shen Garden, talking about the romantic poems of the Song dynasty. It's been a difficult time for Qiangyu, and the Beijing team isn't at the hotel for no reason. He knows better. The power struggle between the 'Youth League' and 'Shanghai Gang' has been coming to a head. The Zhou case could be what the Beijing team uses to break through. Yet, after the death of Detective Wei, I was still out there, pushing the investigation forward in earnest but not in a direction they controlled. Who knew what the possible fallout would be? That's why Qiangyu couldn't let me remain in my position at the police bureau. Your boss might be someone he can trust, but I'm not. In fact, if I stay at the police bureau, there's too much at stake for Qiangyu and his people."

"You are scaring me, Chen."

"No, I'm not. What happened to Detective Wei could happen to me, but I've found something they're after—the information Zhou left behind. What I have could make the whole bunch of live, monstrous crabs inseparable, and their fate inescapable. And these are not just small crabs like Zhou."

"In other words, you're in a position to prove Zhou didn't act alone, but with the help of people above him. You have evidence that they were all involved in corrupt deals involving Shanghai's land allocation and housing development?"

"Not only that, I can prove that the death of Zhou in the hotel wasn't suicide."

"How?"

"You know the expression 'a chain of crabs,' don't you?"

She nodded.

"Zhou must have expected the other 'crabs' to get him out of trouble, since they were all bound together—not by a straw rope, but by the secrets of their shared corruption. But the evidence unleashed in the human-flesh search was too strong. And it came out at a time when the Youth League faction in Beijing was gearing up to annihilate the Shanghai Gang, so the other people in the corruption scheme had to throw Zhou overboard. Shuangguied in the hotel, all alone in the dark, believing that they had left him in the lurch, he must have complained too loudly or threatened them in some way. After all, he'd secretly saved evidence of their involvement, and if he fell into hell, he could drag all of them down with him. They believed they had no choice but to finish him off, and it wasn't unimaginable, they thought, for a shuangguied official to commit suicide. Usually, the police investigation after a shuanggui case is just for show. It was only because of Party Secretary Li's obtuseness, however, that Detective Wei was chosen to handle the case, a cop too conscientious to perform according to their script."

"Zhou's entanglement with other corrupt officials above him might explain why he was murdered," she said deliberately. "But it still leaves the question of how it was done in such a well-guarded hotel."

"Remember the lead that Detective Wei mentioned in his phone call?"

"You said he said something about the interview with the hotel attendant. What did you learn from the attendant at the hotel? Did you talk to her?"

"No, not exactly. Detective Wei walked into that fatal ambush because of his overt move in that direction. I tried not to make the same mistake. I listened to the tape of the interview God knows how many times, and I even brought it with me all the way to Shaoxing," he said, with a sudden sigh. "That night, after the festival dinner party, I tried to call you, but your cell phone was turned off, and you weren't registered at the hotel."

"I took the night train back to Shanghai before the party was even over. I thought you were just too busy to notice me," she said, draining another cup, her face burning under the light. "I'm sorry, Chen, but I didn't know how serious your situation was."

"No, you don't have anything to be sorry for." He, too, drained his cup. "Anyway, I couldn't fall asleep in the hotel, so once again I thought through the sequence of events the night Zhou died, as described in the hotel attendant's statement. Then something occurred to me. That night in Shaoxing, when I stepped into my hotel room, the bedcovers were already turned down and there was a small bag of chocolate and a 'Sleep well' card placed on the pillow."

"That's not uncommon with a luxury suite in a five-star hotel. That shouldn't be surprising. And does that relate somehow to the interview tape?"

"To something on the tape. According to Jiang, he left the hotel Monday afternoon for an important meeting and spent the night at home, all of which has been confirmed. But according to the statement from the hotel attendant, when she tried to turn down the covers for the other two guests on the third floor, both Liu and Jiang were in their rooms.

"Now, with turn-down service, usually an attendant knocks on the door and asks the guest inside if they want their bed turned down. If the guest isn't in, she might let herself in and prepare the bed. Just like the attendant had done in my room earlier that night in Shaoxing. But if the guest is in, he'll answer loudly, without opening the door, that it's not needed, and then the attendant will leave. In other words, there had to be another man in Jiang's room when the attendant knocked.

"If that's true, then why and who? From the very beginning, there was something we took for granted. Jiang and Liu were the shuangguiing Party cadres, and as such, they were above suspicion. What made us further rule them out was that Jiang wasn't at the hotel at the time and had a solid alibi, and Liu, a short and feeble old man, seemed physically unable to do such a thing. Building B is well guarded. Anyone who enters has to sign in, and then sign out when they leave. There is also a surveillance camera over the landing to the third floor.

"I managed to obtain copies of the register pages for building B for that Monday and Tuesday. To my surprise, I found a man named Pan Xinhua had signed in Monday afternoon, visiting Jiang in his room. Jiang left the hotel about an hour later, but there's no record of Pan signing out that day. Pan could have stayed in Jiang's room and could have been the one who spoke to the hotel attendant when she came around six fifteen. Several hours later, he could have sneaked into Zhou's room, where Zhou was in a deep sleep after having taken sleeping pills, strangled him, and staged the room to make it look like Zhou had hanged himself from the beam.

"From the same source, which I have to protect, I was able to get the surveillance camera tape for those two days. On the video, Pan can be seen coming up to the third floor on Monday afternoon, but there's no sign of him leaving later that day. The next morning, when the commotion broke out after Zhou's death was discovered, Pan was caught by the camera walking down the stairs shortly afterward. It was total chaos then, with many people coming and going in a hurry, so no one paid any special attention to him—"

"I have to interrupt with a question, Chen. Did he stay in Zhou's room the whole time? Or did he return to Jiang's?"

"No, I don't think so. After killing Zhou, Pan probably left Jiang's room and stayed somewhere else. There were three unoccupied rooms on that floor. He waited until the morning, then during the pandemonium he slipped out of the room, and the building, without even signing his name to the register."

"That's unbelievable, Chief Inspector Chen, but you've solved the case. Congratulations."

"No, not entirely—"

There came another knock on the door.

TWENTY-SIX

THE DOOR OPENED, AND the waitress stepped into the room, carrying a large silver tray.

"I'm sorry for the interruption, sir. There's one special course before the hot dishes. We thought you might enjoy that."

She placed a white plate in front of each of them, and then a large platter in between. Each plate had on it a deshelled steamed blue crab, still in crab shape, with the legs and claws arranged meticulously. The platter contained chunks of liquor-immersed raw crab.

"It's not river crab season yet," the waitress said, introducing the course, "so we use live blue crabs flown in special from the sea. The deshelled crab is a favorite among Western customers here. The liquor-immersed crab is a celebrated dish in Shaoxing cuisine. We use live crabs, plus Maotai liquor, and it's stored at fifty degrees, so there's no need to worry about the freshness of it."

"Thank you. Liquor-immersed crab is my mother's favorite."

"Why not have it boxed and take it to her?" Lianping asked.

"Good idea. I hardly touch raw seafood myself." He turned to the waitress, "We're in no hurry for the hot dishes."

"We can box the crab for you after you finish dinner. It's seven now," the waitress said, "and we'll wait for your order to start cooking the hot dishes."

She left, again closing the door after her.

Outside, the glittering splendors began to surge up along the Bund. Across the river, the ceaselessly changing neon lights from the jostling skyscrapers projected intoxicating fantasies of the new century on the shimmering water.

Lianping sighed. "What a feast!"

"I have no idea how long it takes to deshell a crab like that."

"By the way, do you know the Internet joke about a river crab? 'River crab' in Chinese is a homophone for 'harmony.' When an online post is banned, people will say it was harmonized, deleted for the sake of harmony of our socialist society. Now they simply say the post has been river-crabbed."

"The connotations are unmistakably negative, just like they are in the idiomatic expression about the chain of crabs."

"Mr. Gu certainly went out of his way to have the Shaoxing style meal prepared for you," she said, picking up a glistening white crab leg with her slender fingers. "But you were saying that there was something else left to resolve in your investigation."

"Yes, there was another part. Remember the other clue in Detective Wei's phone call to Party Secretary Li?"

"You mean the visit to *Wenhui* he planned to make?"

"Yes. From what his wife said, I thought it might have had something to do with the picture that got Zhou into trouble in the first place. That was certainly the focus of Internal Security, and to some extent, of Jiang too. For me, this part is still mostly guesswork."

"So . . ."

Chen helped himself to the golden crab roe, which was displayed like a dainty chrysanthemum petal on the white plate. It tasted scrumptious, just as he remembered it from many years ago. It wasn't an evening, however, for him to savor delicacies.

A shrill siren blared all of a sudden from a distance and reverberated along the darksome water.

"It's an aspect of the case that is not only informed by a lot of guesswork, but also involves some people that you or I may know. Still, I wanted to tell you about it tonight—and not as a cop."

"This is intriguing," she said uncertainly.

"As I may have told you, it can be tiresome to be stuck in one's professional role all the time. So for the sake of convenience, we might as well switch to something different, more like storytelling."

"Storytelling?" she said, surprised by his sudden shift in manner. What was the enigmatic chief inspector up to?

"Do you remember what you suggested with regard to the poems you wanted me to write for *Wenhui*? You suggested that I adopt a persona. A persona that didn't have to be the writer himself. Adopting such a persona has helped me with a couple of poems. It's a pity that I don't have more time for poetry." He poured himself another cup of the aromatic and heady rice wine, which he drained before he went on. "In a police report, in some situations, people may be referred to as John Doe or Jane Doe. Or in some novels, characters might be referred to by letters such as C or L."

"So . . . tell me a story, if you like," she said, the wine rippling in the small cup in her hand, "Chief Inspector Chen."

"This story flows more smoothly if it's told from a third person perspective. More important, remember that you're listening to something fictional. As such, the narrator doesn't have to worry about possible liability and the listener doesn't have any responsibilities. For the record, I'm just a storyteller at the moment, not a cop with any professional obligations, and you are just listening to a fantasized scenario, nothing that concerns you as a professional journalist."

Whatever Chen was about to say, Lianping thought it would

have direct bearing on her. She thought she should have guessed as much earlier.

There was a subtle change in his tone as he started to tell his story.

"C was a cop investigating the death of a shuangguied corrupt official named Z. It was a complicated case with different people from different agencies investigating different aspects, and needless to say, each of them had their own agenda. One of the aspects of the case concerned the subversive role in today's society that the most devoted Internet users—the netizens—can play through those increasingly frequent human-flesh searches. The case in question could be said to have started with a picture posted online, which prompted just such a search, and which in turn exposed Z.

"As a cop, C didn't think that the person who originally sent the picture to the Web forum did anything wrong. On the contrary, C had his reservations about the government's control of the Internet. As for the other investigators, including Internal Security, they were focused on punishing the 'Internet troublemaker' in the name of maintaining social stability. But their target was clever and had sent the picture from a computer at an Internet café, thus making it impossible for them to track down the sender."

Chen paused to pick up his cup again. She reached out, unexpectedly, and snatched the cup out of his hand.

"No, you're drinking too much."

"I'm fine, Lianping," he said with a wan smile. "In the course of his investigation, C came to know a young journalist named L. He was drawn to her, not merely because she was attractive and intelligent but also because she was passionate about justice in socialism with Chinese characteristics. To his pleasant surprise, she helped him with the investigation, familiarizing him with the Internet users' resistance to governmental control of the Internet. She introduced him to a computer expert who was able to break down some barriers for him. In the meantime, in some of the pictures she sent to him and his friends electronically, C came upon clues that had eluded Internal Security. While he was picking up some e-mail from her, C happened to discover a loophole in the new Internet café regulations. From there, he was astonished to learn that the identity of the original picture sender was none other than L." Chen paused for a moment, then started up again. "Now, what was C going to do?

"As a cop and a rising cadre, he was supposed to report this to the higher authorities, but L didn't post the picture out of any personal grudge. She was merely upset with the brazen, widespread corruption that was taking place while those responsible were pretending that their actions were in the Party's interests. Her desire to cause Z trouble was, in fact, a spontaneous protest against the injustices of an authoritarian society. Her action led to a call to dig into the background of Z, which in turn resulted in a flood of responses. What happened to Z subsequently was beyond her imagining, and for which she wasn't to blame, C concluded.

"So, if what she did was done on the spur of the moment, did he . . ." Chen trailed off.

In the silence that ensued, they heard footsteps moving closer to the door, and then trail off down the hall.

"So that's it, the end of the story?"

"Yes, that's the end. As I mentioned earlier, for C, that was an aspect of the investigation he has to wrap up, a missing piece to the puzzle. But there are things above and beyond playing one's part in the system. Things far more important, like justice, however partial and paradoxical, in the present society. Of course, the persona in this narrative doesn't have to be a real person. It's just a story between you and me."

Chen then produced an envelope containing the page he'd torn from the register at the Flying Horse Internet café and handed it to her. "Oh, this is for you. I almost forgot."

"What is it?" she asked, as she opened the envelope. She looked briefly at the name "Lili" on the register page, and her face drained of color. Only a few knew that was her childhood name. Her ID card bore her new name, but the people in the Internet café in the neighborhood knew her well and never noticed or bothered about it.

"I don't know what to say, Chen."

"*What we cannot speak about we must pass over in silence.* I think it was Wittgenstein who said that. A fitting paradigm. After all, exposing the original picture sender wasn't the aspect on which C focused at all."

He reached out to pour himself another cup of wine, but she didn't stop him this time.

"But enough of that story; let me go back to the case that I've been working on. What am I going to do?"

"Chief Inspector Chen?"

"You've gotten lost in this story, Lianping," Chen said, taking a deliberate sip of wine. "As a cop with professional commitments, I'm supposed to report developments in the investigation to Party Secretary Li. Alternatively, I'm required to report to the Shanghai Communist Party Discipline Committee. But then what?"

"Then—"

"You can easily imagine. There's no need for me to get into the possibilities."

"What if you choose to do nothing?" she asked with bated breath. "No one else knows any of this."

"If I do nothing, then Detective Wei died for nothing. I would never be able to look you in the eye again, not with any self-respect as a cop."

"Then—" Impulsively, she reached across the table and grasped his hand, only to quickly withdraw hers, the diamond ring dazzling on her finger.

"You mentioned hearing something about the mission of the Beijing team in Shanghai, Lianping."

"No one knows about these things for certain," Lianping said, her eyes downcast. "It's possible that what I heard was all hearsay."

"Maybe or maybe not. This might be my last case as a police officer, and I want to go ahead."

She looked up in confusion and alarm.

"I don't know how things really stand at the top levels in Beijing, but as a Party member, I'm also supposed to report to the Central Party Discipline Committee in Beijing."

"I've heard of your personal connection to Comrade Zhao, the retired Secretary of that Committee," she said.

"Don't believe what people may have said about the connection. Believe it or not, the Beijing team has never contacted me. For me, it has been just like the proverb about a blind man riding a blind horse to a fathomless lake in the depths of a dark night. Incidentally, I thought of that back at the Shaoxing hotel. I don't know what will happen to me, but I have to take the plunge."

She stared at him, and then lowered her head into her hands. When she looked up a few seconds later, her eyes were glistening.

"You make me feel so wretched," she said in a wavering voice. "Here I am, trying to be smart and sophisticated, trying to realize the Shanghai dream, seize the moment, go with the flow, and lodge an occasional protest on the sly. That's about it. But here you're putting your career on the line . . ." She stopped to wipe her eyes with the back of her hand.

"There's no need to say that," he said, tapping her hand, soft, yet a little wet. He touched the trail of a tear on her cheek before he reached again for his cup. "Perhaps it's time for me to think of finding another job. I might not be too bad a translator, as Gu just told you. Well, something else for your 'biography' of me is that I've been translating some additional classical Chinese poems, also on the sly. Poems such as this one by Wang Han, from the eighth century: '*The mellow wine shimmers / in the luminous stone cup! / I'm going to drink it on the horse / when the Army Pipa suddenly starts / urging me to charge out. // Oh, do not laugh, my friend, / if I drop dead / drunk on the battlefield. / How many soldiers / have come back home?'* "

"Please stop, Chen—"

"I cherish your friendship, Lianping, so I'm going to ask you to do one thing for me. But you can certainly say no."

"Tell me."

"When I give the evidence left by Zhou to the Central Party Discipline Committee in Beijing, they might choose to act on it, or to do nothing at all. Whatever they do, it'll be what is in their political interest at that moment, possibly for all the right reasons, or maybe for all the wrong ones. For them, justice is like a colored ball in a magician's hand; it's capable of changing in a heartbeat. That's why I need you—to make sure the truth comes out, in case my quixotic attempt ends up like a rock sinking silently to the bottom of the sea. With your computer and Internet skills, I believe you'll know how to do it effectively, yet safely."

"I'll do anything you want me to do," she said with a catch in her voice, her eyes locking his.

"And you'll do it without risking exposure. Promise me, Lianping."

"Yes, I know how to do that."

She reached across to clasp his hand. The starry night came streaming through the curtain that rustled once, and once only. The candle-projected shadows flickered in the background.

Fair waves of the moon fading, / a jade handle of the Dipper lowering, / we calculate by counting on our fingers / when the west wind will start blowing, / unaware of time flowing like a river in the dark . . .

They once again heard a melody drifting over from the big clock atop the Shanghai Customs House.

"It's 'The East Is Red' again," he said, "a song proclaiming Mao as the savior of China."

"Yes?"

"The customs house used to play a different melody a few years ago. When they changed it back, I don't know. Time really flows—in the dark."

"It seems as if I've known you for years, Chen," she said softly, "but then, as if just meeting for the first time."

"I remember when we met at the Writers' Association. Professor Yao was giving a talk, titled 'The Enigma of China.' It reminded me of a painting I'd seen in Madrid."

"What painting?"

"*The Enigma of Hitler* by Salvador Dalí. It is a singularly haunting painting. I saw it years ago, but the memory of some surrealistic details has never faded from my mind. The wilted tree, the torn photo of Hitler on the empty plate, the gigantic broken telephone with a teardrop, perhaps symbolic of the ideological control of people. Here, today, we could simply change the telephone speaker to an Internet cable, and the photo of Hitler to one of Mao. In the painting, I remember there's also a shadowy figure emerging out from behind an umbrella. But what does the figure represent? It could be anybody or even a projection of the collective illusion. But I've never really figured that out. It could be me or you. Yesterday, my mother said something truly enlightening. 'You never really see yourself in the painting.'"

"A painting called *The Enigma of China*?"

"For too long, I've been in the painting—or in the system, as you might well say. Perhaps it's time for me to get out of it."

"But I doubt that, Chief Inspector Chen," she said. "Enigma or not—"

There came another knock on the door.

They were both startled.

"What!"

"Mr. Chen, is it time for the hot dishes?"